The Termination
Annette Mori

The Termination

Annette Mori

Affinity
eBook Press
NZ
2017

The Termination
© 2017 by Annette Mori

Affinity E-Book Press NZ LTD
Canterbury, New Zealand

1st Edition

ISBN: 978-0-947528-35-5

Editor: JoSelle Vanderhooft
Proof Editor: Alexis Smith
Cover Design: Irish Dragon Designs

Acknowledgments

A huge thank-you to all my beta readers, Gail Dodge, Cathie Williamson, Ameliah Faith, Carrie Camp, and my sister, who made great suggestions to improve the initial draft. Of course, once again I have to acknowledge Erin O'Reilly, who is a constant support and encouragement to me. I am honored to call her a friend and have her support me in my journey. I would also like to express my gratitude to Affinity Press and the wonderful trio (JM Dragon, Erin O'Reilly, and Nancy Kaufman) who continue to provide feedback to tighten up manuscripts that need assistance and publish my sometimes-unconventional work.

I am eternally grateful for the opportunities they give me to let my stories see the light of day. My other family members who are also very supportive include my nephew Aaron, his wife Chelsea, my little sister Kim, and my father, who struggles to read my books with one eye.

I always enjoy working with the beta editor, and Kay helped to improve my story. Thanks to JoSelle Vanderhooft for her magic as the final editor to tighten the story even further. Inevitably there are those pesky final errors that slip through, and I am thankful that the final proof editor, Alexis Smith, caught those before the book went to print. Nancy Kaufman is a rock star with her covers. Nancy is also a promoter extraordinaire.

A huge thanks to all the other readers and fellow writers who have sent personal emails, written reviews, and posted nice things on Facebook (you know who you are). The Affinity authors are an especially supportive group and often share posts or send words of encouragement. Finally, my wife, Jody, continues her support even when it interferes with our weekend time.

Dedication

To my father, who loves to talk politics and will definitely appreciate the satiric twist in this book. To my wife, who I love dearly for her patience and her ability to take care of me when I fail to do that myself. To Karen Davidson Boatman, who I hope is surrounded by books in heaven. She was a wonderfully supportive reader and will be dearly missed.

Table of Contents

Also by Annette Mori

The Review

The Ultimate Betrayal

Locked Inside

Out of This World

Asset Management

The Incredibly True Adventure of Two Elves in Love
(Affinity 2014 Christmas Collection)

Love Forever, Live Forever

The True Story of Valentine's Day

Vampire Pussy…Cat

Nicky's Christmas Miracle X3
(*It's in Her Kiss*, Affinity's Charity Anthology)

Chapter One

Codee sat behind her obnoxiously large desk. Her company contracted with a well-known office supply chain to provide all the furniture in the hospital. The salesman called it engineered wood and extoled its virtues as he proudly relayed the fact it was the greener choice. She would have preferred a smaller desk made of solid oak, but the design committee only played at asking her opinion.

Some days Codee really hated her job, and today was one of those days. At least it was Friday afternoon and she could leave after this last, distasteful task. She pinched the bridge of her nose and sighed as her employee relations coordinator, Sharlie, poked her head in the door.

"You almost ready?"

The levelheaded young woman was joining them for the meeting and she was thankful for that established protocol. Maybe she could talk some sense into Hilda, the admitting supervisor, who definitely fit her name. Whenever Codee heard Hilda's name, she imagined a mean old witch, and the hard-edged leader could give the worst boss in the United States a run for his or her money. To date, the numerous coaching sessions hadn't managed to change Hilda's perspective on anything, because once she made up her mind, no one could sway her.

"Remind me again why we're conducting a pre-termination proceeding on last month's employee of the month. For God's sake, the woman has more caring cards, star awards, and general accolades from patients, coworkers, and administration than any other employee in the brief time I've been here." Codee took a sip from the water bottle on her desk.

"I know, I know, but after Hilda put that blasted audit log in place, she jumped on Sawyer every time that she didn't meet the ninety-eight percent standard set for the department. Hilda has already gone through the first three steps in our process." Sharlie ran her hand through her hair.

"Half her staff can't meet the standard, so why is she holding Sawyer to that impossible expectation?" Codee grabbed the package of gum next to her monitor and pushed against the foil back to pop out one of the little white squares. Fearing her breath reeked of coffee, she popped the mint gum into her mouth, hoping to mask the odor.

"She argued that the others are too new and need more training, but because Sawyer has been here a year, she should be able to register patients with that level of accuracy. I don't agree and I tried to steer her in a different direction, but she was adamant."

"So what's Sawyer's accuracy rate?"

"Ninety-seven percent."

"You're kidding, right?" Codee asked in exasperation.

"I'm afraid not."

"This is getting out of hand. She's the third person this year Hilda has terminated. I need to talk to Tim. My recommendation would be to give Hilda a severance agreement

2

and find a new supervisor. The turnover in that department is not coincidental. She either fires or chases away every good admitting clerk we hire. I wish that social services position would open soon. Isn't Sawyer a social worker?" Codee grabbed a yellow pad and selected one of the pens in the mug next to her phone.

She scribbled on the pad to make sure the pen worked. She didn't know why when one stopped working she placed it back in the mug instead of tossing it in the trash. It was just one of her small quirks. Sharlie often chastised her for her inefficiency when she did things like that but never in a mean-spirited manner.

"Uh-huh. She finished her master's degree about six months ago, but we haven't had a position open or else we would have transferred her in a heartbeat."

"Okay, that's the angle I'll try to take with Hilda. We can encourage her to wait a little while longer because I heard we're about to post a job in that department. I just need a couple more days. Come on, you can back me up on this."

Codee stood and walked around her desk. She grabbed her down jacket on the way out of the office. She flashed to a mental image of Sawyer crouched down at eye level with a young boy who had scars from severe burns on his face and hands. His body had been tense until Sawyer's low, rumbling voice seemed to transform him. His joyous laughter after whatever she had whispered to him filled the waiting area and brought forth Codee's appreciative smile. Sawyer's impact on patients was nothing short of a miracle.

Codee remembered when she'd met the enchanting woman in new-employee orientation. Sawyer had pulled her long, chestnut hair back into a neat ponytail, and the gentle waves cascaded down her back. Although Sawyer had just finished a twelve-hour night shift, those soothing, green eyes never wavered in their intensity as she appeared to hang on every word. Her thoughtful answers to the questions she tossed out to new employees, accompanied by a hint of mischief in her smile, had Codee continuously seeking her reaction while she did her dog and pony show during orientation.

Codee knew she created a compelling and entertaining first impression, but she'd often felt like a phony when some of the stories she told were embellishments of the truth. Yet, the only way to truly illustrate a point was to create that connection to her audience with an intimate anecdote. She should have been an actress because the whoppers she told at these orientations were compelling. Not everything was untrue, but even the genuine experiences were enhanced for effect.

Codee wasn't great with names, but Sawyer's stood out as unusual, particularly for a woman, and whenever she passed the young admitting clerk in the hall, she made a point of saying hello and having a brief, albeit superficial conversation with her. She wished she had the ability to get to know her on a personal level, but that was out of the question. As the HR executive, she needed to maintain a strictly professional relationship with all the hospital employees—without exception.

Sharlie chuckled. "I don't think I'll have any impact on this at all. Hilda doesn't listen to peons like me; you have a better shot at getting through to her than I do."

On their way out of the cluster of offices that housed the HR department, Codee informed her receptionist, Clare, that they were heading to the preterm hearing. She was going to have to do something about the very black-and-white receptionist who wouldn't know the color gray if her job depended on it. Against her better judgment she'd hired the dour woman who'd come with excellent references. She'd tried to get her to understand that sometimes HR needed to view a situation from many angles and adhering strictly to policy wasn't always the right answer, especially if the policy needed changing, but Clare wanted no part of that.

"We'll be back in about an hour, Clare. Can you please call the social services department and try to get a definitive date on the posting of that new social worker position? I want to know what they're waiting for. I heard Tim gave his final blessing," Codee directed.

Clare nodded. Codee noted the lack of animation from her. No smile, no other sign of acknowledgment, but at least Clare was efficient and would do as she asked. That had to count for something, she supposed.

†

Winter in Moses Lake had been particularly harsh this year. As Codee pushed open the door to the separate office building where the campus housed both the human resource and marketing divisions, a wintry blast of cold air hit them squarely in the face.

She shivered, pulled the collar of her coat close around her neck, and began a brisk walk to the main hospital. The first patch of ice that connected with her high heels caused her to slip and slide, but she managed to catch her balance before she fell on the unforgiving pavement.

"Why haven't the plant guys salted yet? I'd hate to add to our crappy workers' compensation stats with my own claim after falling in the parking lot," Codee grumbled.

"We should have grabbed a pair of Yaktrax before walking over."

"Yeah, hindsight. I never seem to remember. Spring cannot get here soon enough for me."

Patches of snow and ice swirled throughout the parking lot like two different kinds of ice cream in a cone, and if they weren't so hazardous, Codee might have appreciated the

5

beauty in the patterns. When she turned to ask Sharlie another question about the upcoming meeting, her slick sole hit a patch of ice and she went down like a ton of bricks. Flailing her hands, she tried to brace her fall, but her head ended up bouncing on the pavement. The last thing she heard before the blackness enveloped her was Sharlie's gasp.

✝

Something cold and wet brushed Codee's cheek and she struggled to register what had just occurred as she met the concerned gaze of her colleague. Codee looked at the gray sky as the large snowflakes landed on her eyelashes. She blinked once and focused on Sharlie's wide-open, hazel eyes.

"Oh God, Codee, are you okay?"

Codee lifted her head and rubbed the spot that had struck the pavement. She could feel a large lump starting to form. The pulsating pain was almost more than she could bear, but she didn't want to make a big deal about her fall. "Yeah, I'm fine. Maybe I can grab some aspirin from the employee health nurse on the way to the meeting and then ice my head afterward. I'd rather not reschedule. Sawyer is probably petrified at this point, and I don't want to cause her any undue stress."

"As much as I don't want to admit that you're right, because I really think you should go to the emergency department, Sawyer's predicament is far direr than yours. I'd want to know the outcome as soon as possible if my life were hanging in the balance." Sharlie shivered and wrapped her wool scarf around her neck.

Codee knew that while being terminated was an unpleasant experience, it wasn't the end of the world. On a few occasions, it had been the spark to ignite a much-needed change in a person's life. This was especially true for employees who weren't in a position that was a good match for their personality or skillset.

Sharlie held out her arm, Codee grabbed ahold and used it as a leverage to lift herself off the ground. She didn't want to admit that her elbow hurt almost as much as her head, but she would take care of that later. She suspected she had a small fracture and would have to protect her left arm until she had a chance to go to the ED and get an x-ray. Codee thought she was fortunate to be right handed, so she could write her notes without difficulty.

Sharlie bent to pick up her notepad and pen, then she handed them to her boss as they began their trek to the main building.

"Are you sure you don't want to go to the ED and get checked out? The grimace on your face tells me you're in pain."

"No, I'd really rather get this over with."

Sharlie looked a little frightened, and Codee wondered what caused her reaction. She guessed she sounded harsher than she intended. "I'm sorry if I was short just now."

"I just don't want you to think I was being insubordinate, since that's an offense that results in an immediate termination."

Codee chuckled. "You, insubordinate? Never. Besides, you know I prefer when my staff challenges my decisions, except when I do something boneheaded like falling on the ice and deciding not to seek medical assistance right away, of course."

"I know, but there are eyes and ears everywhere, and I wouldn't want you forced into doing your duty." Sharlie's eyes shifted left and right as though she was looking for spies.

Codee shook her head. The conversation was starting to turn extremely odd. She'd never seen Sharlie act like this before. *Paranoid* was the word that came to mind. Something very strange was happening, and she couldn't quite figure out what that was.

As they passed the admitting area, Codee heard a loud commotion as a young Latina woman wailed, "My baby, my baby."

"Ma'am, if you would please provide proof of citizenship, we can take care of your child," the admitting clerk explained.

"Please save my baby," the woman pleaded.

Codee wanted to intervene. She wasn't sure why the clerk was asking for proof of citizenship. This was a public hospital, and they treated everyone regardless of their ability to pay or citizenship. She believed that if anyone required corrective action, this rude clerk was the more likely recipient than Sawyer.

Sharlie gently pulled on her arm. "Please, Codee, you can't intervene. We need to get to the hearing. It won't look good for you if you're late again." Codee thought she saw a desperate plea in her expression before Sharlie looked away.

What the hell is going on? Sharlie wouldn't meet her eyes, almost as if she felt guilty about something. Codee couldn't imagine what might prompt that reaction. Something very strange was happening, and she couldn't quite figure out what that was. She almost felt like she'd landed into an alternate reality and shook her head at the impossible notion.

†

The conference room where Sharlie had scheduled the pre-termination proceeding seemed drearier than Codee

8

remembered. The gray walls and institutional furniture made it look like a modern-day dungeon. She couldn't remember conducting a meeting in this little-used, bleak basement room without windows.

"I guess you weren't able to get one of the conference rooms in the education center, huh?" Codee commented.

Sharlie had a puzzled look on her face. "No, we always do the termination hearings in this room. Are you sure you're okay?"

"Yes, I'm fine. Does Sawyer have a union rep coming?"

"Union rep? What are you talking about?"

Codee thought Sharlie looked completely perplexed but ignored the inner alarm sounding loudly in her head. Before she could explore her confusion further, Sawyer shuffled into the room followed by Hilda.

Sawyer's grim expression and Hilda's blatant smirk disturbed Codee more than she would admit to. In her humble opinion, Hilda was a bully who enjoyed wielding the considerable amount of power the CFO, Tim, had given her over the last year.

Codee tried to remain objective, but the very first moment she'd lain eyes on Sawyer she felt a tinge of attraction, and with every interaction she'd been increasingly impressed with the younger woman's compassion and ability to connect with just about everyone. Codee knew she'd be perfect in the social sciences department, where Sawyer's true calling lay, if only that damn position would hurry and get posted.

Hilda strutted over to one of the hard metal chairs, pulled it out from the table, and sat heavily with an expectant look on her face. "Well, can we please get this over with? I have a very busy day."

Codee glanced over at Sharlie, who shrugged. She pointed to one of the empty chairs, directing Sawyer to have a seat.

After Sharlie sat in the other empty chair across from Hilda, Codee selected the seat across from Sawyer. She placed her notebook on the cheap wood table and poised her pen to begin writing.

"Sawyer, why don't you please share your perspective and provide me with some information that would alter our initial thoughts about separating you from employment," Codee began.

"You mean termination," Sawyer whispered.

Codee looked up and captured Sawyer's soulful eyes. "Well, yes, but that isn't my first choice of words to use with this process. Unfortunately, I haven't been able to change the policy language yet. I'd like to hear from you before a final decision is made."

"I don't really have much of a defense. The emergency department was very busy that day, and I suppose the number of interruptions caused too many errors. I guess I'm not very good at being an admitting clerk, but I do think if a transfer to social services is possible, that would be a better fit for me. I know you're just doing your job and I don't want to get you in trouble. If you can do something else and still adhere to President Trison's directive, I would try very hard to meet the standards until I'm able to transfer." Sawyer clasped her hands in front of her on the table.

"President Trison?" Codee scrunched her face. This day was evolving into one mystery after another. If she didn't know any better, she'd have guessed she was having some strange dream or more accurately a vivid nightmare.

David Trison was an outrageous Patriot Party leader vying for the United States presidency, but to her knowledge, he didn't have a snowball's chance in hell.

"What about what you did for that Mexican woman's baby? You blatantly defied the executive order and you pulled Dr. Smith into your deception. He had no reason to believe he was treating an illegal. You not only risked the hospital, but his medical license," Hilda sneered. She leaned forward, and the aggressiveness of her response played out on her face. Her grimace and puckered lips reminded Codee of the Wicked Witch of the West.

"I'll never apologize for doing the right thing, and I don't care what the laws say, that was the right thing to do. If that means termination, then so be it. At least I will leave this world with a clear conscience. I'm not the only person in this hospital that defies that repugnant law." Sawyer's intense gaze bored into her, as though there was a private message she was trying to communicate.

"We're wasting time. Sawyer's admitted to violating the law and just displayed a level of insubordination that would stand on its own as grounds for termination. Our path is clear. Sharlie, I believe it's time to escort her to the holding cell." Hilda smiled.

Codee saw pure evil in Hilda's grin, and she wasn't sure at what point she'd lost control of the meeting, or her mind for that matter. Nothing seemed to make sense anymore. Maybe she'd hit her head harder than she'd thought.

Sawyer stood and Sharlie escorted her toward the door. There was something in Sawyer's defiant posture that Codee admired. She wasn't sure what they were referring to with the situation with a Latina patient, but Sawyer clearly felt as though she'd acted in a principled manner and her values ruled whatever decision she had made.

Nothing made sense to Codee, but she would take a different tack with Hilda. Instead of termination, she thought Sawyer would accept a separation agreement. She would encourage Sawyer to resign, and in exchange the hospital

11

would agree not to fight unemployment. Of course, Sawyer would also have to not file a wrongful termination claim. The hospital would also pay out her vacation time and that should give Sawyer a little money to tide her over until a social services position opened, and then she would call her personally to apply.

"I'll get Vernetta. She's the best at administering the injection," Sharlie relayed before exiting the dreary room with Sawyer in tow.

Injection? What the hell is she talking about now?

"Well that's thirty precious minutes of my valuable time I'll never get back. Just send the paperwork through interoffice mail and I'll sign it." Hilda stood and started to walk toward the exit.

"Wait. So you'll be fine if I offer a separation agreement?" Codee asked.

"Just do the damn paperwork so I can move forward." Hilda slammed the door, and Codee shook her head.

"That woman is the most despicable human being I've ever worked with. I really have to talk with Tim before things get out of hand." She gritted her teeth.

Sharlie shuffled back into the room a few minutes later as Codee was still trying to process what had just happened.

"Codee, are you okay?"

"This day just keeps getting stranger and stranger. I almost feel like Alice falling down the rabbit hole. Maybe I should pinch myself to make sure I'm not having some weird dream."

"Sawyer has asked that you specifically spend the final moments with her. I know this is hard for you, but I'd probably want you to be with me too." Sharlie wouldn't meet Codee's eyes.

12

"Of course. I always walk them out the door and make sure I've answered all their questions. I don't care what Hilda wants, I'm offering Sawyer a separation agreement, and the minute a social services position comes open, I want you to let me know. I plan on calling her personally."

Sharlie scrunched up her face in confusion. "I don't know what you're talking about. I really think you need to get your head checked out, because you keep saying strange things. But Sawyer needs you right now, so I suppose that has to take precedence."

"Okay, lead the way, and I can take care of the documentation later." Codee pushed herself up with her good hand and followed Sharlie out the door.

Hilda was waiting just outside wearing a satisfied, contemptuous grin.

†

Sawyer sat quietly in the metal chair. She wasn't afraid of dying, but she was disappointed she hadn't been able to follow through on her plans to get Codee involved with the mission of her rebel group. They needed an HR executive on their team, and she was perfect for the job. She had the right personality to make a difference, and Sawyer knew the engaging professional was sympathetic to their cause.

Sawyer remembered the first time she'd seen Codee, in orientation. She'd been dead on her feet after a long shift in the admitting department, but didn't have any trouble at all staying awake for the half-day session. Not only was the HR leader a beautiful woman, but something in her intelligent, gray eyes touched Sawyer. They sparkled with excitement as she wove her gripping yarns, yet Codee had a sadness beneath the twinkle that not many people unearthed. It showed through on the other occasions when Sawyer ran into the magnetic woman. Codee always took the time to speak with her, even though their conversations never penetrated the wall of polite, inane small talk.

The beautiful woman was exactly Sawyer's type, and she'd chastised herself on more than one occasion when she'd allowed her mind to drift, wondering what weaving her hands through Codee's thick, blonde hair, which had just a hint of red streaked throughout, would feel like. Normally women lost that strawberry-blonde color as they matured into adulthood, but either Codee dyed her hair, or she was one of those rare individuals who retained it. Sawyer knew the woman was out of reach, yet because it was common knowledge she was a lesbian, a relationship was remotely possible—of course, that was before the termination hearing.

Unfortunately, it was the end of the line for her, and Codee couldn't do much about it at this point. She wondered if her small part in the resistance had all been worth it. She decided it had. The baby had lived, and she could take that comforting thought with her to the other side. Dr. Smith knew the baby was undocumented. He was another sympathizer, but when confronted, he'd revealed his collaborators because he hadn't been willing to accept the consequences. She couldn't really blame him. He'd rushed to explain to her that he could do more good by touting his ignorance and continuing to save people the hospital would otherwise turn away. Far more workers were willing to ignore the law than anyone suspected. The rebel network was growing.

Vernetta entered the dreary room and looked nervous as her gaze seemed to shift around, never quite landing on Sawyer. She clearly felt sorry for her. She knew that administration always asked her to perform the termination because she was skilled at ensuring the injection didn't cause any unnecessary pain. Vernetta was a sympathizer as well but kept her role in the group well hidden. Sawyer needed to ensure no one blew her cover.

She only had a few minutes with Vernetta before Sharlie and Codee arrived for the final dispensation.

"Vernetta, look at me," Sawyer directed.

"Oh God, Sawyer, I don't know if things are going to work out. There's rumors that we're compromised, and if Sharlie stays in the room, I don't know if I can do this." Tears welled in Vernetta's eyes.

"You have to. We need you here continuing to work behind the scenes. I'm expendable. You're not." Sawyer touched her arm.

The creak of the door interrupted Sawyer, and she looked up to see Sharlie and Codee standing in the doorway, appearing guilty and confused, respectively. In the shadows she saw Hilda, who resembled a statue waiting in the wings to come to life when her prey least expected it.

"Vernetta, why are you here? I'm not sure giving Sawyer her flu shot right now is entirely appropriate. Besides, you're not the employee health nurse," Codee noted.

"Flu shot? What are you talking about? I'm here to administer the lethal injection."

"I'm sorry. I thought I just heard you say 'lethal injection.'" Codee chuckled. "Boy, I really need to get the wax out of my ears. It sounded like you're some kind of death-penalty executioner. I had a fall earlier, and things aren't firing quite right for me."

"I suppose that's a pretty good description of what they always ask me to do," Vernetta answered. The disgust in her voice was palatable.

Codee turned her head and looked at Sharlie. She immediately looked away, and her penetrating gaze landed on Sawyer. "She's not kidding, is she?"

Sharlie looked up and shook her head. Her expression was a mixture of confusion and compassion. "Vernetta administers most of the lethal injections after a termination hearing. I don't usually stay. I don't have the stomach for it."

Sharlie turned and nearly ran out of the room, covering her mouth. She slammed the door shut on her way out, and Sawyer heard the rumbling of voices echo down the hallway. She imagined Hilda gloating all the way back to her office with Sharlie in tow.

"Look, I don't know what the hell is going on, but there is no way I'm going to authorize a lethal injection. Vernetta, you go back to your unit and let me talk with Sawyer." Codee leveled Vernetta with a look that left no room for misinterpretation.

Sawyer was mildly impressed with Codee's command of the room, but wondered what cost to her personally, her directive might bring. "You can't, Codee, they'll find out and then you'll be terminated."

"Codee, we don't have much time. I don't know what's going on with you, but the arrangements are the same as always. The morgue driver is part of the network. She'll help us again." Vernetta turned her gaze to Sawyer. "All we need to do is get a stretcher and transport you out of here. We can get Dr. Smith to verify that I administered the injection and you expired without complication. He owes you and he's done this before for us. Codee, you'll verify that I did my job. You mentioned the last time that we don't need to worry about Sharlie. Is that still true? She looked awfully guilty just now."

"Honestly I don't know anything at this moment. This is like one big nightmare, but I'll do whatever I need to do. We are getting out of here—alive. I have a place I can take Sawyer, but I might need a doctor to check out my head, because nothing makes sense to me. I think I have a fracture in my arm as well, but that is the least of our worries. I'm in, and you can explain everything to me later." Codee turned her penetrating gaze back to Sawyer.

"I don't think it's wise for you to get personally involved." Vernetta shifted her feet, appearing nervous. "I've been hearing rumors a slimy little mole is ratting us all out. Something feels different lately."

"All the more reason for me to do this. I'm taking Sawyer to my cabin in the woods, and that's final. I just need to get a few things at my house first. Do you think you can drive my car and meet us there? It's the only Prius in the management parking lot...." Codee rattled off the address, dug into her coat pocket, retrieved a set of keys, and tossed them to Vernetta.

"Okay, we don't have time to argue. I'll get the stretcher." Vernetta spun on her heel and exited.

Codee looked dazed, but Sawyer was too surprised at the turn of events to say anything. She wasn't sure whom to trust, but it seemed like everyone except Sharlie and Hilda were on her side.

When Vernetta came back with the stretcher, Sawyer crawled under the sheet and they wheeled her through the back hallway to the hearse waiting in the circular drive. Since they made it to the transport vehicle without incident, Sawyer assumed no one was paying attention to their mad dash to freedom. Thank goodness most people were creeped out by death and tended to avert their eyes whenever the funeral home sent the morgue driver for a pickup. She wondered when they would stop bothering to make a show of treating the bodies with respect and begin to simply dump them in an open pit.

Chapter Two

Codee was rubbing the back of her head as the long, black vehicle skidded to a stop in front of her house. She was a little unsteady on her feet when she opened the door and met Sawyer's concerned gaze as she climbed out of the back. The converted station wagon sped away as soon as the women stepped onto the pavement.

"Are you okay?" Sawyer asked.

"I'm fine. Let's get inside, and we can talk while I pack up a few things we'll probably need."

Sawyer appeared at her side and put a steadying hand on her uninjured arm. It wasn't an entirely unwelcome touch, so Codee let her provide that small amount of physical support.

She walked carefully to the back door and picked up the small rock with her extra house key hidden inside. When she glanced at the house next door that shared a driveway with her home, the light in the living room turned on, and a twitch of the blinds revealed that Erma had taken note of the strange vehicle dropping off her and Sawyer.

"I think your neighbor is watching." Sawyer frowned. "Codee, you should have let the network take care of things. Why didn't you?"

"I don't know. Instinct, I guess. It just seemed as if this was the right thing to do. I can't explain my reasoning. I just know it was the only answer."

Codee felt her cell phone buzz and pulled it from her jacket pocket. When she read the message, the hand holding it began to shake.

Compromised. Gone underground. Watch your back. Car not coming, will try to send help. V

"I think our timeline just got cut in half. Come on. You'll need to help me pull together a few things."

"Is Vernetta okay?"

"I think so. She mentioned going underground and that she would try to send help, but I think we're on our own." Codee shoved the key into the lock and pushed the back door open, gesturing for Sawyer to enter.

Normally she would worry about the state of her home when visitors came calling, but that was definitely the least of her worries now. The extra pieces of mail strewn over her kitchen counter and an afghan haphazardly crumpled on the couch where she'd left it before going to bed last night gave her home a lived-in look.

Codee hurried to the master bedroom and began pulling warm clothes from her drawers like a madwoman. She pointed to the closed door on the left that led to the master bathroom. "The walk-in closet is attached to the bathroom. Can you please grab the large backpack propped up in the corner?"

Sawyer nodded.

Ding-dong ding-dong

"Shit." Codee hurried to the blinds and tried to peek out to see who was at the door.

Sawyer appeared by her side. "Someone you know?"

"It's Erma, my next door neighbor. She's harmless and a good friend."

Sawyer raised her eyebrow but didn't say anything.

"I've got to answer. She knows I'm home."

Codee rounded the corner to open her front door.

Erma was wide-eyed, and her gray, wiry hair sprung out in every direction as if she'd been running her hands through it nervously.

"I saw a peacekeeper with Sharlie. They swung by your house about five minutes ago. I came out and told them you weren't home yet. I lied and said you'd asked me to meet you in town at the bistro because you needed my help, and that I'd said I couldn't get involved. I let him believe you were meeting someone else there. Sharlie looked scared, but I don't think she led them here. You need to leave soon, Codee. I think they know. Is that young woman you're with one of the people you've saved?"

This new world she'd been thrust into didn't make sense, but she had zero hesitation about trusting Erma, whom she regarded as a surrogate mother—of that she was certain. *Peacekeeper*, she wondered. The term sounded like something right out of *The Hunger Games*. She loved those books, but she wasn't at all interested in living in a world that even remotely resembled that dystopian society. She'd ask Sawyer about the peacekeepers later when they had more time.

Codee absently nodded.

"I thought so. I'll get the motorcycle you hid in my garage. Hurry, you probably have less than fifteen minutes. I'll get ahold of the network and see what they can do to get supplies to you. Cabin, right?" Erma scurried over the lawn to the shared driveway and her own garage.

"I don't know how everyone knows all of this about me, but yes, I suppose I'll need every bit of help I can get,"

Codee muttered before realizing Erma was already out of earshot. She sighed.

Sawyer appeared next to her again as if by magic and touched Codee on the shoulder. "I saw the already packed bags that I presume you attach to a motorcycle. It's got cash, a gun, warm clothes, and two pairs of boots sitting beside it. I think you may have anticipated something like this happening. I don't think we need to try to pack anything else. Time to go, Codee."

"I hope one of those pairs of boots fit you."

"They do." Sawyer pointed to her feet and handed her the other pair that she'd been dangling from one hand.

Codee noticed Sawyer had on a pair of leather pants and a heavy leather jacket. Slung over her other arm was another pair of leather pants, a thick sweatshirt, and a Kevlar motorcycle jacket. She set down the riding gear on the floor.

Codee kicked off her work shoes and pulled the leather garb over her dress pants, ignoring the twinge of pain in her arm. She was thankful the leathers were a size or two bigger than she normally wore so she didn't have to change in front of Sawyer. However, when she lowered herself to the floor, using both arms, she grimaced in pain as the likely fracture once again made itself known. "Damn."

"Here, let me help you. I've noticed how protective you are of your left arm." Sawyer pulled out a pair of heavy wool socks from her jacket pocket and began to gently tug them over Codee's thin dress socks.

Codee looked into Sawyer's moss-green eyes and saw nothing but compassion and kindness. She felt nauseous thinking about what had almost happened. She needed everything to return to normal so she could do what she'd always done and smooth the rough waters, making the job-termination experience less devastating to the frightened employees. However, for the time being, that wasn't possible, and somehow she was already deeply embroiled in this underground organization they referred to as "the network."

Codee shifted her attention to her favorite neighbor when she heard her cough. *When did she return, and did she just let herself in?*

"Codee, please, you have to hurry. They'll be back soon. I hope that metal monstrosity of yours starts right up. I didn't realize how heavy it was. Maybe you can meet me halfway as soon as you put the rest of your gear on. These old bones aren't as strong as they used to be. It might take me a bit of time to push that heavy bike up the drive." Erma turned and scurried away, shutting the front door on her way out.

Another sharp pain traveled down her arm as she gingerly grabbed for the bulky jacket and started to put it on. Her grimace wasn't lost on Sawyer, who slipped Codee's right foot into the boot and laced it up.

"Any chance you know how to drive a motorcycle? I'm afraid my left arm is going to be a problem."

"It's been a while, but yes, I think I can manage. It's going to be a very chilly ride, but I suppose that's preferable to the heat in the depths of hell." Sawyer grinned.

The dark humor lifted the heaviness of their situation.

"Somehow, I don't think you'll ever be heading to hell."

"Well, that's a very different perspective from President Trison's."

"I know I've got a lot of catching up to do, but I just can't imagine David Trison won the candidacy for the Patriot Party, much less weaseled his way into the presidency."

Concerned green eyes bored into Codee. "You really have lost your memory."

Sawyer finished lacing up the left boot, stood, and pulled Codee to her feet by her good arm.

22

"A slip on the ice and a bonk on the head will do that to a person."

Sawyer grabbed the bulging gear and led the way out the door.

Codee turned back to look at her house and wondered if she'd ever be able to return. Before walking out the door, she left her cell phone on the table where she usually tossed her keys when she came home every night. Instinctively she wondered about the so-called peacekeepers' ability to track her via GPS. She hoped Vernetta was smart enough to use a burner phone and briefly considered smashing it to try to remove any discovery of the text message, but Codee didn't believe simply smashing it would do the trick anyway.

The two fugitives met Erma in the middle of the driveway as she huffed and puffed, struggling to wheel a Harley-Davidson Fatboy down the drive. Two shiny, black helmets dangled on the front handlebars.

Sawyer secured the travel bags to the back of the bike and then grabbed the helmets and handed one to Codee, who struggled to pull it over her head, leaving the shield pushed up. After helping Codee secure her helmet, Sawyer jerked the protective gear onto her own head.

"Shit, I gave my whole set of keys to Vernetta. I don't have keys to the bike," Codee lamented.

Erma furrowed her brow and held up a set of keys. "You gave these to me three months ago and told me to keep them in case you needed to scoot out of here real quick someday. I'd say today is that day."

Sawyer stepped forward and took them from her. "Codee hurt her arm and has a nasty bump on her head from a slip on the ice. I'll be driving the monstrosity. Thank you for helping us. I hope you won't get into trouble because of it. I don't think I could live with myself if they came after you." Sawyer straddled the Harley, pushed the key into the ignition, and took hold of the handlebars.

Erma waved her hand. "I'm an old woman and not afraid of that prick Trison and his so-called peacekeepers. They're all a bunch of bullies who haven't learned the lessons of history. We continue to make the same mistakes. I'll not support that type of world and be proud to die fighting for something better."

Codee leaned over and kissed the old woman's cheek. "I may not remember everything, but I do remember you, old woman, and that serious potty mouth of yours. Although I have to agree that David Trison is the biggest prick our country has ever known."

Sawyer turned the key, pushed the throttle forward, and Codee heard the distinctive roar of the Harley's engine. It sounded strong.

Codee quickly climbed on behind Sawyer. The night air was going to get frosty on the way over to the cabin, and her hands were particularly vulnerable to the cold. She was glad Sawyer had found two pairs of motorcycle gloves as she easily pulled on her left glove with her uninjured right hand and used her teeth to secure the other on her right hand. She flipped her shield down and took a deep breath as she snaked her right arm around Sawyer's middle and gently laid her left arm around Sawyer's other side. She would have to hold on tight with her right side and hope the jarring vibrations wouldn't cause her too much pain.

Erma yelled over the loud engine, "Go, I'll try to get word to you."

Sawyer pushed her own shield down over her face, shoved her hands into the thick, insulated leather gloves, and asked, "Are you ready?"

"As I'll ever be. Just head out and I'll guide you where to go."

Sawyer turned her head and called out, "Are you sure about this? There's no turning back now."

"I don't understand everything yet, but I couldn't be surer than if I was walking down the aisle marrying the woman of my dreams."

†

Sawyer had been chilly before, but this was an entirely new experience. Never had she felt the wind in her face on a cold winter's day while traveling fifty miles an hour down a winding road on her way into the mountains. The protective shield barely made a difference as the bitter temperature somehow snaked inside. The patches of snow and ice made their escape particularly harrowing as she tried to avoid the slick areas. She didn't think Codee normally traveled by motorcycle in the winter, but then all the gear was neatly stacked by the travel bags. Sawyer suspected Codee had planned for this contingency because she knew circumstances would force her to make a life-changing decision.

The frigid air seemed to ignore the heavy layers of clothing as it seeped into her core and left her feeling like a giant ice cube. Her entire body felt numb. If she didn't get hypothermia on this trip, she didn't think she ever would. However, none of this was as concerning as the passenger snuggled behind her who was risking her life and was undoubtedly equally chilled to the bone.

Sawyer imagined the cabin had a fireplace and when they arrived they'd get it started and return their body temperature to normal. The vision of a crackling fire helped to distract her from the mind-numbing cold and focus on the instructions she had to strain to hear over the roar of the Harley's engine.

After an hour and a half, Codee directed Sawyer to turn onto an old logging road, and she struggled to navigate the slippery path. When the lane became too treacherous to continue, she pulled over to the side and tried to turn her head while she planted her booted foot in the layer of snow.

"How much farther is your cabin? I don't think these tires were made for snow and ice."

"It's not too much farther. Maybe a quarter of a mile, and then the turnoff to my cabin is another half a mile or so."

"Okay, but don't blame me if we both land on the side of the road and leave a couple of snow angels as proof we made it this far."

"I trust you." Codee tightened her grasp.

Sawyer eased back onto the road and kept her legs out in case she needed to steady the bike. Fortunately, the snow-pack on the ground had lessened, but that didn't make it any less slippery.

Enormous evergreens camouflaged the small log cabin. Sawyer was sure that if someone didn't know where to turn, they would never find the place. She noticed the stone chimney and breathed a sigh of relief that they would be able to quickly build a fire and thaw their aching bodies. She hoped some amount of cut wood was already stacked inside.

Sawyer's foot broke through the thin layer of snow, landed on frozen ground, and she was able to engage the kickstand so it burrowed into the soil and was stable enough to get off.

She waited until Codee climbed off the bike before she dismounted. She flipped up her face shield and was glad she didn't have to shout. Sawyer's nature didn't include raising her voice, even if the reason was to speak loud enough so a person could hear her over blaring music or deafening machinery. This was the primary reason she never went to bars—the atmosphere didn't suit her personality.

"Your cabin is beautiful. I don't even have the words to express how grateful I am that you've taken me to a place I imagine is a special refuge for you."

Codee smiled. "Something tells me I won't ever regret this decision. Come on, I don't know about you, but I'd rather not have someone mistake me for a human Popsicle. I think I left some wood by the fireplace. Once we have a fire going, the place should heat up relatively quickly. We can get the bags later."

†

Stomping her feet, Codee opened the door to the cabin and stepped inside. Sawyer followed, pulling off her gloves and quickly removed her boots so she wouldn't track in the wet snow and ruin the beautiful wood floor.

She looked to her right and saw Codee's gloves sticking out of her pocket as she undid the laces on her boots. Sawyer noticed her grimace as she attempted to pull off her footwear. Quickly dropping to her knees, she wrapped one hand around each calf as she gently removed Codee's boots. She shook her head in exasperation, wishing her savior had cared more about her injured arm than a few drops of water on the precious floor.

"Thanks."

"Once we get settled, I think I should take a look at that arm and the lump on the back of your head. Why don't you relax while I get the fire going? Are there matches and paper near the fireplace?"

"Yeah, everything should be right there—kindling, newspaper, and matches. I'd get myself some ice for my head and arm, but the thought of putting anything cold next to any part of my body right now is definitely not appealing." Codee shuddered.

As Codee sat down in the cozy recliner with the afghan lying over the back, Sawyer thought she heard her teeth chattering.

Codee wrapped her arms around her body and she looked so vulnerable. Sawyer wanted to envelop her in a hug and tell her everything would be all right, but she knew that was most likely a lie.

When the fire roared to life and Sawyer heard the crackle of the dry timber, she walked over to Codee and offered her hand.

Wordlessly she placed her small hand inside Sawyer's and walked with her over to the fire. They sat on the cold stone that was quickly heating up, and Sawyer wrapped her arm around the vulnerable looking woman, bringing her in close as they soaked up the warmth from the blaze.

"Who else knows about this cabin?" Sawyer broke the silence.

"Sharlie knows I have a cabin and the general vicinity, but not the exact spot. Actually most of my staff know I have a cabin but don't know where it's located. I just purchased it last year, so the only person who's been here is Erma."

Sawyer nodded. "You know you can't go back to your house or your job now and I'm the reason. They'll hunt you as a traitor, and you'll probably be forced to run for the rest of your life, depending on the generosity of the network. Why would you do that?"

The question hung heavily in the air, floating dangerously above the two women. It was a good question.

"It was the right thing to do, and I don't think I could have lived with myself if I hadn't brought you to a safe place. It was the only option that crossed my mind."

Codee blinked and looked again into Sawyer's compelling, wise, green eyes. It felt like she was looking into the peacefulness of nature made manifest.

"I suppose it's like those ethical questions from college that help students ferret out where their values lie. You know, the one where you have to decide who to save, one person or many. Yet unlike in those false situations, you don't know if that one person is likely to change the world and ultimately end up saving many more people. Somehow, there was a little voice telling me that I needed to be the one to save you because you would be the one to spark a change in a world I frankly don't remember or understand." Codee shrugged as if what she had done wasn't a big deal.

"Boy, that fireplace certainly puts out a lot of heat. I think it's about time I started peeling off all these clothes you let me borrow." Sawyer grinned.

She unzipped her jacket, slipped it off, and set it to the side. The leather pants she'd worn over her dress pants came off next.

Codee decided to follow her lead but struggled with removing her own winter gear as her sore arm reminded her of the earlier accident when she'd slipped on the ice.

Sawyer was quick to help her remove her jacket and the warm leather pants. Although Codee knew the beautiful woman hadn't intended the gesture as a caress, her gentle hands sparked a moment of arousal that surprised her despite acknowledging to herself that she was attracted to Sawyer.

She hadn't been with another woman after the sting of her last relationship three years ago. Five years was a long time to spend with someone without feeling like the person was more than a pleasant companion. Her ex had decided the woman she'd met one afternoon at an art gallery was her true soulmate, and after a weekend with the budding artist, Codee's partner announced she was moving out the next day.

To say she was shocked was a colossal understatement, but if she were honest with herself, she'd admit she was relieved the relationship had finally ended.

Since that time, Codee had buried herself in her work and a steady diet of romance novels. She wanted to read about everyone else who got their happily ever after, even if that would never be her reality. Thankfully same-sex marriage wasn't legal at the time of her breakup, so neither of them were forced to navigate a complicated set of legal dissolutions. She was sure she would have avoided marriage anyway, even if marriage was an option.

Codee shook her head in an attempt to remove the unpleasant memories, and once again saw Sawyer's concerned eyes resting on her. She felt as if Sawyer were looking into her core and noticing every little nuance of her life.

"Will you be okay if I retrieve the bags? I think what you packed might answer a few of your questions. It's clear to me these were your to-go bags and somehow you knew the time would come when you'd be forced to make a hasty exit. I had my own exit plan, but I decided to face my fate without putting you at risk. If I'd not shown up for the hearing, they would have gone after you. I couldn't risk that."

Sawyer's words shook Codee. This person, whom she barely knew, was prepared to risk her own life over the mere possibility she would suffer. She wanted to explore what the young woman had just revealed, but too many other questions took precedence.

"I have a lot of questions I hope you'll be able to answer."

Sawyer grabbed the jacket and put it back on as she stood. "As soon as I get those bags, I'll do the best I can to answer whatever questions you have."

She looked back over her shoulder and smiled as she exited the cabin. Codee felt the warmth of her smile even more than the fire. After Sawyer left to retrieve the bags, she decided to see what she'd left in the pantry from the last time she'd visited. They would need food, and she wasn't sure how long they'd be able to stay in the relative safety of her cabin.

As she opened the cabinets and pantry, she found she'd left the cabin fully stocked with hundreds of cans and jars of food, as well as dried foods and staples such as rice and pasta. Later she'd check out the freezer located in the utility room. She hoped it was full of meat that would last for a long time while they considered their options. Her memory was still very flawed as she tried to remember why she would have left the cabin so fully stocked. When she'd blurted out that she would take Sawyer to her cabin, she must have known in the back of her mind that this would be the most logical place to hide out, but she simply couldn't remember anything, including this strange new world that seemed to permeate the cracks like an insidious poison.

It was as if someone had altered her memory with a scalpel, removing only the parts related to the strange policies of the new administration. Every other memory of her life remained intact. As soon as Sawyer returned, Codee needed to go through the bags and then ask her questions. It was time for her to make sense of this living nightmare.

Chapter Three

Sawyer needed to establish some distance from Codee as she fought the strong pull toward her. She had always been the untouchable human resource executive who just happened to be a very attractive woman. She wasn't exactly unfriendly, but she'd always given out a *don't cross the invisible barrier to my personal life* vibe.

The only time anyone got a glimpse of the person behind the professional curtain was when she'd presented at general orientation. Codee was funny and charming and told incredible stories about her experiences, both personal and professional, as she illustrated what a positive attitude and exceptional customer service looked like.

Sawyer wanted to be a part of this magnificent organization that touted people as its top priority. She'd believed every word Codee had said in that training seminar. But all too soon that bubble had burst and the hospital had a new admitting supervisor. Shortly after that, the executive orders had trickled down to every organization across the country, with the special order for disparate treatment laid upon all healthcare organizations. She was surprised she'd lasted as long as she had before the inevitable termination hearing. She was shocked to learn the HR professional was already an integral part of the network.

She supposed grunts in the organization, like her, weren't necessarily privy to knowing the identities of the other members. Knowing whom to trust was difficult, and she suspected the leaders didn't want the cover of any of their major players blown. Too late for that now, because someone had unmasked Vernetta and Codee, but that person certainly wasn't her.

When the HR executive went to the espresso stand every day to get her double vanilla latte, she'd always made a point of saying hello and smiling warmly at Sawyer, but that didn't mean Sawyer had a special relationship with the enigmatic leader. However, that never stopped her from feeling all warm inside whenever Codee took notice of her. Now due to circumstances neither one of them had ever expected, they were together in a remote cabin, trying to figure out how to survive in this crazy world.

Sawyer took a deep breath before entering the cabin with the stuffed bags and braced herself to fight her increasing attraction for the woman.

Codee was standing in front of the pantry as if mesmerized by its contents. A healthy blaze lit the fireplace, and the flames that licked against the dry logs had already made the cabin toasty.

As she set the bags on the floor in the small living room, Sawyer noticed two large pillows on the cream, ultrasuede couch. She grabbed them and placed them in front of the fire and next to the saddlebags, then sat on one. She shrugged out of her heavy leather jacket, laid it gently on the floor, and when Codee turned around, she patted the second pillow, inviting her to sit.

"Let's see how organized you were. Maybe you had the foresight to pack lots of chocolate," Sawyer joked. "At least if we're discovered, we'll exit this world fat and happy."

Codee smiled as she walked over, and Sawyer hoped she was comfortable as she sat on one of the large pillows. "Don't worry, even if there aren't some tempting sweets in the bags, the cupboards are stocked, and I think I saw a few treats nestled among the food staples."

Sawyer began unzipping the pockets of one of the saddlebags and pulled out several heavy sweatshirts, jeans, socks, underwear, sweatpants, and wool pullovers. As she dug deeper and exposed some of the other zippered compartments, she found several wads of cash, a Glock 17, several boxes of ammunition, a swiss army knife, a Mylar emergency blanket, water purification tablets, waterproof matches, Cyalume green-light sticks, and a premium first aid kit.

"Wow, you weren't messing around when you packed this," Sawyer exclaimed. "A tent and a few sleeping bags and we'd be set for camping out in the woods, although I'm grateful for this cozy cabin for however long we're able to stay here."

"I don't remember packing anything. I remember having a motorcycle and even purchasing the saddlebags to attach to my baby, but none of the rest of those things look familiar to me. I don't even know how to shoot a gun," Codee whispered.

"Fortunately this Glock is one of the easiest handguns to use." Sawyer picked up the gun and examined it.

Codee raised her eyebrow. "You don't seem the type to own a handgun."

"That's pretty intuitive of you to notice. Before all the changes in the world, I was adamantly opposed, but life has a way of teaching harsh lessons. I'm not the same person

I was before President Trison took office. If I had to protect you from harm, I could shoot another person and not feel one shred of guilt. This is a brand-new world, and I'm not afraid of fighting for what I know is right."

"I'm not challenging you or passing any judgment. I've just always thought you leaned more toward the turn-the-other-cheek camp. No matter how much bravado you try to put out there, your gentle spirit shines through." Codee leaned forward and picked up the swiss army knife, raising her eyebrow. "I'm definitely not the hardy, camping type, and I certainly don't remember purchasing this thing. This looks like it could also function as a lethal weapon."

"I've learned there are those who cannot protect themselves, and innocent children are worth fighting for. I'll never cave in and agree to turn away care to the poor or people who happen to have been born in another country. I don't think we're winning with passive resistance or subterfuge. The time has come for a more direct approach, and I'm not afraid to die for my beliefs." Sawyer set the gun down and crossed her arms over her chest.

"The last I remember, David Trison was making a bid to represent the Patriot Party in the 2016 election. The debates were almost a joke, and some of the outrageous things he said led me to believe he didn't have a snowball's chance in hell to win his party's nomination, much less the presidency. Clearly I've lost a major piece of my life. I need you to fill me in."

Sawyer saw the almost pleading look in Codee's eyes and felt a considerable amount of empathy for her. She could understand how confused Codee might be and if she hadn't experienced the whole thing first-hand, she would think she was in some kind of alternate universe too.

"Probably the most impactful event and what set up the US for the draconian policies of the new administration was the worst stock market crash since the Great Depression—only this time it happened on a Monday. The conservative right dubbed it Malfunction Monday. David Trison used this to his advantage and blamed the previous administration's mishandling of the financial sector, immigration, healthcare expenditures, and in general what he called 'outrageous social policies leading to the demise of this great nation,'" Sawyer began.

"Okay, I get that frightened people will grab at straws to attempt to make sense of something so overwhelming they don't know where to turn, but killing citizens that don't perform well in their particular job? That's as crazy as Hitler and the Holocaust."

"The unemployment rate jumped to 24.6 percent in less than three months. The highest rate of unemployment in US history was 23.6 percent in 1932. It took nearly three years to get there after the stock market crash of the Depression, so you can imagine what a panicked state we were in. David Trison offered a solution—a very deadly solution." Sawyer leaned back and propped herself up using her arms. She closed her eyes for a few seconds, gaining her composure.

"It was mass chaos, and his platform caught fire. The masses didn't care how Trison proposed to fix things, they just wanted their comfortable lives back, and if that meant we exterminated hundreds of thousands of people, so be it. Of course, many of the illegal immigrants were the first to go. Without proper healthcare, most left on their own, and the ones that remained have it far worse here than in Mexico. Trison is as masterful a speaker as Hitler, and mob mentality is alive and well in the US." Sawyer sat up and crossed her legs into the lotus position.

"So what exactly are these executive orders I've heard people refer to?"

"I can't quote the exact wording, but essentially he ordered that employers with more than fifty employees must terminate any worker who is not productive or breaks company policy as defined by that employer."

"But that's barbaric. What the hell? It sounds like we're back in the Dark Ages."

Sawyer nodded. "His other executive order is that all healthcare organizations must deny services to anyone who doesn't have insurance or who isn't a legal United States citizen. Regrettably the very institutions that provided care to the sick, poor, and elderly were the ones that terminated the most people. A final order blocked treatment for women needing reproductive care involving abortions or removing a dead fetus even if they've miscarried."

"And no one protested." Codee shook her head.

"Yes, many did. As you can well imagine, numerous workers ignored his second executive order. Trison's newly formed peacekeepers jumped right on hospitals and clinics, and when they began adhering to 'the Termination Law,' the floodgates opened for every business to follow, and the for-profit Fortune 500 companies, who already had ruthless CEOs at the helm, seized on to the new laws and never looked back. Lawsuits against unlawful terminations are extinct now."

Codee's stomach rumbled and the loud reverberation permeated the brief silence in the cabin when Sawyer paused. "Are you getting hungry yet?"

"I could eat."

Codee started to rise, but Sawyer waved her off. "Why don't you let me rustle up some dinner? I can fill in more details while we eat. I haven't forgotten about your arm or your head either. You may want to raid that first aid kit. The sooner you have full use of your arm and less of a headache, the better. We'll need both your brains and your brawn to survive."

"Thanks. My head is starting to cause a bit of a distraction. I saw some pasta and several jars of red sauce in the pantry. That should be relatively easy to fix." Codee grimaced as she picked up the gun and stuffed it back in the bag.

"I may not be a culinary master, but I think I can manage to heat up some sauce and boil a few noodles." Sawyer smiled.

†

Codee opened the large first aid kit and found the bottle of Tylenol. She shook three tablets into her palm, and before she could stand to go to the kitchen for some water, Sawyer walked back into the room and handed her an open bottle. She was glad Sawyer had discovered her stash of bottled water because the stuff from the spigot had an unpleasant metallic taste that always made her wonder if it was safe to drink. She smiled gratefully at the woman who seemed to anticipate her needs and wondered if Sawyer had anyone special to care for and dote on. She realized then she wanted to be that special person in Sawyer's life, but recent events pushed those thoughts to the back of her mind. There was a whole new set of rules to life and ultimately survival, and she needed to learn them quickly or she wouldn't be around long enough to consider sharing her life with anyone, much less this improbable candidate.

She watched as Sawyer methodically retrieved the ingredients for the simple meal. She proceeded to open multiple drawers and then pulled out two pots to cook the pasta and sauce. The cabin didn't have a lot of amenities, but it did contain the basics. Sawyer fired up the propane stove and leaned against the counter. She was staring off into space, and Codee wondered what was going through that beautiful mind of hers.

"Tell me about this network. It sounds like I'm connected, but I can't remember how or what to do to contact them should we need them. Vernetta texted me a warning about watching my back. I left my phone at home, so that won't be an option even if I knew who to call. I did have that foresight, since I imagine they can track us through GPS. Maybe I should have destroyed the phone. I would feel sick if something happened to Vernetta."

"Don't worry about Vernetta, I doubt she used a phone that might be tracked, and your instincts were spot-on. I'm sure that's the first thing they'll do once they confirm we've fled. At first, the phone companies refused to give the government access to the passcodes and locking mechanisms to protect privacy, but after a few very public employee terminations for refusing to follow that executive order, no one was willing to take a chance and they all caved." Sawyer tossed the noodles into the boiling water.

"I have everything but the kitchen sink in the travel pack. Surely I have something to help me communicate with this *network*." Codee started to unzip pockets and search the bags, looking for something that might be a means of contact. Tucked in a corner in one of the hidden pockets, she found a basic cell phone.

She pressed the Power button, and the phone came to life. Activating the Menu button on the old-style phone, she found only one number on the display and surmised this was the contact number. She looked up and met intelligent, green eyes.

"It looks like you may have found the solution to a means of contacting the network. That's probably the number you need." Sawyer turned her gaze back to the two pots, which now had steam rising from them. She stirred the noo-dles first, then stuck the large spoon into the sauce. "Dinner is almost ready."

"I think I can handle setting the table." Codee pushed up from her sitting position, remembering to use her legs and right hand only. She didn't bother to put away any of the survival supplies she and Sawyer had uncovered and that she had apparently tucked away in the travel bags. She'd worry about that later. She set the "go" phone on the side table next to the couch.

She opened the cabinets and drawers, searching for the plates, placemats, and napkins. After finding the place settings for two, she gathered them in her hands. Once the items were deposited on the counter, she began searching for silverware. When Codee brushed closely against Sawyer, a hint of Sawyer's clean citrus smell invaded her senses.

Sawyer smiled when Codee placed her hand on Saw-yer's waist as she navigated around the compact, muscular body in the tight kitchen space. The dance was comfortable, and Codee couldn't remember feeling this at ease with her ex when they prepared dinner. Mostly her ex had pushed her out of the kitchen, complaining she was just in the way. Since her ex left, cooking wasn't something she ever engaged in because what was the point? Preparing a meal for one was never worth the effort. She imagined that almost everyone would shake their heads at the contents of her pantry and re-frigerator at home. That was why she was shocked she'd managed to somehow fully stock her cabin with at least twenty times more food here than she had at home. She was sure of that.

"You've got a pensive expression," Sawyer noted.

"I was just marveling at how I managed to make sure there's enough food to feed us for months at this cabin, but my refrigerator at home probably has a tomato, a jar of

Kalamata olives, and feta cheese. That's it, nothing else. They huddle together on one shelf in all their loneliness. I don't even have a normal person's requisite condiments."

A crease formed between Sawyer's eyebrows. "You're worse than any bachelor I've ever known."

"I know. Pathetic, huh? I don't like cooking for one."

"How about cooking for two?"

Codee nodded. "I used to be a fairly decent cook. My ex was a chef. She did most of the cooking."

Sawyer lifted one eyebrow. "'She'? 'Ex'?"

"Oh I'm sorry, I thought everyone knew I'm a lesbian. I don't hide it, but I also don't flaunt my personal life. Well…didn't flaunt it—past tense. I don't have a personal life right now."

"I did know and wondered how you managed to avoid the more emboldened staff spewing their special brand of hate. I guess that's another thing you've forgotten that President Trison changed. We've taken a huge step back regarding civil rights. It's no longer acceptable to be out and proud. Somehow, the bastard got the Supreme Court decision overturned. No more legal gay marriage. Employers have free rein to fire gay men, lesbians, bisexuals, and transgender people. States and cities aren't allowed to pass their own antidiscrimination laws because it's not in the best interest of…" Sawyer made air quotes "…strong family values." She sighed. "We've slid all the way down that slippery slope—at least fifty years of progress up in a puff of smoke, with more egregious policies just around the corner."

"I think I want to go back to sleep and wake up from this nightmare. I don't understand how something this inconceivable happened. It just doesn't seem possible."

"Honestly I think part of the reason I was on Hilda's radar is because she suspected my sexuality. I never broadcast it or anything, but I think she could tell. I refused to play the game and start dating some guy just to throw people off my trail. Not dating is all it takes to accuse someone. So far they haven't decided to execute homosexuals, but I suspect it's only a matter of time. The radical conservatives are licking their lips in anticipation."

"What does the rest of the world think about our new direction?"

"They think we're nuts, but so far no one is willing to blatantly oppose his policies. However, there are rumblings that Canada and some of the more enlightened European nations are preparing to take military action against the US. Of course, we only get news reports that Trison's tightly controlled media has carefully censored." Sawyer turned off the burner heating the sauce and then picked up the large pot with the noodles. After pouring the scalding water into the sink where the strainer sat, she continued, "The rumors have only served to embolden Trison, and he's made some very outrageous threats to the opposition, should it surface."

Codee rummaged around the drawers until she found the plastic pasta-straining spoon. She handed it to Sawyer, who stood over the sink as the steam from the newly strained noodles rose from it. "Maybe we should all move to Canada. Problem solved."

"Hmmm, a solution you and thousands of others came to before Canada cracked down. They have their own version of an immigration problem now. Personally I'd rather stay and fight the good fight." Sawyer dipped the spoon into the steaming noodles and scooped up a large serving that she deposited on the plate handed to her. "Are you a *bury every noodle under a heaping mound of sauce* kind of person, or a *small glob in the center* type?"

Codee laughed. "I don't think I've ever heard either one of those expressions. You must be some kind of pasta connoisseur. I'll offer a third alternative that is somewhere in

42

the middle. I'm a *leave a small, untouched-by-sauce ring around the outside* kinda gal. I'm going to forage in the pantry to see if I can find that awful grated parmesan in the green container. Regardless of the brand, it always has green on the packaging. I wonder why? Did all the parmesan manufacturers get together at some conference and say, 'Yeah let's go with green, that's a nice color'?"

Sawyer held her stomach as she bent over, laughing uncontrollably. Thankfully she'd managed to set the plate full of spaghetti on the table first. "I never noticed that, but God, I think you're right. It's a cheese conspiracy. We'll have to get the network to attack that right after we manage to overthrow the government."

"Aha. I found it." Codee stood in front of the open pantry and held the shaker up triumphantly. "I suppose conspiracy cheese is better than no cheese at all. Besides, I kinda grew up with this stuff."

"Your plate is already on the table. I'll be right there, so don't use up all the cheese." Sawyer dished up her plate and set it on the table at the same time Codee placed the generic grated cheese in the middle.

"Do we dare chance sharing a bottle of wine, or do you think we need our full faculties in case someone manages to find us out here?"

"I say we live on the edge and have some wine."

Codee pointed to the small wine rack on the counter. "Do you mind doing the honors?" She lifted her left arm. "I think I might be at a disadvantage, and I'd hate to get cork in the bottle."

"Oh damn, that's right. Maybe you shouldn't have any because we still don't know the extent of your head injury." Sawyer frowned.

"Oh no, if you get wine, I get wine. I'll take my chances." She pointed to the wine rack again. "Get busy. I think I saw a nice Sangiovese on the rack."

"I don't know whether to cheer or cringe at what you chose to focus on in the midst of breaking every law and running from the peacekeepers. The magic motorcycle bags have nearly every possible item we'll need, the cabin is generously stocked, and you don't remember a thing, but you took note of what kind of wines are on the rack." Sawyer raised her eyebrow.

Codee shrugged. "What can I say? Wine is important. You do like wine, don't you?"

"Well yeah, but it isn't necessarily the first thing I would have concentrated on as a fugitive." Sawyer pulled out a bottle and then pushed it back, repeating her search method until she pulled out the Sangiovese.

Codee nodded her approval when Sawyer turned the label in her direction.

"I suppose if I don't find a corkscrew in one of these drawers, I can always get that badass swiss army knife you packed." After opening the middle drawer, Sawyer pushed aside several utensils until she found and pulled the corkscrew out.

"I'll get the glasses. I hope you don't stand on ceremony, because I don't think the cabin has wineglasses. Will jelly glasses do?"

"It's the only way to drink red wine."

Codee thought Sawyer looked sexy leaning against the counter with a crooked grin on her face. The dress pants fit snugly over Sawyer's legs. The heat that traveled up her body reminded her of the snug fitting work clothes she still wore and moisture suddenly pooling in her silk undies. Dinner first, and then she could get comfortable in a pair of soft cotton sweatpants. She still had more questions, and Sawyer seemed a willing teacher.

Chapter Four

After dinner, Sawyer had retreated to the bathroom, mentioning shedding her uncomfortable dress pants and changing into something more pliable. When she came back into the main area of the cabin after changing, she noticed Codee had also made herself more comfortable in her own pair of sweatpants.

On her way to the bathroom, she'd noted the cabin only had one bedroom, and she took a deep breath to broach the sensitive topic. She didn't mind sleeping on the couch but worried about leaving the injured woman unattended while she slept, especially since she wasn't sure about the seriousness of the knock on her head. Since Codee couldn't remember a great deal about this year's dramatic political events, Sawyer thought her concerns were more than valid.

"Um...I can take the couch. I noticed the cabin has only one bedroom. I'd like to assess the bump on your head, and if you don't mind, I'd like to check on you every couple of hours. I heard that's the protocol for head injuries. By the way, how's the arm doing? It looks a bit swollen."

Codee reached around to the back of her head and rubbed. "Arm's still a bit sore, and I'm sure the knot on the back of my head is giving my skull an unattractive shape. There go my plans to shave my head and sport the Sinéad O'Connor look. You have to have a nicely shaped head to pull it off."

Sawyer smiled and cocked her head. "I'll bet you could rock the bald look. Besides, it might go along with my newly formed impression of your rebel status. Not many people can manage to go without hair, but with your delicate face and beautiful features, I think it would work. I'll get the clippers."

Codee laughed. "Oh my, a woman who can play along with my demented sense of humor. Be still my heart." She winked while placing her hand over her heart.

"Are you warm enough now that I can strategically place a few ice packs on your head and arm? I promise to avoid doing anything kinky with the ice…for now. And yes, I'm flirting with you, because this cabin lacks the requisite board games, so a woman's got to get her jollies somehow."

"Well, my flirting is a little rusty and I have more holes in my memory than swiss cheese, so maybe we can rain-check any heavy-duty flirting, because you'll win hands down. Can we play the trivia game Fill in the Blanks?" Codee tucked her left leg under her bottom and bit her lower lip.

"I'm not familiar with that game."

Codee patted the space beside her on the couch. "That's the game where, after you set me up with some ice, you tell me more about the network and what we're likely to face in the future."

"Let me get the ice packs first."

Sawyer opened the freezer and surveyed the contents. Frozen peas were always a good choice, but she didn't find anything like that in the cabin's ice box. She pulled open a few drawers and found some freezer bags and dumped a healthy amount of ice into two of them. She made her way down the hallway and into the bathroom in search of a few hand towels to wrap around them.

"Frozen peas make a much better ice pack because they mold so well around an injured area, but I guess these will have to do," Sawyer said. After she had handed them to Codee, she sat down next to her and surveyed the beautiful woman, scrutinizing her for any sign of pain.

"Um, I didn't want to say anything, because it looked like you were on a mission, but I'll bet that first aid kit lying on the floor probably has a ready-made ice pack." Codee pointed to it.

Sawyer smacked her hand to her head. "God, I'm an idiot. I guess I'm not a very good rebel. I do know how to use a gun—my pop made sure of that. He was a hunter, a card-carrying NRA member, and a tree-hugging liberal." She held up her hand. "I know, they don't really go together, do they?"

"I guess the apple didn't fall far from the tree, because you are definitely an oxymoron. Social work is your true calling, yet you don't have any compunctions about fighting. I get the sense you can be fierce when protecting someone you love."

Sawyer tilted her head. "And you've surmised this from the short time we've interacted?"

"I'm in human resources, and we're paid to assess someone quickly. Usually I do it in an interview, but in general I pay attention to the little things, and it always gives me a complete and accurate picture of the person behind the mask. I have laser-like accuracy with first impressions."

"Hmmm, beautiful and intuitive. That's a wonderful combination." Sawyer pushed aside a lock of hair that had fallen over one of Codee's eyes. The blush that rose on her face was nearly impossible to ignore, and she had to do everything in her power not to capture Codee's inviting lips with her own.

Codee shifted, broke eye contact, and leaned back on the couch. She laid her head on the icepack she'd placed on the back of the couch while holding the other pack across her left arm.

"Tell me more about this network. Who's involved? How are they organized? Is there a central location for gathering? Goals? A leader?"

"Whoa. That's a lot of questions, and I don't know that I really have all the answers. We started out as a group of loosely organized passive objectors and then evolved into multiple geographic hubs. It's ironic that we resemble the military in our structure now. Of course we don't call ourselves generals or captains, but there are various levels of leadership."

"What level are you?" Codee lifted her head and the ice pack slid down behind her back. "Ooh, that is cold."

Sawyer reached behind Codee and gently removed it as she inched closer and wrapped her arm around the injured woman's back. She held the pack against Codee's head. "I'm just a grunt. For the most part I stayed under the radar and linked doctors with patients in need. I did that every chance I got and made arrangements outside of the hospital as I helped connect people to the hidden clinics the network created. Those who have access to supplies take greater chances than I ever have."

"Somehow, I seriously doubt that or you wouldn't have ended up on the chopping block ready to die for the cause. So the network has clinics to care for the poor and undocumented; what else?"

"I wasn't privy to most things, but I heard rumors the network was about ready to take arms against the government. They are watching carefully for what Canada and the sympathetic European nations are willing to do. I think they've recruited enough people to make up a rebel force that will give the peacekeepers a run for their money. Some of the peacekeepers aren't aligned with the government either, and many of the city police secretly side with the network."

Buzz buzz buzz

Sawyer shifted her eyes to the vibrating phone on the side table and continued to hold the ice pack.

Codee picked it up and stared at the screen. After reading the message, she put the phone back on the side table.

"Perhaps you know what this means. I got a text stating, 'Grid search is not imminent.'"

"That means we have at least twenty-four hours and they don't have a clue about our exact or approximate location. Sharlie might not be a network member, but she hasn't given them any useful information."

Codee grinned. "I didn't suspect she would. Sharlie's a good person, and I wouldn't be too sure about her not being a part of the network."

"She ran from the room pretty fast. That doesn't sound like someone who's taken a side in this fight. Citizens who sit on the sidelines and allow the atrocities are just as guilty as the people who follow the orders and take direct action." Sawyer shook her head in disgust.

"I don't think we should judge too harshly. There are probably a lot of people who are taking action behind the scenes. Like undercover agents. I suspect that wasn't in your nature, which is why Hilda was on the warpath with you. You aren't designed for subterfuge because your true feelings are always written all over your face, so don't ever play poker. You'll lose your shirt."

"I'll bet you're a good poker player."

"I've been known to school my features so as not to show my true feelings. That also comes with the territory of an HR exec, but sometimes doesn't work out so well in relationships. I've been told on more than one occasion, and I quote, that, I 'couldn't find a real emotion if my life depended on it.' That was the kinder version that my ex threw at me. I think 'f-ing B' was her go-to moniker. It's funny because I've also been told that when I do have strong opinions, my expressions damn near broadcast every thought."

"Still waters run deep, but the purest water lies in those deep pockets of the crystal-clear pools. I'll take purity and sincerity any day of the week. I'll bet when you communicate those feelings, they aren't just pretty words you're compelled to say."

"That's just it, I don't think I've ever fallen madly in love. It's like that old song by Meatloaf, 'Two Out of Three Ain't Bad.' I've wanted women before, maybe even needed them, but never quite loved them in the way they wanted me to. I gave up after some very painful endings."

"I'm sorry," Sawyer said. "Although, I almost wish I had your problem. The old saying, 'It is better to have loved and lost than never to have loved at all,' gets old after your third heartbreak. I always pick the love-'em-and-leave-'em types. I can't even hope for three times being a charm, because number three left me for a stripper."

"You're kidding, right?"

"Nope. I have to admit, she did have a killer body and made a lot more money in her profession than I did, or ever will, even if Trison had never made it to office. Social workers are definitely not at the top of the financial pyramid."

Codee didn't want to seem insensitive, but continuing to discuss their past relationship woes was heading into dangerous waters for her, and everything lately was far too chaotic to try to navigate those rapids. She decided to respond to Sawyer's last comment and ignore the more personal revelation.

"Believe it or not, HR execs do okay—well, did okay in my case. I'm thinking I've pretty much committed career suicide." Codee chuckled. "Let's hope I haven't literally signed both our death warrants. Do you think that little 'go' phone will keep sending hints to us and maybe some directive on what we should do? I guess I didn't think things through very carefully. I just knew I had to get you out of that situation. Long-range planning is not really my forte."

Codee reached behind her head and removed the ice pack Sawyer was holding against it. As her hand brushed against Sawyer, chills traveled up her spine. She was smart enough to recognize it wasn't due to the ice against her head but the effect Sawyer had on her. This was neither the time nor the place to explore her increasing attraction.

"You should really leave the ice on for a little longer." Sawyer brushed her hand over the back of Codee's head. "I can feel the lump, and it's not insignificant."

"I'm okay. My arm worries me more than my head. Although I suspect if it were a more serious fracture, I wouldn't be able to move it at all." She tossed the pack down next to the phone on the table.

Sawyer jumped up and rummaged through the first aid kit until she held up a triangular sling and a wire splint. "Which of these lovely accessories goes best with most of the outfits you'll likely wear over the next few weeks?"

Codee thought Sawyer's impish grin was irresistible.

"I'll take the sling. White goes with everything, and I can probably slide an ice pack underneath."

"I should have pulled this out right away instead of searching for frozen peas." Sawyer held up an instant-cold pack and carefully replaced the splint.

"Can I just put on the sling for now and worry about continuing to ice later?"

Sawyer frowned. "I don't know, it hasn't been anywhere near twenty minutes."

"You've been hanging around too many ED nurses." Codee waved her good hand in the air. "I'm starting to feel chilled again, so I'd rather cut a few corners here and there."

"I'm sure you have some extra blankets hanging around and I can add some more logs to the fire."

"Okay, hand over the insta-ice, but only one and I'll slip it in the sling. I might need your help to put it on correctly."

Sawyer brought over the sling and instant-cold pack, then gently placed Codee's arm in the protective fabric.

Her warm touch was a welcome relief against the chill of the pack as Codee slid her arm into the sling. She sat so close that the enticing scent she now recognized as uniquely Sawyer infiltrated her senses and awakened her burgeoning attraction.

Codee had never wanted to kiss someone so badly in all her life. When Sawyer looked at her with her amazing green eyes, she had to turn away, because she imagined that her own arousal reflected back at her in Sawyer's darkening gaze.

Sawyer cleared her throat. "Um...how's that? Are you still in pain? Can I get you anything else? I think I know my way around the first aid kit now."

"No, I'm good."

Buzz buzz buzz

Saved by the buzz. Codee picked up the cell phone again and glanced at the strange message.

Presume you're at the cabin. Please confirm. Help will arrive tomorrow morning. New orders coming.

"I think we're going to have visitors tomorrow and they're coming with a plan. I assume I'm supposed to confirm our location. Do you think it's safe?"

Sawyer leaned in, and Codee thought she might be reading the message. "It's obvious you packed the travel bags, and since that phone was in there with only one contact number, I think it's a pretty safe bet that the person sending the messages has our backs."

Codee nodded and typed the short affirmation.

"We never quite settled the sleeping arrangements. After the day I've had, I'll probably fall asleep right away. There's no sense in either one of us taking the couch. It's lumpy and uncomfortable, and something tells me we're going to need a good night's sleep. The new-orders part of the message concerned me a bit because it sounds like I'm up to my eyeballs in whatever this network has planned." Codee popped up from the couch and glanced back at Sawyer. "Come on, fellow rebel, let's turn in."

Sawyer returned her smile with that slow, sexy grin of hers. "I'm guessing you're up there in the ranks with the network. That makes sense because of your position at the hospital. Order is important, so I would be remiss if I ignored a direct order. Besides, I really didn't want to leave you alone with that head injury. Do you want to take some more medication before we turn in?"

"No, I'd rather not use up all the Tylenol. I'm still okay right now. A dull ache won't kill me."

As Codee's eyes became heavy with sleep, she thought she heard distant voices calling her name. Dreamland took her away as "Codee, Codee, can you hear me?" echoed in her head as if she were in an enclosed cave where the words bounced around in a distortion of sound.

Chapter Five

Codee had always been a light sleeper. It was a survival tactic that had enabled her to fend off the assholes in the various foster homes she'd lived in as a teen. She'd learned how to protect herself and how to fight dirty because she was often a lot smaller than anyone who came sniffing around.

The guys who would periodically cross the line didn't surprise her, but the first time Sue crawled into bed with her taught her a valuable lesson: always be wary and keep one eye open at all times. Even though Sue protected her as much as she violated her, it was quite a mixed message.

Her introduction to intimacy probably should have had her running in the opposite direction from women, because although she was attracted to girls, she wasn't inclined to have sex with Sue. She hadn't fought Sue's touch, not like she had with the boys. She never returned Sue's interest, but after a while she rationalized that Sue was the lesser of the evils, and since she'd promised to protect her, Codee just accepted her fate without emotion. That wariness of any form of intimacy stayed with her into adulthood and colored every relationship she attempted.

A rustling outside the cabin, although barely noticeable to most, jarred Codee from her light sleep. Sawyer's arm protectively draped around her middle gave her a warm feeling unlike anything she'd ever felt before. It wasn't like the protectiveness that felt more like possession when Sue or any subsequent lover slept with her.

She wondered when Sawyer had crossed the invisible barrier they'd put between them after getting into bed and why Codee hadn't pulled away.

She turned over from their spooned position and brushed her hand against Sawyer's cheek.

"Mmmf." Sawyer's eyes opened slowly, and Codee thought Sawyer was trying to focus on her surroundings as she woke.

"Not a morning person, huh?"

"Mmm, no," Sawyer growled. "What time is it? Because I'm pretty sure it isn't time to start the day. The roosters aren't even up at this ungodly hour."

"We have company."

Sawyer sat up so quickly that all the covers came with her and Codee felt the chill of the room.

"What?"

"Damn it's cold in here." Codee rubbed her eyes. "It's probably whoever sent the text last night."

Sawyer jumped out of bed. "I don't think so. Hurry, we have to get dressed. I have a feeling a welcome party isn't out there at zero dark hundred waiting to shower us with supplies."

Codee swung her feet over the bed, and when she reached for the sweatshirt slung over the chair, she remembered her injured arm. "Shit."

Sawyer already had the leathers pulled over her legs and was headed out the bedroom door. She turned her head. "God, I'm sorry, I forgot about your injuries. Do you need help getting dressed?"

Codee waved her good arm. "No, I'll manage, but I'm not sure how good I'll be in a fight. My fighting days ended long ago when I left the foster system, and besides, I only have one working arm. I do know how to bite and kick, and I play dirty, but if whoever is out there has guns, we're toast."

"You stay here and get dressed as best you can. I'll check it out. Can I use your gun?"

"Of course, but please be careful."

†

Sawyer's bad feeling was confirmed when she peeked through the blinds and saw the four men dressed in peacekeeper uniforms making their way through the foliage trailed by Sharlie. "That little traitor," she mumbled.

The cabin didn't have a back door, but she thought they could crawl out one of the windows. She felt Codee slip beside her and placed her finger over her mouth, then pointed to the enemy progressing quietly through the forest.

The peacekeepers had rifles slung over their shoulders, and Sharlie wore fatigues. She wondered why Sharlie might be dressed that way. It didn't make sense. Leading them to this secret location was one thing, but getting personally involved in their capture didn't seem like Sharlie. She'd always appeared standoffish and not willing to take a stand or get too intimately involved with the more distasteful aspects of a termination.

"I don't honestly know what to make of this. Sharlie does not wear fatigues. Ever. It is inconceivable to me that she might be leading the group." Codee scrunched up her face. "I take it those four gentlemen are peacekeepers."

Sawyer nodded. One of the peacekeepers removed his rifle, set it on the ground, and pulled out a pair of binoculars. Stepping away from the window, she ordered quietly, "Shit, come on. I'll help you with your boots. Good thing I re-packed the bags. Maybe we can double back and get the motorcycle after they've left. When they find the cabin empty, I hope they'll presume we've moved on. I guess the honeymoon is over. Too bad. We were having such a lovely time here before we got company. Back to the real world."

"You're joking right now?" Codee asked in an incredulous tone.

Sawyer shrugged. "Always good to retain a healthy sense of humor."

Codee moved quietly and quickly to her boots by the door. Sawyer marveled at how calm Codee was as she pushed her feet into them and managed to get them tied despite the obvious pain in her arm. Before Sawyer was able to don her own boots and help, the stealth woman was standing with her leather coat in her hand, ready to make a break for it.

"I think the window in the bedroom is our best chance. We'll have to be extremely quiet as we sneak out."

"I can be as quiet as a mouse, don't worry about me." Codee moved gracefully to the bedroom, and Sawyer followed with one bag slung over her shoulder and the other draped across her arm.

When Sawyer reached the window, she set down the bags, slid the latch to the unlock position, and tugged on the frame. "Okay, I'm officially having a shitty day and definitely woke up too soon. It's stuck, and breaking the window is not an option. I'd ask for your help, but with only one good arm, I'm not sure it will do any good."

"One good arm is better than none, and I'm freakishly strong for my size. Let me help," Codee whispered.

"I guess I'm out of options. Quick, on the count of three give it all you've got. One, two, three."

Bang!

The window opened with such vigor that the force caused Codee to lose her balance.

Sawyer was beside her in a second and caught her before she landed on her behind. "Criminy…" She looked up at the ceiling. "Goddess, why do you hate me so? Get ready to make a run for it, because I have a feeling that noise just notified the welcoming party of our location. Go on, hurry, start running north, and I'm right behind you."

Codee turned around and gave Sawyer a look of exasperation. "God, I hate when people use north, south, east, and west when they give directions. I haven't the foggiest idea which way north is."

Sawyer pushed her toward the window. "Just go. Pick a bloody direction and run for your life. Literally."

Codee grabbed one of the bags and scrambled out the window, saying, "Okay, okay, bossy much?"

After grabbing the other bag, Sawyer ducked and crawled out the window. She hit the greenery surrounding the bedroom window and then followed close behind.

They weren't able to escape quietly as they ran deeper into the forest, because at this point they'd already revealed their location and a sneaky getaway was no longer possible.

Sawyer marveled at how fast Codee was. She was barely able to keep up with her, and she'd been a track star in college. She looked over her shoulder and was amazed no one was following.

They ran hard for fifteen minutes, then Codee dodged to the right and crawled through a dense cluster of trees and ferns. She bent over, and Sawyer thought she was trying hard not to give away their location with heavy breathing, but clearly the run had winded her.

"I…need…a few…minutes," Codee gasped.

Sawyer ducked under a branch and surveyed the area. "This is a pretty good location to hole up for a little bit and see if they're following—"

The loud crack that filled the air interrupted Sawyer, and her panicked eyes looked around for the origin of the noise. Two more cracks followed closely behind the first.

"Uh-oh, that was a rifle, Codee. The peacekeepers are shooting at something, but it sounds a fair distance away. Do you think your friends showed at a very inopportune time?"

"I don't even know who my friends are. I suppose I should have asked when I got the text, but maybe they would have seen that as suspect."

"Let's hunker down and wait here for a spell and see what transpires. How's your head?"

"Head's fine, but my feet aren't doing so well. I wish I had my track shoes right about now, because these boots are killing me," Codee said.

"I knew it. You were a track star. Geez, I thought I was following the Road Runner. I had a hard time keeping up and I ran track in college."

"Do you think we should cover ourselves in leaves or something? I saw that in a movie once."

Sawyer shrugged. "Can't hurt, I guess."

Codee began gathering leaves and pine needles and pushed them into a pile as Sawyer collected a few broken branches nearby. She used one to start digging to create a small indentation in the frozen ground. She wasn't making any headway when Codee touched her shoulder.

"I don't think it's worth it to try to create a hole. The ground's still too hard. I think we'll be hidden well enough," Codee whispered.

Sawyer jerked her head up and placed a finger against her lips. She leaned in close and whispered into her ear, "I hear someone coming."

They quickly lay on the ground and pushed as much as they could of the downed leaves, needles, and branches around them and over their bodies and waited. Their fate was no longer in their hands. Sawyer wondered if maybe their luck might change, because things sure hadn't gone very well so far.

✝

Codee strained to listen. Along with the ability to sleep with one eye open, she had exceptional hearing. This was another thing she'd learned in foster care. Listening carefully to the sounds, voices, and other warning signs outside her bedroom door had saved her bacon on numerous occasions.

She knew Sharlie was with the peacekeepers, so hearing her voice didn't surprise Codee. But she was astonished that Sharlie would bring the enemy to the cabin. She supposed she wasn't as good a judge of character as she'd thought.

As the group of men neared, Codee listened to their conversation.

"I told you she took a bad fall and she probably doesn't know who to trust now," Sharlie declared.

"I suppose that's a good thing. Someone might have given the location away, but it's more likely they looked up any real estate purchase records," a deep voice answered.

Sawyer turned her head and gave Codee a puzzled look.

Codee decided it was worth a chance, so she leaned in and whispered in Sawyer's ear, "It sounds like they aren't our enemies. I don't understand what's happening, but I told you I trusted Sharlie."

"She was acting strange after the fall, but I never suspected she would make a run for it with Sawyer. Maybe something caused her to suspect she'd blown her cover," Sharlie theorized.

"Is your cover still intact?" the man asked.

"No, I don't think so, or at least I'm under suspicion now. It was time anyway. I'm ready to take a more aggressive role, and it sounds like Codee is as well. Too bad we can't nick some uniforms and pose as peacekeepers like some of you, but they don't allow women in their sick little group," Sharlie answered bitterly.

Sharlie and a tall man were almost on top of them now. Codee popped her head up. "Sharlie?"

Sawyer sat up, quickly flipped open one of the bags, pulled out the gun, and aimed it in the direction of the man, whose gun remained slung over his shoulder. Her grip on the Glock looked deadly serious, and Codee wouldn't want to be the person in her line of sight.

The man put up his hands. "Whoa, whoa, whoa, we aren't here to hurt you. I can't say the same thing for the three genuine peacekeepers that arrived shortly after we got here, but they're all taken care of. Thank God for reputable intel. Can you please put that thing away? I take it you're Codee."

"What the hell is going on, Sharlie? Why is he dressed like a peacekeeper?" Sawyer asked.

The man grinned. "Because I am one. It's just I don't exactly agree with their policies, but what they don't know…well. I guess I can't claim it won't hurt them, 'cause three of the bloody bastards are dead in their jeep and my buddies are burying them right about now. You need some fertilizer around your cabin, right?"

Sawyer hadn't taken her eyes off the two-person search party.

"How do I know this isn't a trick? Codee may trust you, Sharlie, but I sure as hell don't. You were quick to tuck tail and run at my termination hearing, claiming you 'didn't have the stomach for it.'"

"You dolt, that was for the benefit of Hilda's big ears. She was right outside the door. It wasn't like I could completely do an about-face on my values once that asshole Trison got into office. Playing like I was a person who couldn't stomach it but would follow orders like the rest of the sheep seemed like the safest avenue." Sharlie crossed her arms over her chest and glared at Sawyer.

"I can read people extremely well and there was guilt written all over your face. You could be a double agent or something," Sawyer said.

"Oh for Christ's sake, this isn't Hollywood. I'm just a minor player in this three-act tragedy we've all been forced to participate in, and I wouldn't know the first thing about doing a second double cross. It's been hard enough to take part in the role I have been playing. The guilt was because I couldn't manage to get Hilda to go back to her office prior to the last minute so it was touch and go for a while. I wasn't sure I'd be able to pull it off, and I really couldn't stomach seeing Vernetta have to actually administer the real injection."

The man looked back and forth between Sharlie and Sawyer with keen interest.

Codee pushed Sawyer's gun arm down. "I believe her. You trust me, right?"

"Yeah," Sawyer answered with hesitation.

"Then trust that I know my own staff enough to believe in them and their loyalty. Sharlie's been with me for a long time. I think I know her well enough to have confidence she'd never roll over and accept Trison's barbaric laws."

Sawyer tucked the gun back into the bag. "Don't give me a reason to pull this out, because I swear if you're lying, I'll come back from the dead and haunt you until someone finally sends you to hell."

"A feisty one. Good. We need all the feisty ones we can get if we're going to win this war, because, ladies, make no mistake, we're about to forge into World War III, and President Trison is a dangerous dictator." The man pivoted and repositioned his gun as it started to slip from his shoulder.

Sawyer helped Codee stand and whispered, "Do you think we should ask him his name? I kinda like him."

Codee raised her brow. "Changing sexual orientation on me?"

"Oh no, nothing like that. I just like how he doesn't treat women as lesser fighters."

The man turned around and called over his shoulder, "Derrick, that's my name, and my little sister would kick my ass if I didn't treat her as an equal." He chuckled as he continued to make his way back through the forest.

"Hmmm, I guess he's not the only one with bat ears." Codee grinned.

"Um, not that you don't know what you're doing or anything, but if our location is compromised, how come we're heading back to the lion's den?"

Sharlie took her place alongside Sawyer and Codee as they continued to follow Derrick. "You have a new unit to lead, Codee, and they're only going to take enough time to regroup and be on their way. These guys are your escort service. That's their specialty. Sawyer's now part of that troop."

"Unit?" Codee furrowed her brow.

"The war has begun, and everything has changed overnight. We're on a brand-new trajectory. The new group is smaller and more mobile. It will be easier for you to hide now, and they'll fill you in. I don't have all the details, but I know you'll be able to rest at the compound until it's been determined you need to move," Sharlie explained.

"I don't think I'm fit to lead anyone. Maybe you should promote Sawyer, or you can take over for me."

"Sorry, someone higher than me determined we still need you. You've become the key to the revolution. Sawyer might have grit and passion and I'm loyal, but you're the natural-born leader here. Besides, I'm not really privy to much. I was just a familiar face they thought you would trust. I'm not part of the new unit." Sharlie pushed a branch out of the way, clearing the path for Sawyer and Codee.

"Yep, that's what the uppers told us, boss lady," Derrick added.

Chapter Six

The small, grassy clearing in front of the cabin revealed three men positioned in a triangle formation. All had high-powered binoculars pushed up against their faces as they presumably performed a continuous scan of the area. The rifles strapped across their bodies all had scopes attached at the top, and Codee thought they looked expensive.

She wasn't an expert on rifles, so she didn't know where that thought came from. Like everything over the last couple of days, facts and information seemed just out of reach but vaguely familiar. Codee thought it was almost as if she could pop everything into place if she could just stretch her arm out and pull the various pieces within her sphere of understanding.

"Any more activity?" Derrick asked.

The largest man, who had a shiny, bald head, lowered his binoculars and pierced the group with his ice-blue eyes. "No, but they never just send one team, especially if that unit hasn't reported back within the hour."

"Okay, I'd say quick introductions are in order, and then we need to move out. The bald dude is Cue, as in cue

66

ball." Derrick pointed at a tall, lanky man with blond hair. "That's Surf, because when he's not fighting for the cause, he's talking about his glory days as a professional surfer."

The small, wiry man with round spectacles stepped forward. "It's an honor to meet you. I'm Doc." His voice was so soft that Codee wondered how he had managed to get a job as a peacekeeper, even if he was undercover for the network. He didn't seem to fit the stereotype she'd already formed about the president's lapdogs.

"Don't let Doc's size fool you, he's a mean little fucker when roused," Derrick added.

"How come the other three have nicknames but you don't?" Sawyer asked.

Derrick chuckled. "Oh I have a nickname, but not one anyone says to my face. It rhymes with my name and I earned it. They think I'll kick their asses if they dare to call me that, but I don't take offense. I am a prick, but I'm a prick that's on your side, so I'm your prick. Either is appropriate."

"I think I'll just call you Derrick, if that's all right with you." Codee pointed to the jeep off to the side. "I assume that's your transportation. I don't think two more will fit comfortably in that thing, so we'll follow you to wherever it is we can regroup before someone else is rude enough to crash this private party."

Derrick nodded. "Yes, ma'am. I assume you'll be taking that sweet ride of yours."

Codee nodded and turned to Sawyer. "Will you drive again?"

Sawyer took a step toward the motorcycle. "Love to. I sure hope it's not too far. It's still a bit nippy out."

"Doc and I can take the cycle if you want to cozy up in the jeep," Derrick offered.

Sawyer grinned. "That sounds good to me. Are you okay with letting them take your baby?"

"Oh absolutely. I'm a fair-weather rider and would have never taken her out had it not been an emergency. She's all yours."

"Keys?" Doc asked.

"I think they're still in the cabin on the side table in the living room. We weren't worrying about them when we snuck out. I honestly didn't think anyone knew about my cabin, so we didn't worry about a lot when we settled in last night, but that sure changed quickly for us when we heard the rustling outside. Will there be enough room in the jeep for our bags?" Codee asked.

Doc sprinted away and called out, "I'll be right back."

"We'll make room for the bags. You know, you just made his day." Derrick laughed. "He always feels like people pigeonhole him into the wuss category, so anything to boost his cred, like driving a motorcycle, makes him happy. Between you and me, I'd rather face Cue than Doc in an alley fight, but you can count on every single one of us to make sure you make it out of these woods alive."

"Won't you be missed or something if you don't report to work?" Sawyer inquired.

"We'll explain everything as soon as we make it to the safe house. Your timing was perfect. It's begun, the revolution, and there's no turning back now."

†

Sharlie kept looking in the rearview mirror, and Sawyer knew it was probably because she'd grabbed Codee's hand and given it a reassuring squeeze but hadn't let go yet. Since Codee didn't appear uncomfortable with their fingers laced together, she kept holding her hand. She still had that glazed—or was it a dazed and confused?—look on her face, and Sawyer wanted to do whatever she could to ground her. It didn't seem out of place for her to hold her hand as they made their way to wherever they were going, but then the world had tilted so far off its axis over the last year, not much would feel unusual to her.

Sawyer had paid close attention to the four false peacekeepers and noted Doc regarded Codee with what she could only describe as reverence. The HR leader was clearly a key player in the revolution. These men were loyal and would sacrifice their lives for her safety—that much was abundantly clear. Sawyer knew she was just along for the ride, and if Codee was going to lead them, she would devote her life to make sure she was safe.

"Can you tell us anything about what's happened in the last twenty-four hours?" Sawyer inquired.

Cue turned his head while barreling down the winding road. "The United Nations just voted to impose sanctions on the United States until we decide to reverse our recent policies that are considered a violation of human rights. We've become the new poster child for genocide of our own people. You can't shut down every single media outlet, so it was only a matter of time before the world discovered what was really happening here. That was the spark needed to mobilize the thousands of micro units interspersed throughout the country."

"Well that and your disappearance," Sharlie added.

"The rumor that you'd been executed spread like wildfire, and we did nothing to squelch it. The tide is turning. I even heard a rumor the UN might activate that criminal court to try Trison, but I don't know how that works," Cue continued.

Codee's brow furrowed. "I don't understand. I'm a nobody. Why would my life matter if what I've learned is true, so many have been killed?"

"You left a video and somehow managed to ensure it went viral. You've always been a gifted speaker, but this was a speech as impassioned and impactful as any I've ever heard. It will go down as one of the greatest moments in US history." Sharlie turned around to face the passengers in the back. "My personal favorite two lines were, 'For the masses who stand by and watch as your mothers, fathers, brothers, sisters, children, and dear neighbors are executed summarily, you might as well have delivered the deadly blow with your own hands. The blood of the community rests squarely on the shoulders of every man and woman who remain silent while the atrocities continue.' Just repeating those words gives me goose bumps."

"At first, only the rogue media outlets managed to sneak it through, but somehow the others got the hint and the major news channels blatantly ignored their marching orders from the government and played it in a continuous loop while the network fought the remaining peacekeepers loyal to Trison. Those fighters managed to keep enough stations running the feed that the message got out, and when someone planted the seed that the government executed you for speaking your mind, all hell broke loose." Surf pushed his blond bangs away from his face and grinned.

"The rumor you were dead actually saved your ass because they only learned early this morning that you were still alive. We were the closest unit to your location. We have a few key players high up in the government, and now the perfect storm has arrived. I mean that in a good way because you turned the tide and it couldn't have come at a more opportune time." Cue turned the jeep sharply onto an old logging road.

Sawyer looked at Codee with a sense of awe. She'd heard her lead an impassioned training session on topics such as customer service, but she really wanted to get her hands on that video to see and hear it for herself. She squeezed her hand again for reassurance. "And to think I cooked a regular old spaghetti dinner for the future President of the United States."

"Oh no, I don't want that job. Maybe the other person running against Trison wasn't perfect, but I think we should push her into the role when we manage to boot that sociopath from office."

The jeep bumped along on the frozen road as the dips from the previous harsh winters created a jarring ride for everyone. The vehicle slid to a stop on the snow-packed road, and Surf jumped out to open the massive gate with an impressive amount of barbed wire attached to the top.

The cluster of buildings looked a bit like a paramilitary compound. Not that Sawyer really knew what one of those looked like, but if the Hollywood representations were remotely accurate, that would be her guess.

Sawyer counted at least two dozen men and women in fatigues carrying various weapons. She wasn't sure, but she thought most of them were some type of automatic machine gun. This was a heavily guarded fortress because, as she'd just learned, they had precious cargo to protect.

She scrambled out of the jeep and looked around as she clutched one of the bags. Surf had the other bag draped over his shoulder. At least a dozen buildings were scattered among the trees. Most of them were institutional-looking cement, block-shaped structures with tiny windows. They weren't beautiful, but functional and designed to keep people tucked safely inside.

She noticed Codee taking in her surroundings and thought the whole situation had to be overwhelming for her. Sawyer handed Cue the motorcycle bag, then she did the first thing that seemed natural to her—she took her hand again, and they followed Cue and Surf into the only wood building in the complex. The log home stood in stark contrast to the other bland structures.

When Erma, the elderly next door neighbor, opened the front door with a huge smile on her face, Sawyer felt Codee relax beside her. She eased her grip, and Codee removed her hand. After Codee took several steps toward Erma, she accepted her warm embrace.

"Thank God, they brought you here unharmed. You are unharmed, right?" Erma asked.

"I still have a sore arm and massive headache now, but yes, our escorts made sure I made it here in one piece. How is it you've joined the ball?"

"Oh, I've got connections. I thought you might want to see a friendly face when they brought you here. It's bad out there, what with the fighting flowing from the cities and into the suburbs. It's total anarchy in the more populated areas. Like in the Civil War, it's brother against brother and the rest of the world has taken a page from our sordid history as former allied nations start skirmishes against each other. It's quickly devolving into complete and total chaos. It's unfortunate that some people aren't necessarily taking sides, but using the pandemonium for their own personal advancement. There's a lot of looting going on. In times like these the best and worst of human nature comes out." Erma twisted and gestured to the inside of the large home. "Come in. I have fresh coffee for you after you get settled and cleaned up."

"You are a goddess," Sawyer exclaimed.

"Oh, I like this one. She's cute too. Are ya single?" Erma winked.

A blush crept up Sawyer's face.

Codee nodded. "She is adorable, isn't she? You want to confirm your relationship status for my nosy neighbor?"

"Remember, three times was definitely not a charm. Heartbreak…"

"I remember. Your exes were very stupid women," Codee remarked.

Erma shifted her eyes between the two of them. "Come on, girls. Unfortunately, the house is a wee bit crowded at the moment with these paramilitary types over-flowing from the other buildings, so the two of you will have to bunk together in one of the bedrooms. You don't mind, do you?" Her face blossomed into a huge smile.

"I think the old coot is trying to play Yenta, the matchmaker in *Fiddler on the Roof*," Codee whispered.

"I'm old, not deaf. I heard that, you know."

"You were meant to," Codee deadpanned.

"I refuse to comment and get in the middle of this. For some reason, I think you two do this for sport." Sawyer chuckled.

Codee and Erma flashed twin Cheshire grins.

Chapter Seven

Codee thought the warm fire in the cozy log home felt oddly out of place amid the raging chaos surrounding them as the country danced on the brink of World War III.

Erma led them to a midsized bedroom with a queen bed and smirked as she pointed to the room. "You'll stay in here for a while, unless it's determined they need to move you again. The guys will drop off your bags, and anything you didn't pack, we can get for you. I doubt you packed shampoo, toothpaste, or some of those essentials that make us feel human again. There's a bathroom adjacent to this room. You can use that to freshen up, and then we'll talk." Erma left the room chuckling.

"I don't know anything more than you do at this point, but I'd sure like to see that speech they're all yammering about. I'll bet it was a doozy. I think Doc is just a little bit in love with you from the way he looked at you."

Codee waved her arm. "You know he's not my type. I'd much rather have someone else madly in love with me." She pinned Sawyer with a penetrating gaze.

"How do you know they aren't?"

74

Codee pulled a leaf out of Sawyer's hair. "You picked up a few hair accessories, so maybe you'd like to use the shower first—not that they aren't nice and don't go quite well with your outfit...." She swiped her finger down Sawyer's cheek. "But I don't think this chocolate-colored blush is quite the right shade for you."

"I have mud on my cheek, don't I?"

Codee nodded. "It's sort of endearing. You look like a little kid who just came in from making mud pies."

"I suppose you would understand. You probably played in the dirt as a child every bit as much as I did. No Barbie dolls for us, huh?"

"Actually, no, I didn't. I was too busy keeping myself from an ass whupping. Foster care doesn't allow for much of a normal childhood. I learned how to fight and fight dirty."

Codee had no idea why she continued to reveal bits and pieces of her childhood to Sawyer. Confessions seemed to explode from her mouth around the woman whether Codee wanted them to or not. The compassionate young woman had a way about her that seemed to scream, "Tell me all your deep, dark secrets, and I promise to make it all better." For some reason, she wanted Sawyer to know her on a meaningful level, and that included her painful childhood.

Sawyer pulled her into a comforting hug, and Codee let her hold on for a long time. "That's for every hurt you endured, and thank God you didn't let it keep you from becoming the amazing woman you are."

Sawyer gently disengaged and cocked her head to the side. "How did you possibly manage to escape getting dirt and grime all over yourself? You were right there with me hiding in the forest. Besides, I thought the ground was frozen solid. I can't believe I managed to find the one area that thawed enough for mud to jump on my face."

"A mystery of the universe, I suspect. Maybe you happened to find a place where some animal dug in for the winter, got all cozy, and heated up the spot enough to create a little mud. Or maybe you're so hot, you created the mud." Codee chuckled.

"Are you flirting with me again, Ms. Sorenson?"

"Maybe," Codee hedged. "With the impending apocalypse, I've suddenly decided life is way too short."

"Amen to that." Sawyer removed her shirt and stood in front of Codee in just her bra and pants. She surveyed the room. "I wonder where I should put these dirty clothes?"

She stood gaping at Sawyer's lean, muscular body. *I guess she's not too self-conscious about stripping in front of others.* When Sawyer grinned, apparently catching Codee admiring her, she decided it might be best to join the conversation again. "Um, maybe we can just put them in the corner for now and ask Erma later."

"Okay." Sawyer removed her pants and strolled into the bathroom in her underwear.

Codee was thankful Sawyer didn't completely undress in front of her. After the bathroom door closed, she sat heavily on the bed and sighed. She wasn't sure what had come over her in the last twenty-four hours. She'd acted completely out of character when she'd decided to take a virtual stranger to her cabin. Then she'd begun to reveal pieces of her childhood, and now she was shamelessly flirting and gawking at a woman to whom she was wildly attracted. She never pursued women; they always hounded her. This was entirely new territory and not altogether unwelcome, she thought.

As she listened to the shower, she reflected on all the craziness that seemed to orbit around her. Sawyer wasn't the only one who wanted to view the speech she'd apparently given and left instructions to send to media outlets. She wasn't sure to whom she'd left those instructions and what had triggered the event. The only people who knew she was on the run were Vernetta, the ambulance transport woman, Erma, and Sharlie. It was a riddle she'd be sure to ask Erma about.

Codee sat, folded her hands in her lap, and waited patiently, letting her mind dodge from one thought to another. She didn't know the first thing about leading a unit, especially if they used rigidly defined military rules and training. She'd never been in the military, nor had she ever wanted that kind of inflexible structure. Codee wasn't used to taking orders without questioning their rationale, and she had a jaundiced outsider perspective of the military. She thought there wasn't enough questioning of orders and that was how the United States always seemed to entrench themselves in ethical dilemmas. Her style of leadership was inclusive of various perspectives. If an organization didn't ask others for their opinions and have a willingness to alter their perspective, a company could not reap the benefits of the shared pool of learning.

The bathroom door creaked open, and a puff of steam meandered into the bedroom. Sawyer had wrapped herself in a towel and slicked back her wet hair. It was probably the sexiest thing Codee had ever seen, and she couldn't stop herself from once again staring at the beautiful woman who was at least ten years younger than she was.

"It's all yours. I think I left enough hot water."

I wish you were all mine, screw the hot water. "Thanks."

Codee took her fully clothed self into the bathroom and looked into the mirror. She was thankful she didn't look like something the cat dragged in and puked up on the floor. She looked to the ceiling and silently thanked her mother for hair that she could sleep on and finger-comb in the morning without looking too disheveled. That was one thing she'd dimly remembered about her mother, and if she forgot, she had a single photo of the woman to remind her. Light gray eyes looked back at her. She hoped that sometimes they conveyed compassion, but too often she'd learned they appeared stormy and cold to others, especially those who irritated her. She'd heard it often enough from her exes.

Does she find me as attractive as I find her?

She looked closely at her other features. In the early days of one relationship, her lover had fawned over her full lips. She'd described them as "luscious." Codee thought at the time it was corny and over-the-top, but now she wondered if Sawyer liked full lips. Her mother had always told her high cheekbones and a heart-shaped face were something any successful model would kill for, but she'd been too young to care about that. She shrugged. She'd never felt beautiful, especially after her mother died and she'd entered the broken foster care system.

She heard stirring in the other room and shook herself from her thoughts. She needed to get in the shower, get dressed, and learn more about her current predicament.

†

Sawyer wondered why she didn't hear the shower start. Nearly five minutes had passed before she heard the water run. She'd almost barged in to see if Codee was okay, but she was glad she hadn't because the guarded woman didn't seem to be comfortable changing in front of her. She debated with herself whether she should bring her a new set of clothes. The bags they'd swiftly packed didn't contain many items, so she searched the drawers of the dresser and found some basic fatigues she thought would fit her and a set that might fit Codee.

After donning her own bland, practical ensemble, she decided to set the other uniform of sorts on the toilet while Codee was still behind the protective curtain.

Just as she opened the door, Codee pushed the curtain aside and grabbed the towel Sawyer had discovered earlier and hung on the hook.

"Shit." Codee pulled it to her body. "You scared the crap out of me."

"Oh, sorry. I just wanted to leave this set of fatigues for you. There wasn't a whole lot to choose from, and at least these look comfortable."

"Um, okay. They're fine. It's not like we're about to go out to a fine-dining establishment."

"I'll just set them on the toilet. I'm sorry for violating your privacy." Sawyer began backing out of the small room.

"Don't worry about it. I have an unhealthy habit of placing a barrier around myself, and that includes avoiding getting dressed and undressed in front of others. I haven't even done much of that around lovers, and it was always a point of contention…."

"I'll just wait outside for you, and then we can go on the hunt for coffee. I smell it and it's starting to make me crazy. I've usually had my first cup by now." Sawyer smacked her lips. "I guess we can get some toothpaste and toothbrushes after breakfast. I'm just glad there was shampoo and cream rinse in the shower for us to use."

"It won't take me long. No makeup today. That should shave a good ten minutes from the time it'll take me to get ready. I'd like to blow-dry my mop, though, if you can give me a few extra minutes. I'd rather brush before coffee, but it won't kill me to wait until after breakfast."

"Sure, no problem. Patience is a virtue, they say." Sawyer exited the bathroom and carefully closed the door, making sure she heard the click as it shut. She had to concentrate on taming her racing heart after catching a glimpse of Codee. She couldn't deny her attraction or her growing desire.

Chapter Eight

Sawyer let her nose lead her to the kitchen and the precious black liquid sitting in a carafe on the counter along with two empty cups. She poured the coffee nearly to the rim of one, leaving just enough space to add a small amount of cream and sugar. Pushing aside various beverages in the fridge, including soy creamer and coconut milk, she found her favorite french Vanilla option and grabbed the container. When she turned around to fill her mug, Erma was directly behind her.

"I see you've found the various options to ruin a good cup of java. I like it black myself, but to each their own." She was leaning against one of the kitchen counters, smiling.

"God, you scared me. I can't believe how many choices there are in this refrigerator."

"A good cup of coffee to start the day is a motivating factor that garners the right kind of loyalty. My home cooking doesn't hurt either. These young men and women are easy to please, and I suppose I've become everyone's mom in the process. I used to only come on the weekends, but now I plan to stay here full-time until this whole ugly mess is resolved one way or another. Everyone has a special niche. I found mine and consider what I do worthwhile work for the cause. Of course, I'm not much of a fighter, but then everyone has value."

"You couldn't be more right, Erma."

"So what's your specialty?"

Sawyer shrugged. "I don't know. Some folks say I have a way with people. I can calm the most distraught person."

"Codee's special. She has a rare knack for getting people to follow her. When I heard she hit her head, I got worried. You stick close to her, ya hear, and when she needs that calming, I expect you to be the one to take care of her."

"I'm not sure I'm needed to do that for her—she seems pretty strong to me already—but I'd be honored. I know how special she is, and I didn't even have to hear that revolutionary speech of hers."

"Just don't get distracted by your attraction to her—that could get both of you killed."

Sawyer didn't disagree that she was attracted to Codee, but she wondered how this woman who barely knew her, and hadn't spent a lot of time around the two of them when they were together, noticed this. *Am I that transparent?* Sawyer could almost feel the crease in her forehead deepen as she worried about this revelation.

"I, um, I'll do my best...."

"Now don't get your panties all in a bunch. Codee may realize your feelings and that might scare the crap out of her, but don't let the little shit distance herself from you. I've got a feeling you two are good for one another and together you'll be the spark to getting us on the other side of this nightmare. I think it would be prudent to put your attraction on the back burner for now and concentrate on keeping her safe."

"What an interesting description. It does feel like a nightmare, doesn't it?"

Sawyer heard a soft shuffle and turned her head to watch the beautiful woman float into the room. At least that's what her movements looked like as Codee's presence seemed to fill the kitchen without fanfare or noise.

"Now what are you two jabbering about? I felt my ears burning, so I suspect Erma here was telling some stories. I plead the Fifth." Codee grabbed the other mug and filled it to almost the three-quarter mark, leaving plenty of room to add a healthy amount of cream. "Yum, I'll take that creamer off your hands; it's my favorite." She added the cream until the coffee almost spilled over.

Sawyer peered at the nearly overflowing beverage. "A little coffee with your cream, huh? Well…we were talking about you, but Erma hadn't gotten to the interesting stories yet. Do you care to expand on what some of the more titillating ones might be?"

Codee laughed. "Who came up with the word *titillating*, and does it remind you of a stripper's large breasts, or am I the only freak that goes there?"

Sawyer chuckled. "Um, no, I might go there on occasion—so you are definitely not alone. I'm sure a few adolescent boys and girls giggle when they hear the word too. How can you not when part of the word is *tit*? The history of that word is really rather boring; it goes back to the seventeenth century. *Titillare* is a Latin verb for *tickle*."

"That is a rather boring word origin." Codee leaned down and slurped from the overflowing cup before picking it up and taking a proper sip.

"I've tried to nose my way into Ms. Tight Lip's personal life, but unfortunately she holds things close to the vest, so the only good stories are ones I have to make up when I bother peeking through my curtains and catch her while she's entertaining one of her lady friends. I've got a good imagination though," Erma added.

Codee smacked her on the arm and winced.

Sawyer noted she had used her free, injured arm.

"Cut that out, you're fabricating everything. I have never entertained ladies in my home. You know I've only had one failed relationship since we've been neighbors, and you marched over the minute she moved in and were also quick to point out what a dolt she was the minute she decided I was no longer the love of her life. It might have been more helpful if you'd given me that information before she settled in."

"I don't butt into people's private affairs," Erma defended.

"Since when?"

Sawyer kept moving her eyes back and forth between the two women as if she were watching a tennis match. They clearly had a comfortable friendship and felt at ease teasing and joking with one another.

"Okay, point taken, but I thought my nonverbals were clear. Every time I came over for coffee and the dipshit was hanging out, I'm sure it looked like I'd just sucked on a lemon. You had to know I didn't care for the girl."

Codee grinned. "I did, but it was so much fun watching you try not to say anything. I've gotta hand it to you— you were incredibly controlled. I thought you might burst, but you kept it all inside until you saw the moving van. Damn, that was some tongue-lashing you gave me after the truck pulled away."

"What was wrong with her?" Sawyer interjected.

"Pretty package, but nothing inside," Erma answered. "Only good for a one-nighter, but this one's got too many morals for that. She had to keep the stray."

"You are just mean, Erma." Codee grinned.

"No, just honest. That one latched on to you because she needed a meal ticket, and when she found someone new, *hasta la vista, baby.* The only consolation was that she didn't break your heart. Otherwise, I would have gotten all up in the hussy's grille."

"Where in the world did you learn those words?" Codee chuckled.

"Oh, being around all these young military types is so educational, you know. I have a lot more colorful language I've learned since I joined the network. I know this is all serious business, but I've had more fun in the last twelve months than in my whole adult life. It keeps me young at heart. You girls go on into the living room and I'll whip up some breakfast before I need to fill you in on a few things." Erma frowned. "Something surprising just came my way, and I need to prepare you, Codee."

"Hmmm, sounds intriguing. I'll be waiting with bated breath." Codee glanced at Sawyer and motioned in the direction of the living room with her head. "Shall we?"

"Right behind you."

Chapter Nine

Even though Codee wasn't cold, she was happy to see a healthy blaze in the fireplace. Fire always mesmerized her and created a calming influence—a lot like Sawyer had done since the onset of her confusion and spotty memory. She lowered herself onto the couch that was perpendicular to the hearth, and Sawyer joined her as they set their coffee on the table in front of them, almost in unison.

"Erma seems like a good friend. You must be close."

"Honestly, she's a jewel, and has been like a second mother to me. Mine died when I was young and none of the foster mothers were very motherly. Erma seemed to worm her way into my heart. There was a huge hole from losing my parents I don't really remember my father much and...." Codee hesitated. There was something in her memory that was barely on the fringe. She knew she should remember it, but couldn't quite put her finger on it. She shook her head and continued. "One day he was there, then...I don't know exactly what happened. I was pretty young and clung more to my mother than my father. How the heck do you always manage to get me talking about myself, yet I know virtually nothing about you? Come on, give me a little bit so I don't feel so vulnerable."

"You already know the highlights. I fall in love quickly and trust easily. It's not worked out all that well for me so far. I grew up in a typical middle-class family and knew I wanted to do something with my life that had meaning. Since my parents didn't have a lot of money to help with school, I delayed getting my master's degree until I'd saved up enough money to finish. That's why I took the job in admitting." Sawyer shrugged. "It was a way to pay the bills until I got a job in social services."

"So do you have any brothers or sisters?"

"I have one older brother who is overbearing and overprotective. Every time one of my lovers dumped me, he threatened to track them down and pluck out their eyelashes. He's a good guy and has some kind of role in the network, but I'm not exactly sure what it is. He's been pretty tight-lipped about it. My parents have also done some work behind the scenes. I'm fortunate to come from a family who is very socially conscious and always taught kindness is an equal-opportunity value. My dad has the right mix of toughness and compassion. I think I learned most everything from him. I was definitely a daddy's girl. I followed him around like a puppy dog."

"I guess I should feel like I missed out not remembering my father, but honestly it's my mother I miss more. Tell me a story about you and your father."

"I'm not really sure why I wanted to go with him because I hate even the thought of shooting defenseless animals, but my dad used to take me hunting. I'd dutifully follow him into the cornfields, and he gave me a shotgun and told me to point it at the pheasants when he flushed them from the brush. I didn't get a whole lot more direction than that. So when I pulled the trigger, of course I missed and the kickback caused me to land on my ass. I was only eight."

Sawyer looked up and smiled at Codee. "When I came home with a bruise on my shoulder, my mom lectured my dad for over an hour about his irresponsible behavior. I never picked up a shotgun or rifle again. Watching *Bambi* pretty much locked in my view on hunting, and I stopped following my dad into the fields."

"Yeah, I can't see you enjoying killing an animal even if you were going to eat it."

"The funny thing about my dad is that he's this big, macho guy when it comes to hunting, fishing, and his military experience, but when he watched *Beauty and the Beast*—you know, the Disney classic—with my nephew, he cried. He's just a big mush ball."

"You're lucky your parents are still alive. I used to dream about my dad coming to find me in one of the homes to take me away. Before Mom died, I asked her about him. She seemed exceedingly distraught over the question, so I dropped it. When I understood relationships later in life, I just figured they'd lived in sin and he decided he wasn't cut out for parenthood after all. How did your parents react to you being a lesbian?"

"It was a nonissue for them. They wondered when I would figure it out because they'd suspected since I was very little. I turned up my nose to all things girly, gravitating toward what I considered more interesting, like climbing trees, playing softball, and making mud pies. If I wasn't following Dad around, I was hanging around with my brother and his friends. I was willing to push the envelope a lot more than many of his pals. The more daring the challenge, the more I wanted to participate. How about you? Did you get any support in the foster homes you grew up in?"

"Now that depends on how you define 'support.' I wasn't broadcasting what I suspected about myself and waiting for them to shower me in gold stars, if that's what you mean, but I did learn a bit about sex and sexual orientation from a fellow foster kid. She took a very special interest in me. I had my first girl-on-girl experience at the ripe old age of twelve."

"That doesn't sound too positive."

Codee shrugged. "I was conflicted. I knew I liked girls, but I wasn't necessarily into this particular girl. It was a very confusing time for me. It always felt wrong, and twelve isn't the right age to lose your virginity, especially with someone you don't have strong feelings for. I guess I'm still searching for the person who will feel just right."

"I guess we aren't completely dissimilar, because I haven't found Ms. Right quite yet either. I just thought I had several times."

†

Erma walked into the living room carrying two heaping plates of pancakes. The steam was still rising off them as a healthy square of butter melted on the top of each mound and oozed down the sides.

Sawyer noticed the dark blue dots woven into the cakes and assumed Erma had filled them with blueberries. "Yummy, blueberry pancakes. That's one of my favorite breakfasts. Sometimes I even have them for dinner."

Erma set the plates down on the coffee table. "I'll get the syrup for you girls. Would you like some juice? We have grapefruit, orange, and apple."

"Apple sounds good to me, but I don't need any syrup," Sawyer answered.

"I'll take the same, but I need some syrup. It's down-right un-American not to have pancakes smothered in butter and syrup."

Sawyer jumped up from the couch. "Let me help you. I don't think you can carry all three items. Besides, where's your plate? Aren't you going to join us?"

"I thank you for the assistance, and yes, I am going to join you, and then I really have to explain a few things before the rest of Codee's new unit arrives. I don't want her going into cardiac arrest."

"What? It's bad enough I banged my head and can't remember a whole bunch of very important developments, and now there's something that will possibly shock me further, sending me down a new rabbit hole?"

Erma held up her hand. "Just hang on a minute. We'll be right back."

Sawyer squeezed Codee's shoulder and smiled reassuringly. "It'll be okay. I promise. Whatever is coming down the pike, we'll face it together. I promise I won't leave you to overcome anything alone."

†

Codee couldn't imagine what could possibly be more shocking than Trison's two executive orders Sawyer had already told her about.

She was jolted from her thoughts by three short raps on the front door, and a woman strode confidently inside. She focused her attention in the direction of the woman but only managed to view her profile.

When the newcomer turned around, Codee gasped. She blinked and stared at her reflection, but she wasn't in front of a looking glass. The eyes that stared back at her were a mirror image of her own. Spiky, chestnut hair adorned her head, and her generous lips quirked up in an expression of warmth and joy. *This woman is the butch version of me.* "You….you…could be my twin."

A deep-throated chuckle erupted from inside the woman.

Erma rushed into the room carrying the syrup and her plate of pancakes. Sawyer followed closely behind, juggling three glasses of juice. Sawyer's eyes widened as she moved her gaze from Codee to the stranger.

"Aw shit, Chynna, I told you to wait a few minutes. I wanted to prep Codee, you bullheaded imp," Erma shouted as she set down her plate, napkins, and three sets of utensils.

"It's after eight thirty. What the hell have you been doing? Playing tiddlywinks? Ya know we've got a war going on right now and don't have much time to pussyfoot around. Yep, I'm your twin, Codee. You probably don't remember me, but I remember you, and Pa talked about you all the time. Well at least in his *lucid* moments. Promised me we'd come get you someday and he'd fix what he'd broken, but then he lost track of you and Ma and his illness got much worse."

"Is he…is he still alive?" Codee managed to ask.

Chynna's smile faltered. "Nope, he was terminated six months ago. He was in one of his less productive cycles, and that was all it took to initiate termination at the garage where he'd managed to get by for several years. The new owner didn't appreciate Dad's special quirks. When he was on a roll, he'd do the work of five guys and barely go to sleep because he spent so much time at work, but when he crashed, well, it wasn't a pretty sight." The corners of her mouth turned up, and Codee thought she saw amusement in her expression. "Your speech was brilliant, by the way. I wished I'd heard it six months ago. It took Pa's early retirement to shake me out of my complacency. Most people chose to stay under the radar and hope no one keyed in on them or one of their loved ones, just hoping the evil wouldn't touch them or their families. But as you stated more eloquently than anyone else, no one is safe and if you aren't part of the solution, you're part of the problem."

Codee wasn't sure what to make of this newest revelation. She thought she heard admiration in Chynna's voice. "Chynna?" She rolled the name around in her mouth. It tasted familiar. "I have a sister," she said in amazement.

"A twin sister," Chynna corrected. "I'm the bigger, more badass version of you. Pa always said you had the brains and I've got the brawn."

Sawyer put the juice on the table, sat next to Codee, and grabbed her hand, squeezing it. "Having a sibling is a really good thing, and your sister seems like a nice person."

That small gesture created an instant calming effect. When she dug inside herself to determine how she felt at this moment, one word came to mind—*joy*. Regardless of whatever else was happening in the world and the fact her parents had allowed her and Chynna to be separated, she had a sister. She'd always prayed, dreamed, and pretended she had a long-lost sister out there somewhere, and now her dreams had become reality.

Despite her joy, anger invaded her mind as she was unable to understand why Erma hadn't told her before today. "Erma, you knew this all along and never told me?"

"I only learned about this last night when I hightailed it to this compound after you two made your escape. Chynna saw the newsfeed and knew instantly who you were. She demanded to join your unit, and I was about to prepare you for the shock before she preempted me."

Codee sighed. "Okay, you're forgiven. Mainly because I'm starving and that stack of pancakes is getting cold. I hope you have some more warming in an oven for Chynna, because I'm not sharing," she joked as she wrapped her arms around her plate.

"I've got plenty, but I think it might be a little crowded now in the living room. Can we move to the dining room table?" Erma asked.

"Yum, pancakes. They're my favorite. I guess growing up thinking you were an only child didn't teach you how to share." Chynna winked.

"Unfortunately I didn't exactly grow up as an only child and I learned the hoarding rule instead," Codee blurted out before she could censor her confession.

Chynna's forehead furrowed, but she remained quiet.

Sawyer moved her hand to stroke gently, once again giving her the silent support she needed.

The group picked up their plates and juice, and meandered over to the large, rustic table in the wide-open floor design. It looked a bit like one of those old farm tables with scratches, dents, and other marks that supposedly gave it "character." It wasn't exactly her style, but she did appreciate that look and wondered if the owners used it as a remembrance map. Memories were like that—something small could trigger either a positive or negative recollection. She searched her own mind for positive memories of Chynna. She knew they were there somewhere, because this woman didn't cause the hairs on the back of her head to rise. Instead, a warm feeling spread through her system, almost like a sip of soothing tea. The sensation was there on the edge, but somehow she wasn't able to pull it back into focus.

Chynna stared at Codee. "You're trying to remember me, aren't you, little sis?"

"I'm sorry, neither you nor Dad are clear in my mind. I vaguely remember asking Mom about him, but I can't imagine why I wouldn't have done the same about you. Maybe Mom was just so hurt by my questions, I decided not to ask anymore. I never liked seeing her cry. Wait, 'little sis'? What am I, one minute younger?"

"Yep, Pa always said I couldn't wait to get out and probably pushed you aside."

Erma waved her fork in the air. "Come on, girls, eat up. The rest of the crew will be here soon." She pushed it into her own large stack and separated a big chunk.

The room was quiet for a few moments while the group began to eat. Sawyer broke the silence after finishing her first bite. "These are wonderful, Erma. Thanks for cooking for us. Can you tell us where we go from here?"

"Well basically we're planning to overthrow the government, and Codee's unit is supposed to head to the Westin hotel where Trison is making an appearance soon," Erma answered.

Sawyer raised her eyebrow. "Are you out of your mind?"

"Nope, her specially picked unit has some former and current Navy SEALs and other Special Forces types. There's also a key insider helping us."

"And what exactly are we planning to do?" Codee asked in exasperation.

"Take President Trison into custody and try him for war crimes against his own nation. Rumor has it that if we're able to capture him, the United Nations will step up to the plate and convene the International Criminal Court. Even though this isn't a part of the UN, there's an agreement that governs the cooperation between the two organizations." Erma took another bite of her pancakes.

"Yep, that's what I've been told too. I studied this in War College. Basically, the UN adopted this back in 1998 at a UN Diplomatic Conference. It's based on the Rome Statute, which was a treaty negotiation within the UN to create an independent judicial body. I suppose this is their way to create a checks-and-balances system, kind of like the one we supposedly have in the US that Trison has trampled all over with his narcissistic, power-hungry ways," Chynna added.

"There's a war college?" Codee asked.

"Sure, in order for someone to achieve the higher ranks in the military, you've got to pass War College. Pa didn't exactly jump for joy when I joined the Army, but I think he was proud of me in the end. I might not talk like I'm a scholar, but I did manage to climb the ranks quickly and obtained a graduate degree compliments of Uncle Sam. I also made it into the elite Army Rangers."

"What's your rank?" Sawyer asked.

"Lieutenant colonel," Chynna proudly answered.

"Wow." Sawyer whistled. "That's impressive."

Chynna puffed out her chest. "I used to be proud to serve my country, and when they abolished Don't Ask, Don't Tell, I was able to perform my duties openly, which made it all the sweeter to follow the commander in chief, but now…." She shook her head. "Until I heard your speech, I felt like a traitor. Now I know I'm doing the right thing, and sometimes ignoring an immoral order is what we have to do, even if it comes from my commander in chief."

"Did they tell you I hit my head and don't remember anything? I don't know what I said in my speech, or even how it was distributed to media outlets. I really don't think I'm qualified to lead any unit. You seem to be the more appropriate choice here. Maybe we can fool everyone into thinking you're me and I'm you."

"Oh, I'm the one who distributed the videos—right after you and Miss Cutie here sped off on your cycle. I was following your very specific instructions. You may not be able to remember everything, but you're the best damn strategist I've ever known. I think the two of you should combine powers. Kind of like those Saturday morning cartoon heroes, you know, *Wonder Twins*. Only you two are both women, as it should be," Erma exclaimed.

Codee chuckled. "Well, at least that's one mystery solved. I wondered who released the video to the media. Well, Sawyer, you're not getting off that easy. I'm involving you in the plans, so I suppose we'll have to become the Three Amigas instead of the Wonder Twins. I'll need Chynna's military expertise and your ability to read people."

"Whatever I need to do, I'm in." Sawyer grinned. "I just have to get used to seeing double."

"Oh, I think you can tell us apart. I'm the butch twin, but try not to fall in love with me too; I'm taken. My partner is also part of the unit, and you won't meet a tougher, more badass person. The other guys stay clear of her every time she has her period. She's a Navy SEAL, one of the first women to make it through the program when they opened the doors this past year," Chynna exclaimed proudly.

"How many people are in this unit I'm supposed to lead?" Codee asked.

"Including you and Sawyer, there are a total of twelve." Chynna took another big bite of her pancakes. "Mmm, this really hits the spot,"

"When is the rest of the unit arriving?" Sawyer asked.

"Oh, not for three more hours, because I wanted to get the surprise out of the way first. I wish we had more time to catch up, but we'll want to have some kind of plan in play before the others show up. We'll have plenty of time for me to fill in the blanks once we bring that bastard to justice." Chynna set her fork down and pierced Codee with a penetrating look.

Sawyer made a quick connection with a short caress on her arm. "How's your head and arm this morning? Maybe whatever plan is devised should include you directing on the sidelines but not taking an active participation in any snatch-and-grab heroics."

"The best leaders are the ones that personally lead their men and women into battle. A few more Tylenol and I'll be good as gold. Erma, is there an office with a large conference table so we can spread out, maybe look at maps and building plans? I suspect our inside person has provided some of this information along with the best times to attempt a capture. I imagine Trison has an army of Secret Service agents and peacekeepers surrounding him 24/7," Codee said.

Chynna frowned. "Look, I don't really know why they wanted a nonmilitary person to lead this mission, but I do trust the person who made the decision. I guess they want to use you as the face of democracy, freedom, and human rights, but they didn't say you should personally be involved in the actual abduction to acquire our own war criminal. I agree with Sawyer."

"Sorry, whatever plan we devise, me being a part of it is non-negotiable. If they want me to be the face of this for publicity purposes, then those are my requirements." Codee looked directly at Chynna, who nodded once.

"I do have the maps, building plans, and other details you need in my jeep. I've always been willing to give my life for my country, but I'd gladly sacrifice it to protect my sister, and so would Jac, my wife. I can't wait for you to meet her. Most people can't see the two of us fitting because we're both strong-willed women, but it works." Chynna chuckled. "Just don't instigate any debates on which branch of the armed forces are the bigger badasses. We never agree on that."

Chapter Ten

The small group of women finished going over the plan. Codee had asked Chynna what she would do, and that started a lengthy brainstorming session that incorporated bits and pieces from everyone until they all agreed the strategy gave them the best option of success. She had never been one to have just one plan and insisted they have backup options for every stage in their mission. She voiced her concerns that the inside person may be a plant to draw out the network's key players and floated out the idea of an exit strategy in case their contact double-crossed them.

The only people she trusted implicitly were Sawyer, Erma, and her sister. She told them she preferred they keep some parts of the plan under wraps, especially their contingency plans and different exit strategies. The success of their mission depended on key individuals in the White House staff giving them access to parts of the Westin that were normally well guarded and controlled by the Secret Service during a presidential visit. Unfortunately for Trison, he'd made a lot of enemies, some of them were very close to him. His policies had inadvertently affected some of his trusted staff, and she wondered how someone as cunning as Trison was blissfully unaware of the trickle-down effect of his termination orders. He had to know that eventually this might happen, so she wondered what he had put in place to counteract this possibility.

President Trison might be a narcissist and a sociopath, but he was far from stupid, and that's what worried her. Something niggled at her brain, telling her that they were walking right into the lion's den and he was just waiting to snap his powerful jaws.

Codee stood and stretched her back. After bending over the documents for so long, she'd started to stiffen. She turned her head toward the door when she heard a commotion in the hallway.

"So where is your little *love bunny*? I thought for sure you two would arrive together," a male voice boomed in the hallway. A deep belly laugh followed.

"If I didn't love you like a brother, I'd knock the shit out of you for calling Chynna my love bunny. I wouldn't say that around her though, because she doesn't consider you her brother. You know that coupon for saving your ass was already used; you don't get a second one," a husky female voice answered.

Chynna ran out of the room and Codee heard her yelling, "Dirk, you smartass, you knew I would hear that, but you know what? I'm gonna let it pass because you're just jealous you don't have your own little love bunny. Bet it chaps your hide that I'm getting some every night and you're not getting any—well, at least every night my *love bunny* is with me."

Codee walked into the hallway and witnessed Chynna kissing an extremely muscular woman with short, dark hair, chiseled features, and expressive, dark brown eyes. She was what some might describe as a very handsome woman.

"You must be Jac. Chynna didn't tell us how attractive you are, only that you're a badass Navy SEAL and all hers. I'm Codee." She stuck out her hand and shook Jac's.

"It's an honor, ma'am."

"What's with the 'ma'am' bit? You're Chynna's wife, so that makes us family."

Sawyer stepped up beside Codee and offered her hand. "It's great to meet you, Jac, and I think I heard Chynna call you Dirk." She shook both Dirk and Jac's hands.

"Oh darn, how rude of me. Hello, Dirk, it's good to meet you as well. I assume you're part of my newly formed unit?"

"Yes, ma'am, I am, and I'm very proud to serve under you." Dirk barely moved as he acknowledged her greeting. He reminded Codee of a giant old Sequoia, tall and straight with a thick trunk. His closely cropped red hair and square jaw screamed "military."

"Would you all please stop calling me 'ma'am'? It makes me feel old, and I don't like feeling old."

"Okay, ma...,"

Dirk and Jac started to reply, stopped, and then responded in stereo. "Jinx."

"Oh jeez, these guys are incorrigible, but they're the best two-person scout team the SEALs ever trained. They've single-handedly eliminated over fifty potential threats in an earlier mission, so we couldn't ask for a better unit to go in first." Chynna smiled broadly at the pair. "Where's the rest of the team?"

"They're waiting in building F. Are you ready to brief us on our mission? I get the feeling this isn't going to be a run-of-the-mill rebel strike. From the looks of the rest of the team, they're the cream of the elite forces. I recognize some of squad, and their reputations definitely precede them. This is big, isn't it?" Jac asked.

Codee swayed as she realized the magnitude of what they were about to do and hoped another day might provide her with the confidence she needed to pull off their hasty plan. Too much was at risk for them to fail. If the country left President Trison to continue his rampage on humanity, more innocent people would lose their lives, and she could not stand by doing nothing.

Sawyer quickly steadied Codee with an arm around her waist. "I'm right here. You can do this. We'll have another couple of days to mentally prepare for D-Day. If you need to barricade yourself in the bedroom and meditate without distraction, I'll make sure you aren't disturbed," she whispered.

Codee took a deep breath. "Nothing is going to happen until the day after tomorrow. We have a small window of opportunity, so I'll meet with the unit and explain everything. That will give everyone time for some R and R to mentally and physically prepare. Chynna, will you lead the way to building F, please?"

†

Sawyer scanned the large bunkhouse and watched as nine pairs of eyes stared straight ahead, waiting for Codee to speak. The people they belonged to were all rigid in posture, and she recognized the sign of strict military training.

Codee looked at her sister with a wide-eyed stare. Sawyer imagined this situation was a foreign world to her. It wasn't all that familiar to Sawyer, either, but she had rubbed elbows with some of the hard-core military types after joining the network, so at least she'd become used to them after Trison rose to power.

Sawyer noted that Doc, one of the fake peacekeepers they'd met earlier, was looking more intently at Codee than the rest. He was clearly in awe of her.

Before Chynna stepped forward, she seemed to focus on Doc and hesitated a few seconds before addressing the group. "I don't think my sister is familiar or comfortable with military protocol, so we're going to do things a little differently. Y'all can relax while we do some introductions and brief you on your mission."

"I apologize in advance if I forget your names, because that's never been my forte. Please don't take offense. I'm delighted to meet all of you and applaud the sacrifice you're about to make, because I don't think this mission will be a cake walk. I have a nagging feeling we're walking into someone's trap, so we need to prepare for every possibility. Which is why we'll be laying out backup options for every step. I'm guessing you know who I am, so will you just give me your first names? If you prefer using a nickname, by all means shout that out. Hello, Doc, it's good to see you again." Codee's voice was soft but commanding.

Doc's smile took over his face as she addressed him.

"I thought you were only on the escort team, Doc. How'd you end up in this unit?" Chynna asked.

"It was a last-minute change and I volunteered. Hardgrove got the flu, and they don't think he'll be ready to move out in the next couple of days."

Chynna narrowed her eyes. "No offense, Doc, but this unit was specially picked for the mission, and if this last-minute change fucks things up, you're gonna wish you never volunteered. I know you're top-notch, but I haven't worked with you before."

Jac stepped forward and touched Chynna's arm. "I'll vouch for Doc. He's one of the quickest thinkers I know and able to adapt to any situation. I think he'll be an asset."

"He's also a fast little bastard and the only one to ever best me in hand-to-hand-combat training," Dirk added.

Doc grinned. "That's because the bigger they are, the harder they fall."

Sawyer liked Doc, but she wasn't sure how she felt about his clear affection for Codee. She was surprised to recognize that what she was feeling was jealousy.

Chynna pointed to the man standing next to Doc. "Names. Take a step forward and spit them out. If your nickname is crude, give your first name. My sister is not some lowlife grunt."

The man who looked like a World Wrestling Entertainment star took one step forward. "Hulk, ma'am."

"I hope you're referring to my sister when you say 'ma'am,' because I'd really rather you not call me that," Codee announced.

"Yes, ma—I mean, Ms. Codee."

The rest of the team stepped forward one by one, introducing themselves.

"Mac."

"Blackie."

"Cind."

"JT."

"Hellen. I won't let them shorten my name even though I resemble hell when someone pisses me off." The final member of the team smirked.

Sawyer surveyed the group. Counting Chynna and Jac, two other women—Cind and Hellen—made up the twelve-member unit.

"I don't suppose I could get you to wear those stick-on name badges for the next couple of days until I learn your names. You know, the ones that say, 'Hello my name is'...." Codee grinned.

"I can send someone out to get some," Dirk answered.

"It was a joke, you dipshit." Jac punched his shoulder.

"Ow. I think it's kind of a good idea."

"Oh brother." Chynna rolled her eyes. "Come on, let's quit screwing around. I'd like to get this briefing over so I can spend a little time with my sister before we jump into the fires of hell."

"Let's head over to the table and I'll lay things out. At three o'clock on...."

Chapter Eleven

Codee was exhausted after the meeting. She just wanted to hide away in the room they'd set aside for her and Sawyer. Normally she needed a lot more time alone to process things and wind down from a stressful day at work, but after a light dinner Erma had prepared for the team, Sawyer asked if she wanted to take a walk around the grounds. Codee had surprised herself by saying, "Yes, I'd love to."

She meant it too. She hadn't agreed just to be polite.

When Sawyer took her hand, she hadn't pulled away. She knew where things were heading between them, and she couldn't think of one single reason she shouldn't let it progress naturally, unless she counted her shitty track record with women.

Sawyer had told her that she fell in love easily, and Codee didn't want to hurt her, but they could both be dead in two days and she wanted to feel her gentle touch. It wasn't about sex for her, it was about connection, and she felt a deep bond to this woman who had the ability to calm and encourage her with a single touch.

The nature trail around the sterile, functional build-ings felt out of place to Codee as she noted the beauty that surrounded the compound. Although snow hadn't fallen in a while, the grounds still looked pristine as the evergreen trees made a stark contrast to the snow that remained on the ground.

Neither had gloves on and the air still had a chill to it, but Codee didn't want to release Sawyer's hand. Instead they stuck their free hands in the pockets of their warm leather jackets.

"Your sister seems so...protective. You don't re-member her at all?" Sawyer broke the semi-quiet as her voice combined with the crunching of their boots on the snow-laden gravel path.

"I was so young when they left. I've tried so hard to recreate those memories, and it's like they're just out of reach. I wanted to sit down and talk more with Chynna, but it sounded like she hasn't had much time with her wife lately and I couldn't bring myself to interrupt them." Codee sighed as she stepped over a fallen log and Sawyer followed.

"I'm sorry about your father."

"I don't really remember him either. When my moth-er died, my whole world came crashing down. Honestly I didn't believe anyone would come to my rescue, and I sup-pose my experiences in foster care might just be my saving grace for what we have planned. I have a sixth sense about trouble and can almost smell it. I don't suppose your normal childhood prepared you for what we're about to face, but then again, you've been living this hell for the last several months and I can't remember a damn thing about it."

Sawyer stopped and gently tugged Codee against her as she wrapped her arms tightly around her body and gave Codee one of the most soothing hugs she'd ever experienced. When they separated, Sawyer leaned in and barely brushed

Codee's lips in an almost-chaste kiss. "We complement each other."

One brief taste of Sawyer wasn't going to do it for her. When she reconnected their lips, there was nothing chaste about the kiss as she explored every inch of Sawyer's mouth with her lips and tongue and then wove her way inside. Codee excelled at kissing women. She made it an almost-religious experience—or so her past lovers had informed her.

"Wow," Sawyer exclaimed.

"At least this whole nightmare of a world we now live in provided this opportunity. I never would have pursued you at the hospital. You know that, right?"

Sawyer smiled. "Maybe I would have pursued you until you acquiesced to my charms. I've always been one to pursue a woman completely out of my class."

Codee linked her arm with Sawyer's, clasped her hand again, and pulled her along the path. "That isn't why I wouldn't have dated you, because you are definitely not out of my class—because I have no class." She grinned. "There's that whole nepotism policy that HR is supposed to uphold. Dating a coworker is strictly a big no-no when you're the HR exec, because we have to be a role model. Of course, ferrying them away after a preterm proceeding isn't exactly kosher either." Codee laughed. "I suppose that's one way to resign. Do you think they got that we both won't be showing up to work on Monday morning?"

"I haven't seen your little video yet, but I'd say that was probably your definitive resignation."

"My job was getting boring anyway. I guess it's time to start anew. Maybe I'll run for some political office after this is all over—if we survive. Apparently I have the gift of gab."

"Just so you know, I'm not expecting anything when we get back to the house. I didn't want to waste an opportunity to kiss you even if it only happened once. I've wanted to do that ever since I saw you in orientation. You mesmerized me then, and you still do."

"Don't believe everything you hear. Most of the stories I told were completely embellished for effect."

"You just had to burst my worship bubble, didn't you?" Sawyer bumped her shoulder while keeping their arms looped and fingers entwined.

"I never want to be on a pedestal or someone's object of worship. A relationship never works when there's an imbalance. If we even have a chance at pursuing some type of relationship after this is all over, we have to stand side by side as equals."

Sawyer stopped walking again and pulled Codee close as she held up her free hand, bringing her thumb and forefinger an inch apart. "Not even a tiny bit of worship?"

Codee laughed. "Only if I can also show you a tiny bit of adulation too. Come on, my goddess, it's getting a bit nippy out here and I'd like to see if Erma will make us her special hot chocolate while we sit beside the fire. Maybe Chynna and Jac will have had enough time to reconnect and I can prod her for more information about her childhood before we turn in for the night."

"You know she's going to be just as curious about you. Are you willing to reveal as much about your life after they left as you are interested in learning?"

"Good question. I don't know. Until I met you I haven't ever really talked much about my foster care experiences. Erma is the only other person who knows anything, and Sharlie doesn't even know I grew up in foster homes."

Codee stumbled on a root that had pushed through the gravel. She thought it was a symbol for what she was struggling with now—faltering over how much to share with her newly found sister as her revelations and emotions continued to push to the surface. For the first time in her life, she wanted to reveal more about herself to not only her new friend, but to her newly acquired sister. *Friend? Is that what Sawyer is, a friend, or is something more developing?*

"You look like you're pondering the meaning of life." Sawyer chuckled.

"No, nothing that profound, but honestly, I was thinking about us and what's happening. Are my evolving feelings just a byproduct of our shared experience right now?" Codee laughed. "I can't believe I just blurted that out. I'm never that open about my thoughts. You seem to be a confession magnet."

"I've been practicing since I was a little girl...." Sawyer grinned. "You wouldn't believe the secrets my Barbie dolls told me. Skipper was secretly in love with Tiff and not Scott, but she was expected to uphold all those darned societal expectations."

"Somehow I can't imagine you playing with Barbie dolls. I see you more as the climb-a-tree, toss-a-softball, or kick-a-soccer-ball type."

"Ah, you caught me. Okay, I wasn't going to admit this to anyone, but my soccer ball used to spill her guts to me all the time. She said she snuck out one night with Ms. Softball and met up with Ms. Mitt, and boy did they wreak havoc on my mother's windows. I got blamed, of course."

Codee bent over laughing and brought Sawyer toppling to the ground with her. With only inches between their lips, her injured arm forgotten in the moment, she took advantage of this opportunity and captured Sawyer's lips in a searing kiss. Breathless, they broke apart and stared at one another as they lay on the frozen earth.

"You, Sawyer, are undoubtedly going to present a big problem for me. I like you far more than I should, and I don't have a very good track record with women. You deserve someone who can open their heart and commit, and honestly, I don't know if that's in my DNA. Too bad my twin is taken; she'd be a much better choice for you."

"I don't mean to be adversarial, but I disagree. She's not my type, but you are." Sawyer gave her a quick peck on the lips, pushed off the ground, and offered her hand to help Codee up.

The two women resumed their walk, turning and heading back to the main house. The sweet scene they happened upon when they entered the cozy cabin brought a smile to Codee's lips. Her twin had her arms wrapped around the tough Navy SEAL and was whispering in her ear as they toasted themselves in front of the fire. The look of bliss on Jac's face told the whole story. These two women were deeply in love with one another, and Codee wanted what they had. A brief thought fluttered through her mind, reminding her that maybe Sawyer was the one to bring what seemed an unreachable dream close enough to grab, if she would only let it happen.

†

Sawyer was having a hard time keeping her emotions in check. First, there was that passion-filled kiss Codee had initiated, and then the brief brush against her extremely tempting lips. If she didn't absolutely know without any reasonable doubt that the guarded woman would run screaming for the hills, she would have confessed to her that she was once again falling for someone who was probably going to break her heart. Only this time it felt more real and more mature. Maybe she was wrong and this would be the time it stuck. Surely she deserved to find the kind of love Chynna and Jac so clearly had.

When they'd returned to the house, she hadn't missed the beautiful scene of Jac and Chynna cuddling on the couch. She and Codee shared a look, and Sawyer thought that maybe she was wondering the very same thing. *Could this be us in the near future? Would fate be so kind to allow us a similar love before life's cruelty takes it all away?*

Sawyer squeezed her hand and gave it a quick tug to lead her to their bedroom, leaving the reunited lovers to their special moment before the impending storm hit.

"I know it's a little early, but maybe we can head to the bedroom and just chill for a bit. It looks like Chynna and Jac are cozy in their own little world right now."

"Yeah, I think you're right. That's a good choice for me because I generally need quite a bit of down time without having to interact with people after a draining day of having to communicate as much as I did today."

"Oh I'm sorry, do you need me to get lost for a bit? I can find something to entertain myself and leave you alone."

"No, please don't. I'd like you to join me while I wind down. That is, if you don't mind. For some reason, you don't drain my energy and I don't feel like I have to be on stage with you. I can relax and be myself."

Sawyer was immensely grateful Codee felt comfortable with her, and that gave her a sliver of hope that maybe this time her heart wouldn't shatter into a million tiny pieces.

✝

When they reached the bedroom, Codee looked through one of the bags to find a T-shirt and sweatpants. She still felt somewhat exposed and started to take the makeshift sleepwear into the bathroom to change. She wondered if

Sawyer thought that was an odd quirk. After all, they had shared several sizzling kisses, so surely changing in front of one another shouldn't be a big deal.

"Um, I'll just go change into sleepwear."

Sawyer's penetrating gaze never left her as she gave a slight nod before Codee walked into the bathroom and closed the door.

When Codee finished changing into her sweats and brushing her teeth, she ventured out into the bedroom and noted Sawyer was pulling her T-shirt down over her head. She got another glimpse of her sculpted stomach and couldn't help the instant reaction. Sawyer was a beautiful woman in an equally attractive body, and she'd have to be blind not to notice.

Sawyer had been the one to remember to ask for toothpaste and toothbrushes after they'd finished breakfast, and Codee assumed Erma had laid them on the bathroom counter. She hadn't remembered stacking them side by side after their earlier use, but maybe Sawyer had done that. Everything was still a blur to her, and she was trying her best to adapt.

Sawyer silently passed her, moving her hand down Codee's shoulder and arm in a gentle caress. Just that small touch of reassurance before she went into the bathroom was enough to put a smile on Codee's face. She heard the water and presumed Sawyer was brushing her teeth. They'd both have minty-fresh breath, and maybe more kissing would transpire before they shut off the lights and turned in for the night.

The door to the bathroom was slightly ajar, and when Sawyer pushed it open she looked almost unsure of herself as the corners of her lips turned up in a shy smile.

"So…what small talk shall we engage in before falling asleep?"

"I'd like to hear more about your normal childhood since I don't really know what that looks like." Codee walked to the bed, turned down the covers, crawled in, and propped herself against the headboard.

Sawyer scooted under the covers next to Codee, turning her head to face her. "Normal is relative, you know. What is ordinary to one person may not be to another. I think in today's world there's a whole lot of diversity in families. At least there was until Trison started upsetting the apple cart. Fortunately, the barn door is already open and it's pretty difficult to go back entirely to the way things used to be."

"Point taken, but I'd still like to know what it was like to grow up with a mom, dad, and sibling. Was it as wonderful as I always imagined when I was young?"

"Meh, sometimes, and other times family can get all up in your business and drive you crazy. Don't get me wrong, I love my brother, but he is so overprotective, he scares the crap out of me when he meets a new girlfriend. I can't imagine how they felt. My mom is even worse. She has that stink eye when she doesn't like someone, and she didn't like any of my former lovers. I'm still waiting to bring home someone she'll approve of. My parents are intellectual snobs, and if a person didn't have an advanced degree, they were automatically discarded as not the right partner for me. Of course, neither one was ever impolite to the person's face, but I sure heard about it later."

Codee cringed. "If we make it through this ordeal, I don't think I want to meet them. Can we just have a glorious affair and never reach the meeting-the-parents part?"

"Oh no, they would love you. You have everything on my mom's list of partner attributes. She's written it down for me and e-mailed it several times. Every time I've been dumped, I get the list in my inbox again."

"Okay, I've got to hear this list."

"Number one is 'makes more money than a social worker,' because you already know they make diddly squat. Then there is having an advanced degree. I'm not sure how she judges kindness and unpretentiousness, but they're on the list. Cat lover is a plus, but wanting to have children is an absolute non-negotiable requirement in her book."

"What about in yours?"

"Oh, I'd love to have children someday with the right person, and only if we go back to pre-Trison days where the country seemed to be heading in the right direction. I refuse to bring children into a narrow-minded, draconian world, or worse...."

"Honestly I never thought of having children. I've passed the age where doing that is safe, but I have considered fostering a child, especially an older child. I'd want someone to have a different experience than I had. I'd also want to adopt the child I foster, no matter what, to give the message that you don't have to be perfect for someone to want and love you. I know that may seem ideal, but too many times, foster parents don't stick it out with the children and run away at the first sign of difficulty. That is far more damaging than people realize."

"Sounds like you speak from experience. I can't imagine you being anything other than a perfect little girl."

"I had my moments, just like any child who suddenly has their whole world drastically change overnight. Either you act out or you get eerily quiet. Sunny little children who reach out right away to their new parents are the adoptable ones, not the sullen, scared children who shy away from everyone. I didn't want a new mom, I wanted my mom back, and I had no idea what having a father was like."

"When I heard you speak in orientation, I would have never guessed. The things you said about choosing a positive attitude really resonated with me. Somehow, you managed to work through your experiences, because I would definitely have pegged you as that sunny, outgoing child."

"Smoke and mirrors…." Codee shifted in the bed and repositioned herself to lean on her side. "I had a very instrumental teacher early on who encouraged me, and doing well in school became my primary focus. It paid off, and the scholarship that followed allowed me to get to the place I am now. I really wish I'd remembered Chynna. I would have done everything in my power to find her and reestablish some semblance of a family."

"What doesn't break us…makes us stronger, huh?"

"Amen to that, and hopefully that lofty notion will pan out as we embark on our mission. I'm glad we have this time to settle and take advantage of Trison's presidential tour before he arrives in our state. Can I ask you something?"

Sawyer rolled to her side and was face-to-face with Codee. "Of course."

"Does it seem a bit strange how easy our rebel forces are making everything sound with the inside track regarding the Westin employees and the Secret Service agent?"

"Hmmm, I'm not really a master strategist, but I suppose it does. Although I'll bet our first hurdle is getting through whatever traffic blockades are in place for his upcoming visit to Seattle."

"I just get an uneasy feeling, and whenever that's happened before with me, I've always regretted not listening to that inner voice. Foster care nurtures paranoia."

"Not to make you nervous, but, Codee, they *are* out to get you and that's not paranoia, that's a fact."

"Well aren't you a cheery little thing. I think I'd prefer to be delusional versus paranoid. Delusions of grandeur sound very appealing right about now."

Sawyer wrapped her arms around Codee and pulled her close, kissing her forehead. "God, I'm an idiot. My job is to keep you calm, so I should be fired." She pulled away and left some space between their bodies so they could still talk.

"Oh no, that's what got us in this predicament to start with...your impending termination. I think I'll keep you in that job, because it's a perfect match for your skills. Believe it or not, you do keep me calm. Just a touch from you and I'm instantly in Zen land."

"Well, I don't know if I am uniquely suited, but I can tell you that I love my new job," Sawyer smiled as she stroked Codee's cheek. Codee leaned into the touch and briefly closed her eyes.

As Codee opened them, she found nothing but love and compassion staring back at her. She wasn't sure how she knew those were Sawyer's emotions, she just knew. "God, you would be so easy to fall in love with, if I had the psychological composition to do that. I could also surrender to making love with you, but I'd better settle for a more judicious form of touch. Maybe we can just hold each other and allow for some amount of touching but not enough to let our passions run wild. I think I need the human connection. Is that all right with you?"

"It's perfection in a bottle."

"Why in a bottle?"

"Because then I can keep it and take a sniff every once in a while when I need the boost."

"I know that smell is a precursor to taste, but if it's in a bottle, I want to roll it around on my tongue and let my taste buds burst with joy when that perfection lands on them." Codee closed the distance and began moving her hands along Sawyer's body before she ensnared her lips and began nibbling on them as she thoroughly explored Sawyer's bottom lip.

Sawyer opened her mouth, and Codee's tongue danced inside.

Codee felt Sawyer's hands reach the small of her back, then move lower to cup and stroke her behind. Sawyer's hips rose and moved in rhythm with the strokes. Everything was like an explosion to her senses. If she didn't stop, she would seize this woman and allow herself to be taken right now.

They were breathing heavily when Codee broke from the kiss and their heated caresses. "Sorry, sorry, my bad, and I'm the one who established the rules of engagement for the evening."

"Rules, smules, you know rules were meant to be broken or at the very least bent almost to the point of breakage. I vote for breaking some rules tonight," Sawyer hastily added.

"You are an evil temptress."

"Bwahaha," Sawyer chortled and rubbed her hands together. "But will evil win tonight?"

Codee shook her head. "I want to face myself in the mirror tomorrow, and if I take advantage of this dire situation we're in, I won't like myself very much. You deserve so much more than a quick roll in the hay."

"No, I don't. I'm not complaining. I'll take whatever I can get, and then we can see where it goes after we rid the world of the evil force—you know, the other evil force. Bad-to-the-bone temptresses are always needed in the world." Sawyer winked.

"Oh hell, restraint is overrated when you're facing a possible end of the line. You win, evil temptress."

"I like the sound of that." Sawyer tugged on Codee's T-shirt and gingerly pulled it over her head, letting her fingers brush Codee's sensitive sides.

Codee felt the tingle of a thousand tiny goose bumps as they created a wave over her body. She returned the favor, and they were skin to skin as their breasts came together. The gyrating motion of their bodies moving together as one was like a synergetic collection of grace.

The additional layer of clothing separating the two women had to go. She began to urge the removal of Sawyer's sweats.

Sawyer responded quickly by lifting her behind and pushing them down with one hand while reaching out to nudge Codee's bottoms down. Both women were pleasantly surprised when they found the other had foregone underwear. They struggled to remove the clothing that had gathered at their ankles, stubbornly refusing to separate from their owners without awkward embarrassment. The clumsy de-robing was only a minor nuisance.

Stereo giggles penetrated the quiet of the evening as they finally freed themselves from their nightwear.

"I swear I really have done this before. Perhaps my smooth moves will improve now that we're both naked." Codee ran her hand up and down Sawyer's breast and hip as they lay side by side.

"Do you hear me complaining? No way. You can continue to do that for, oh, how about an eternity?"

Codee stiffened and stopped her exploration. "Um...."

"Oh shit, I meant to communicate that what you're doing feels very nice and to please continue."

"I'm sorry. I know I have commitment issues, and honestly I just don't know what tomorrow will bring."

Sawyer brought her hand to Codee's face and pushed a lock of hair aside as she stroked gently. "I'll take whatever I can get, and if tonight is it, then so be it. I'm not asking for your hand in marriage—yet...." She grinned, and Codee understood the joke, or at least she hoped Sawyer was joking.

"Sawyer, what a fine girl, what a good wife you would be, but alas, my love and my lady is a good cup of tea…." Codee laughed as she sang.

"That is a horrible butchering of a great old classic. I'm seeing a completely new side to you, and I like it." Sawyer closed the distance between them and began to kiss her with a passion Codee had never experienced before.

Three years had passed since Codee had made love with any woman, and then it had seemed almost mechanical. Part A, her middle finger, went into part B, her partner's vagina, and she moved it around a bit while part C, her tongue, lubricated the other woman's clitoris. Codee nearly burst out laughing as her mind took this mini journey, but whatever Sawyer was doing to her suddenly garnered all her attention, and her arousal went into the stratosphere. She no longer had any coherent thoughts other than, *Oh God, please don't stop what you're doing.*

Sawyer was making her way down Codee's body, not leaving any part untouched as her rain of kisses and caresses created a sudden flow of moisture down below. When her hot breath barely made contact with the sensitive bud, Codee's thoughts became words after a low, long moan.

"Oh God, Sawyer, please touch me. I need to feel you."

Sawyer didn't waste any time as she made circles on Codee's clit with her tongue while she slowly entered her with one finger, then two. Hips rose to meet the teasing tongue, and Sawyer began to suck and nibble, causing Codee to moan loudly.

Codee had never been a vocal lover, but Sawyer was playing her like a fiddle, bringing her to the brink and then backing off just enough to hold her in that state of ecstasy right before falling over the edge.

"No more, please no more teasing," Codee begged.

Sawyer increased the rhythm and sucked just a bit harder, and Codee exploded into the most intense orgasm she'd ever experienced. The waves of pleasure continued for what felt like minutes but were probably only several seconds. After the final twinges ended, Sawyer slowly removed her fingers and kept gently stroking her body with reverence. Codee had a feeling of floating, and peace flooded every part of her body.

"Wow, just wow. I'm reconsidering that whole offer to touch or be touched like that for all eternity. Is that still on the table?" Codee pulled Sawyer closer and kissed her, tasting herself on Sawyer's lips.

"I believe the request was for you to continue touching me for all eternity."

"Oh right, no wonder I balked. Somehow I knew deep inside I needed to hold out until you revealed your own cards. I do believe you distracted me from my earlier mission, you evil temptress, and now I'm a tad overwhelmed. Just give me a few minutes to recover, and then you must lie back and become a pillow princess for me."

"Never. I will never be a pillow princess."

"Do I need to tie you up to get you to behave?" Codee wiggled her eyebrows.

"Do you want me to strut out there in my birthday suit and ask your sister for some rope? I'm sure she'd be happy to find some for us, or maybe Erma would want the honors?"

Codee swatted Sawyer's behind and then rolled her over. "Shush now. I'm suddenly ravenous, and I need to keep up my strength. You wouldn't want our upcoming mission to go awry because you're a cheeky little temptress that won't behave."

"Oh, no, never. I'm happy to provide whatever sustenance you need."

. Codee pushed up with her good arm and traced her finger around Sawyer's nipple, causing it to pebble. She leaned in and gently bit and sucked until Sawyer moaned. On her way down to the spot she was eager to taste, she rolled her tongue around Sawyer's belly button, eliciting another sound of bliss.

She parted Sawyer's folds with her hand and found glistening moisture as she glided her fingers along the edges, barely touching Sawyer's clit. Instead of entering Sawyer with her fingers, she continued to stroke along the edges and dipped her tongue into Sawyer's opening, pushing gently inside.

"Oh, holy hell…my God, woman…." Sawyer hips rose from the bed, and it didn't take long for her to cry out and for Codee to feel the contractions on her tongue.

When her spasms subsided, she carefully slithered back up and returned to their previous skin-on-skin, full-body contact. It felt right to lie there with Sawyer for a few more minutes. She quickly pressed her lips to Sawyer's and then moved to the side. She began to draw lazy circles on her stomach.

Sawyer remained on her back with a satisfied smile on her face. "I've never had anyone do that to me. To say it was heavenly would be an understatement. I think if I died right now, I'd feel like I hadn't missed a single thing. Thank you. I know people describe intimacy as an out-of-body experience for them on rare occasions, and I just thought they were making that shit up, but now I'm a believer. I'm such a believer, I'm ready to start breaking out in that oldie but goodie Monkees' song from the sixties." Sawyer turned her body to face Codee.

"Ooh, I love that song; go right ahead. I'd like to think I'm not the only one who breaks out in song at the oddest times."

"I've always been a big fan of combining intimacy with play. Too often people get in this serious, 'I gotta do this right' groove, and it makes the whole experience stressful and mechanical."

"That's so funny you should say that, because earlier I was thinking the very same thing. Sex had become so mechanical for me, even though it's been so long, I can barely remember what it felt like." Codee laughed.

"No regrets?"

"Surprisingly, no, Sawyer. You are an easy woman to love and be intimate with. I'm not necessarily offering a long-term commitment, but I want you to know I'm not closing off the possibility and, in the very short time I've known you, I feel such a connection to you that I'd be crazy not to keep my options open. Let's get through the next few days and then we'll see."

"I'll take whatever you're willing to give. No pressure. You know we're not done for the night, right?"

"I was counting on you to have more stamina because it's way too early to fall asleep," Codee assured her.

Chapter Twelve

The newly formed unit traveled along I-90 in three separate vehicles. They were meeting other members who had arranged for them to infiltrate the Westin Hotel disguised as various staff. They just needed to get close enough to President Trison to incapacitate his Secret Service agents and cut off any escape route that would certainly be in place. The Secret Service always had contingency plans for removing any threat and transporting the president to a secure location.

Doc drove the SUV that carried Sawyer, Codee, Jac, and Chynna. He kept looking in his rearview mirror at Codee, and Sawyer felt just a smidgen of jealousy. She didn't think anyone missed how she was holding Codee's hand in a gesture both of support and intimacy. Erma, Jac, and Chynna had teased the two women when they'd emerged from their room that morning.

Erma was the worst with her kissing sounds, heavy breathing, and mocking words. "Oh God, oh God, oh God, don't stop, Sawyer."

Codee had given her *the look* and she'd taken pity on the two new lovers, but then Chynna took over and began her teasing, which she wasn't able to stop with a look.

Sawyer had had to pull Chynna aside and convince her that teasing about something else may be more appropriate if she wanted to stay on the good side of her newly discovered sister.

Sawyer would have almost welcomed the teasing while driving to their destination, because the inside of the car was now eerily quiet as each member of the team mentally prepared for what they needed to do. She imagined a tomb was livelier than the vehicle.

The silence was broken when Doc whispered, "Oh shit."

The three-car caravan stopped behind a long line of vehicles. Peacekeepers had established a blockade on the highway three miles from the turnoff to Interstate 405 that led into Bellevue. They would definitely recognize Codee after her video had been aired by every major news station. They needed to activate plan B.

A quick text to the lead car and they were speeding along the shoulder, looking for a quick exit.

"I always wanted to be a redhead and who needs long hair anyway?" Codee nervously joked.

"I think you'd look hot with a buzz cut," Doc answered.

"I have to agree with his assessment," Sawyer chimed in.

"How'd you know we might need to camouflage you with a quick dye job and buzz cut?" Chynna asked.

"Easy, if I was charged with protecting the president, I'd have roadblocks looking for me, especially since he's scheduled to visit my neck of the woods. I still get the feeling this is all for show and they're creating the illusion that it will be easy to get to him. I smell a trap, but I can't put my finger on where the odor is coming from," Codee answered.

"I agree, and I can't get a handle on the stink either, but it's there, just beneath the surface," Jac added.

"So what do you propose we do to combat this feeling both of you have?" Chynna turned to face Jac, Sawyer, and Codee, who were riding in the backseat.

"What can you hide in your clothes that can be used as a weapon if we get in a tight spot?" Jac asked.

Chynna grinned. "Fountain pens have sharp stabbing points and are relatively innocuous. I never leave home without one. Stab in the right place and you can incapacitate just about anyone."

"I don't need no stinkin' weapon; my two hands is all I've ever needed," Doc boasted. "Jac, I'll bet you can take out a few peacekeepers with your bare hands and whatever makeshift weapon is in the vicinity. You and I need to stick to Codee like glue. We can't let anything happen to her, agreed?"

"Agreed. Chynna, you have Sawyer duty," Jac directed.

"Wait one damn minute. Maybe I don't have military training, but I have other life skills, and if I need to, I can surely take care of myself," Codee insisted.

Sawyer pointed to Codee. "What she said."

"Oh for fuck's sake, a few days ago you didn't even remember that Trison was president and Sawyer was on the verge of termination, so excuse us for analyzing our current situation and determining what's needed," Jac huffed.

"Ooh, you don't really want to piss Jac off. I know. It ain't a pretty sight. Can you please just humor us, or ignore our chatter?" Chynna pleaded.

"Fine, but don't count out my ability to fight. Growing up in foster care taught me a few things that will help if we get in a bind." Codee crossed her arms over her chest and glared at Jac.

Jac ignored the defiant gaze as she pointed to the right. "There, go ahead and pull into that gas station and let's get this done quickly. We're on a tight schedule here, and we only left a sixty-minute window of extra time to get into position."

Sawyer glanced out the window. "Where did the rest of the team go?"

"They were tasked with setting things up and clearing the area to ready our team to take Trison into custody," Chynna answered.

The car careened into the gas station and came to a screeching stop in front of the restroom. Chynna jumped out and jogged into the small minimart.

The rest of the group remained in the car until she strolled out a few minutes later, holding a key attached to a large wooden block. When Sawyer and Codee emerged from the vehicle, she handed the key to Codee.

"Who has the scissors and clippers?" Sawyer asked.

"I put them in the bag in the back," Chynna responded.

Codee's eyes went wide. "Wait. I was kidding about the buzz cut. A short haircut, yes, but you aren't going to shave my head GI Jane-style, are you? It hardly seems necessary to dye my hair if you aren't planning on leaving any behind."

Sawyer grinned. "Spoilsport. I think you would rock the GI Jane look."

"I'll let you use the clippers right after you shave your own head," Codee retorted.

Jac emerged from the vehicle. "What the fuck is going on? We're not having a damn tea party; can you please talk about appropriate hairstyles another time? I don't give a shit what you two decide on, but you have exactly five minutes to get it done."

Codee shrugged. "God, she's bossy."

"Aren't you glad I'm your girlfriend instead of her?" Codee looked at her in shock, and then a shy smile blessed her beautiful face and Sawyer wondered if maybe she was warming to the idea of a potential relationship.

†

Codee felt an increasing sense of unease as the small team made it through all the various roadblocks and checkpoints before arriving at the Westin's employee entrance. Sawyer had done a good job of dying and cutting Codee's hair. She had to admit, it didn't look that bad.

A middle-aged woman escorted the five-person team into a back room where catering uniforms were laid out on a table, and she waited patiently for them to change. The head server didn't expect them to join the rest of the servers for another fifteen minutes, and at that time they would receive instructions on the presidential state dinner. Since this event was unusually large, even for the Westin, hiring additional servers was not out of the norm and the lead server expected that new faces would arrive.

Everything was going like clockwork, and while Codee was the first to admit she was often cynical about most everything, things were going far too smoothly for her liking. Something still felt amiss.

When they headed to the main area, she spied the gathering of the rest of the servers. Codee thought she saw her receptionist, Clare, from her former place of employment before she'd abruptly left with Sawyer in tow. She squinted, trying to get a better look, but the older woman who resembled Clare was already out of view as the woman turned the corner with two peacekeepers on each side of her. Codee shook her head, convincing herself she was seeing things. After all, why would Clare be at this event?

She felt Sawyer's light touch on her arm and refocused her attention on the rest of the team as she followed them across the enormous ballroom. As they reached the group of servers standing next to the large kitchen, Codee heard the clinking of plates and imagined the bustle of chefs working frantically behind the scene to produce a gourmet meal for one thousand.

Codee knew they wouldn't be assigned to the main table where the president was dining, but that wasn't necessary for their plan to work. The hard part was over; they were in. They still had to disable the large Secret Service contingent and the peacekeepers milling around the room. She'd seen at least twenty as they'd meandered over to their coworkers for the evening. Jac, Chynna, and Doc were obviously surveying the room and taking in every little detail. Codee was sure they knew exactly where every entrance and exit were located. She hoped the mission wouldn't come to a glorified kidnapping of the president until they reached their contact at the UN, but they needed to prepare for every contingency and making sure they knew about every possible escape route was crucial to their success.

Chynna reached into the pocket of her uniform and retrieved a cell phone, "What?" she barked into the device. "Are you fucking kidding me? Well, how long? What the hell do we do with him in the meantime? Okay. Okay." She shoved the phone back into her pocket.

"Bad news?" Codee asked.

"There's been a slight delay with the meet and greet with the UN rep. We'll need to find a way to either delay the grab and go or find a secure location to hole up in while we wait. Codee, what do you think?"

The whole team was staring at her waiting for her wise words and nothing surfaced. This brave group of men and women depended on her and she didn't have the right answer for them. Flip a coin? Circle A or circle B? She didn't have the slightest idea which option would guarantee success. She wondered if they were doomed no matter which directive she gave. Codee braced herself for the frigid waters and dove in. "We go now, take our chances, and find a hole to wait it out."

"Good choice," Chynna acknowledged.

†

The plan got off to a slow start, not at all like Codee had envisioned when all hell broke loose. She turned to see a platoon of peacekeepers accompanied by men in black suits file into the staging area where the catering supplies were located. They pointed dangerous-looking assault weapons at the group of servers. It was a trap neatly set for the small team that not even Rambo would have been able to escape from. Fate was not smiling on them today.

"Okay, plan Z might have to come out of hiding. For right now, we're outnumbered, and I suggest we just go along quietly and pretend they've won. This is just the first skirmish; this war is not yet lost," Jac whispered to the tightly knit group.

"Not to state the obvious, but right now it looks like they might win the war and not just the first battle," Sawyer quipped.

"Oh ye of little faith." Chynna grinned.

Codee didn't share Chynna and Jac's optimism. They'd clearly been compromised, which meant someone was a big fat double-crossing rat.

The biggest, meanest-looking man amid Trison's henchmen waved his rifle to the left, as if forming words in his tiny pea brain took too much effort, she thought in an uncharacteristic lack of grace for another human being. The absurd scene unraveling in front of her reminded her of a day-care worker admonishing a three-year-old for stealing a favored toy from another tot as the teacher encouraged the child to "Use your words, please." She didn't think it would help to remind the intimidating man that verbal directions might help.

The rest of his army quickly closed ranks, and each member of their five-person team had an assault weapon pressed against their backs.

"No need to be rude. Do you see any of us resisting, you overgrown caveman?" Doc's snarky question didn't earn the team any brownie points as the peacekeepers led them to a small, yet remote conference room where President Trison waited.

Before Trison won the presidency, political cartoonists had had a field day with him. He reeked caricature with his comb-over hair and perpetually arrogant smirk. He was a narcissist and a sociopath—a dangerous combination. His hands were folded on the table in front of him, and his eyes narrowed when the rebels entered the room with their fifty heavily armed escorts.

"Ah, Miss Sorenson, we meet in the flesh. I must say you're a lot shorter and surprisingly more attractive than in your video. Although, I suppose the beauty that did reveal itself on tape made you all the more appealing to the masses." Trison licked his lips. "I'm just surprised how attractive some dykes seem to be these days. Such a waste." He shifted his eyes to Sawyer. "Hmmm, I can almost see why you would try to save her, Miss Sorenson. I presume you're the spark that set this deadly blaze across our great nation.

You'll be the first person we terminate, as we need to right a grievous wrong. Your execution, I hear, would have occurred three days ago if Miss Sorenson had been performing her job as required by law." He directed his cocky smile back to Codee. "Your receptionist, Clare, has been so instrumental in enlightening us about your traitorous leftist leanings. I've made this nation great again by getting rid of the riffraff. You and all those bleeding-heart liberals are what got us into the mess before I took over. You should be thanking me," he shouted.

"Go ahead and do what you will, because I won't be the last or most lethal thorn in your side. I'll be happy to play the role of martyr and pave the way for the revolution," Codee announced.

"Oh, we have no intention of terminating you, Miss Sorenson. We have other plans that will help us continue our wave of persuasion. We'll not make a martyr of you."

"Bastards," Sawyer muttered.

Trison nodded and the lead peacekeeper raised his weapon, squeezed the trigger, and sprayed Sawyer with several bullets as she crumpled to the ground. He swung his gun at the remaining rebels and one by one he picked them off like sitting ducks in a second-rate carnival game.

"No…!" Codee cried before her world went black.

Chapter Thirteen

Beep beep beep beep

"It's only been three days. I don't think we should automatically arrange for her to go to Columbia Crest just yet. She must have some family we can confer with."

"Look, this is only your first day in the department. Patients have to be transferred to the appropriate level of care, and we can't do anything more for her here."

"But she's one of our own. What if it was your sister? Would you say the same things?"

"Sawyer, I know you have good intentions, but we have to follow hospital policy on this."

Sawyer's name penetrated Codee's foggy brain as she listened to the whispered argument. She thought she recognized the voice of the social services supervisor who in her opinion had always been a bit abrupt, especially for her role in the organization.

She wondered if someone had attached weights to her eyelids. They felt so heavy as she struggled to open her eyes, and then she felt it—that familiar touch to her hand.

"A few more hours, that's all I ask. My shift just ended, so I can stay with her while you make the arrangements. I'd like to go with the transport vehicle in case she wakes up and is confused about where she is and where she's going."

"Okay, Sawyer, two hours. That's all you've got."

Sawyer, did she say Sawyer? But she's dead. I saw them shoot her.

"Sawyer...," Codee croaked as her eyes fluttered open.

"Oh Lord, that is the most welcome sight I've seen in days. You're finally awake." Sawyer's hand squeezed Codee's.

"Where am I?"

"You're in the hospital's advanced care unit. You've been out for three days now. Since you didn't have any advance directives on file, or an emergency contact for us to call, we didn't know how to proceed."

"I have a sister, but she's dead and you're dead too." Codee began to cry. "You're a bloody hallucination that my guilty conscience is conjuring up right now. Where are all the peacekeepers, and what special hell did Trison decide to send me to?"

Sawyer crinkled her nose. "Trison? Are you talking about David Trison, the Patriot Party frontrunner?"

"Yes, President Trison," Codee replied in exasperation.

"Oh, hon, bite your tongue. Boy, you really did bang your head good, not that I didn't already know that after you wouldn't wake up for the first forty-eight hours. God help us if that imbecile gets into office."

She looked down at her hand linked with Sawyer's and moved her thumb in an intimate caress. "You're real."

Sawyer chuckled. "Yes I am, or at least I think so. Reality can be elusive, can't it?"

133

Codee tried to push herself up and felt an immediate pain travel along her arm. She glanced at the source of it, and her eyes traveled up and down the length of a cast starting from her elbow and nearly covering her wrist. Her fingers looked like large, fat sausages. "What did I break?"

"Some little bone in your arm, I think. I can't recall the proper name for it. You probably shouldn't try to push yourself up. Let me raise the bed for you."

Sawyer removed her hand and started to fiddle with the controls on the side of the bed.

She felt the immediate loss of their connection. Coming out of the fog a certain level of coherency returned.

Codee let out a sigh of relief. "It was all a dream, or rather nightmare. In my dream, my injured arm didn't require a cast. I'm probably not making a lot of sense, am I?"

Sawyer raised her eyebrow but didn't respond.

"Why are you here?" Codee blurted out.

Sawyer slapped her hand to her chest. "I'm wounded." She winked. "Look, Sharlie told me what you planned to do before the preterm hearing and she made sure I was transferred to social services before I got the ax, which was your intent. It's the least I could do. You advocated for me, so it was my turn to advocate for you."

"I think I'm getting whiplash from all the radical events happening around me. First, I'm ready to attend a preterm proceeding and offer to delay things until the social services position opens, and then I'm in this alternate universe where we're on the run from some very bad people."

Sawyer wiggled her eyebrows. "I was in your dream?" She pushed a button and the bed moved to an upright position.

"Thanks. Yes, but it was more like a nightmare."

"Wow, that must have been some dream—I mean nightmare."

"It seemed so real. You were there. Erma, my next door neighbor, was on the side of the righteous and helping us out. I had a unit, as in a military unit to lead, and I found a long-lost twin sister I never knew I had." Codee paused. "It all seemed so real," she repeated. "I know this sounds crazy, but maybe I do have a sister out there. For some strange reason, I think my subconscious is trying to tell me something."

Sawyer touched her hand again. "Listen, I need to get a doctor now that you're awake. They'll want to check you out. I can't tell you how relieved I am to see the whites of your eyes, with that lovely shade of smoky gray in the centers. Maybe after the doc checks you out, you can write everything down as a detailed dream diary. Record as many specifics as you possibly can." She squeezed once and then pivoted and left the room.

Did Sawyer just flirt with her, or was she still in her dream where they'd moved their professional relationship to a personal one? Damn, that was clearly against hospital policy. *I can't really get involved with her, can I? What would that mean to my career? There's something about her that I'm inexplicably drawn to.* Codee shook her head as that thought snuck in before she had a chance to censor it. The smile that blossomed on her face was hard to control.

†

Dr. Smith smiled as he approached the side of the bed. "Welcome back, Codee. I know they overwork HR execs, but maybe next time you take a nap, you could make it just a tad shorter."

"You were a sympathetic ED doc in my dream, not the hospitalist, but you'll be happy to know you were one of the good guys."

"Glad to hear that. Okay, can I do a few quick tests, please?"

"Sure, Dr. Smith. It's 2016 and I'm in Moses Lake General Hospital. That asshole Trison is not in office. How am I doing?"

Dr. Smith chuckled. "Well, I wasn't going to ask you about your political leanings, but"—he leaned in—"I have to agree with your assessment on Trison. What an idiot. Surely they need doctors in Canada if they put that twit in office. I'm beginning to wonder about the collective intelligence of our nation. We won't be the big bad super power we are for much longer if we let the rednecks take over."

Dr. Smith pulled a pen light out of his pocket and shined it into Codee's eyes.

She blinked a few times. "They're pretty sensitive. Is that normal?"

He nodded. "I'm not concerned about the light sensitivity. How's your head feel?"

"Like a thousand woodpeckers decided to settle in for the winter."

"Okay, I'll order up some medicine that should help with the pain. I'd like to run some more tests, maybe get another CT of that noggin of yours. Perhaps if you behave yourself, I can discharge you tomorrow, but you need someone to stay with you or no release from hospital prison." He winked.

Codee often wondered why there weren't more hospitalists like Dr. Smith. He always seemed to talk to his patients without using medical jargon and creating more stress and tension. His down-home style and joking made patients feel more comfortable.

"I can stay with her," Sawyer blurted out.

Codee jumped in her bed. "Shoot, where did you come from? I think my dream missed its mark; I should have cast you as some CIA-spy type."

Sawyer smiled sheepishly.

"Done. I'll come by a little later after I get that second scan back," Dr. Smith interjected.

"Wait, don't I get any say in this? I don't want to inconvenience you, Sawyer. You might have a hot date or something."

"Nope, no hot date. I lead a very boring life."

Codee was celebrating this last comment before she sobered and thought again about her position in the hospital. Screw it, it wasn't as if she was sleeping with Sawyer—well, at least not in real life. She smiled to herself as she noted that part of her dream wasn't a nightmare. In fact, it was the hottest sex dream she'd ever remembered.

Dr. Smith waved. "I'll let you ladies work out the details. I've got to finish my rounds."

Sawyer stepped farther into the room and shuffled her feet, looking uncomfortable.

"Um…my offer was sincere, but if I've overstepped any boundaries by barreling into your private life, I'll back off. I really don't have anything on my social calendar that would interfere, and I want to help out. I guess you don't really know me very well, but I swear I'm not some crazy stalker."

Codee chuckled. "I believe you, and for once in my life, I think I'm going to just take a leap and graciously accept your offer. You had a starring role in my dream, so maybe we were meant to be great friends." *Or more.*

"A starring role, huh? Care to expound on that a bit?"

She could feel the heat in her cheeks. "Um, no, at least not until I get to know you a bit better."

"Why do I get the impression I'm going to like hearing the details of that dream? I reserve the right to come back to this at a later date."

"So if they spring me from this joint tomorrow, do you think they'll allow me to drive my own car? I hope they haven't towed it from the employee parking lot."

"No, they didn't. I wouldn't let them. I was still hoping you would wake before they transferred you to the long-term care facility. You know, you really should appoint someone as your medical power of attorney."

Codee frowned. "I don't have any family that I know of, and the only other person I'm close with is my next door neighbor, Erma. Unless there's something to my dream and I really do have a twin sister. Something keeps bugging me about that possibility. I was very young when my father left and don't really remember anything, but the name *Chynna* does seem to ring a bell. Do you think it's possible?"

Sawyer smiled. "Anything is possible. Not to pry, but what about tracking things through your mother? Although I assume she's no longer alive."

Codee furrowed her brow. "I wouldn't know how to even approach that. She died when I was young—well, not as young as when my father left, but still young enough for the details to remain somewhat hazy about where we lived and where I was born. You know, those things that would help me research my family tree. I must not have had any living grandparents because foster care is where I ended up. They couldn't have been successful at tracking down my father or I probably would have ended up with him. To my knowledge I don't have any aunts or uncles, either, unless there are some on my father's side of the family."

Sawyer clasped Codee's hand and wove their fingers together in an interlocking puzzle. "Hey, don't worry, we can figure this out together. I think I know of a place to start. Do you trust me?"

"I do."

Sawyer released Codee's hand, reached over to the nightstand, and picked up a pad of paper and a pen the hospital staff provided for patients in case they had questions they wanted to write down to ask the doctor during rounds.

"I don't suppose you're ambidextrous, are you?"

Codee shook her head.

"Well then, I guess I'll have to play secretary while you dictate the details of your nightmare. There may be a few golden nuggets we should get down on paper while it's still fresh in your mind. Are you up for it?"

"Sure. The scary part of the dream began when I realized the pre-termination proceeding with you wasn't a typical separation from employment, but termination in the literal sense…."

Chapter Fourteen

Sawyer offered to drive Codee's Prius after the doctor discharged her with the stipulation that the reluctant patient could not drive. Codee had mildly protested when Sawyer revealed she'd asked for a few days off to help out. She could have kicked herself for mentioning it. Her boss hadn't been very happy with her, considering she'd just started the new job yesterday, but taking care of Codee was far more important to her. She supposed taking time off so quickly after the transfer wasn't the best way to secure a happy future in the hospital's social services department, but something drew her to the beautiful woman who seemed so vulnerable and not at all like the confident HR executive she'd come to admire. Losing her job wouldn't have been the end of the world since it wasn't where she ultimately wanted to be, but she felt indebted knowing the HR leader had advocated for her.

Rather than sending her home in the clothes she'd worn the day of her fall, the hospital had provided scrubs, and Sawyer had brought along an extra winter coat she had hiding in the back of her closet. The worn-out leather jacket over the thin scrubs added to Codee's look of vulnerability. The blood from her head wound had managed to seep onto her work clothes, and Codee had instructed them to just toss the shirt. She'd pulled Sawyer aside and told her that she didn't want to wear her nice pants or put on dirty underwear, so the option of scrubs was readily accepted.

Codee provided directions to her home, and as they pulled into the driveway, Sawyer noted the light dusting of snow surrounding the beautiful residence with the lake creating a perfect backdrop. Although the sun was shining on the ice-encrusted water, the temperature was still below freezing. The shared driveway veered to the left, and her house sat above the slight rise to the right.

Sawyer noticed the blinds move in what she presumed was the main living area of the house that partially shared Codee's driveway. Just as she pressed the button below the rearview mirror to open the garage door, an older woman barreled out of her home.

"I think your neighbor is coming for a visit, and she looks a bit frantic." Sawyer eased the car into the garage.

Codee turned her head. "She probably doesn't know where I've been for the last four days. Erma is like a second mother to me. She's the closest thing I have to family because she takes pity on me during the holidays and brings me into her fold. I get to enjoy her fabulous cooking on nearly every holiday I choose not to work."

"Yeah, I think I saw you at the hospital when I was working an admitting shift this past Christmas. I wondered about that." Sawyer pushed the button to shut off the car.

"Oh, holidays can be a great day to catch up on the thousands of emails I get, because no one responds right away. It allows me to decrease the ridiculous number of the darn things. I feel like I'm making progress, even if it only lasts one day." Codee pressed the button to release her seat belt, pulled on the door lever, and carefully emerged from the car. Although she had some difficulty opening the door by reaching over with her left hand, she managed to hide the awkwardness from Sawyer.

By the time they got out of the vehicle, Erma was approaching the garage. "Who are you?" She directed her irritated look at Sawyer. "And where the hell have you been, Codee? You two don't look like you've been on a long weekend away, and I didn't know you had a new girlfriend."

The embarrassed woman coughed. "Um, Sawyer's not my girlfriend. I had a small accident and was indisposed for a few days."

Sawyer looked down.

"Okay, you"—Erma pointed to Sawyer—"fill in the gaps, please, because this one"—she waved her arm at Codee—"tends to gloss over important details."

Codee sighed. "Care for some tea, Erma? Come on inside and make yourself at home while you give Sawyer the third degree."

Sawyer winked. "Now this ought to be interesting. I've never been interrogated by anyone other than my mother. Let's see if you're any good at it."

"Oh Codee, I like her, and she's cute too. If she isn't your girlfriend, maybe you should rectify that. I get a good feeling about your new friend." Erma grinned.

Codee playfully backhanded her with her good arm. "Stop it, you're embarrassing my guest."

"No, she's not. Just for the record, I'm single, disease free, and officially applying for the position if it's vacant."

Codee's mouth opened to reply, then she shut it quickly and led the two women inside.

†

Codee started to notice the little things about Sawyer that made her irresistible to want to get to know better. The minute they'd entered the kitchen, Sawyer made a beeline to the teakettle on the stove and filled it using the water dispenser located in the mud room. She hadn't argued because both her head and her arm were throbbing and she needed to sit down before she passed out.

"If you give me a hint about where you keep your tea bags, I won't have to embark on a treasure hunt to find them. Not that treasure-hunting isn't fun, but I think Erma is squirming to get on with her interrogation."

"They're in the cabinet to the left of the stove on the middle shelf. Erma prefers the cinnamon apple, and I'll take some chamomile, and, by the way, thank you." She lowered her body to the couch and leaned her head back on the cushion, momentarily closing her eyes. When she opened them, she saw the concerned eyes of her neighbor staring back at her. "No questions. I'm not in a very good place to survive an inquisition from you."

Erma patted her good arm. "You know I just worry about you. You're like a second daughter to me, and goodness knows you're a helluva lot nicer to me than my own evil offspring."

"Aw, she's just sowing some wild oats. She'll calm herself down in a few years and let you know how much she's loved your not-so-gentle advice or attempts at it."

"I suppose I can be somewhat overbearing at times, but, like you, she seems to pick the biggest schmucks she can find. In her case, I think it's on purpose to irritate me. In your case, well, I don't know why you've chosen the dimwits you have."

"Be nice, Erma, or I won't let you grill my new friend."

"She seems interested, you need to jump on that," Erma whispered.

Codee shook her head. "She works at the hospital, so, unfortunately, that's an unlikely possibility. All the good ones are either taken, straight, or work there."

"Excuses, excuses. I think you look for reasons not to open up to someone."

"Can we have this tired old argument another time? My head is killing me and you're adding to it."

"I promise I wasn't trying to eavesdrop—okay, maybe I was—but why don't I bring you some medication to help with the pain," Sawyer called out from the kitchen.

"Oh yes, she is definitely a keeper. Did you hear that, Sawyer? Because you were meant to." Erma laughed.

Codee groaned. The teakettle began to whistle, and she was glad for the interruption.

Sawyer lifted the kettle and poured the steaming water into two cups. She opened the jar of honey and asked, "Would either of you care for honey in your tea, or do you prefer cream and sugar?"

"Honey," Codee and Erma called out in unison.

"No more side comments from you, or I'm sending you back to your house without an explanation of where I've been," Codee whispered right before Sawyer crossed the room and set down the tea.

"Aren't you having a cup, dear?" Erma asked.

"No, ma'am, I'm strictly a coffee gal."

"I do have coffee in the same cabinet, with the grinder and a french press."

Sawyer grinned. "I know, I saw it and was very happy indeed. It will save me a trip in the morning to my favorite coffee place. I only allow myself one cup—a very large one, mind you, but just one in the morning, so I'm good for now."

Yes, you most certainly are. She shook that thought from her head as Sawyer sat down next to her and then reached into her pocket and retrieved two small pills, which she presented in her palm.

Codee accepted them, tossed them in her mouth, and attempted to wrap the string around her tea bag. She had started to become frustrated with her swollen hand when Sawyer gently removed the tea bag, wrapped the string around the spoon, and squeezed out the extra hot water. She placed the discarded item on the saucer.

"Thanks," Codee mumbled and screwed up her face as the two bitter pills started to dissolve in her mouth before she had a chance to pick up the cup and take a sip.

Erma tilted her head and focused on the two women. She picked up her own cup, which she'd already removed the tea bag from, took a sip, leaned back in her recliner, and seemed to wait for Sawyer to fill her in. "Okay, spill, cutie, what kind of accident? I presume she's been in the hospital the past four days."

"Shortened version is she slipped on the ice, bonked her head, and remained unconscious until yesterday. They kept her one more day for good measure, and now I'm her get-out-of-jail-free card because I assured the doc I would be here to watch over her for the next few days."

Erma sighed. "You never designated me as your emergency contact, did you? For Christ's sake, Codee, you work at a hospital. You know how important it is to have your advance directives in place in case something happens. Besides, why'd you bother to ask me if you weren't going to follow through?"

"I got busy," she sheepishly replied.

"Oh really? And it takes, what, weeks to fill out the damn forms?"

"Point taken, okay? I forgot."

Sawyer's eyes drifted back and forth between the two arguing women. "I work in the hospital and I haven't submitted my advance directives yet. Am I helping your case, Codee?"

"Oh do not help her, because then I cannot properly chastise her."

"I'm sorry, I promise I will rectify the situation as soon as I go back to work. Sawyer can help me fill out the paperwork." Codee lifted her cast. "Typing on my keyboard is going to be a total pain in the rear. At least in my dream, my left arm was injured versus my dominant right. I wonder how or why I conjured that up instead?"

"Dream?" Erma asked.

"Yes, she had a dream—well more like a nightmare from what she dictated to me—but you and I had starring roles. I get the sense I played a pleasurable role from the way she blushed when she referred to my part in it." Sawyer wiggled her eyebrows.

"Ooh, I wish the little tight-lips would spill about that, but Codee keeps her cards close to the vest with certain topics. Romance and sex are two things she won't blab about no matter how much I beg. Over the last three years, I haven't even been able to imagine her having hot monkey sex with anyone, because Miss Boring stopped dating. She's such a stingy thing, not letting an old woman live vicariously through her hot neighbor."

Codee rolled her eyes. "This one has absolutely no sense of decorum. She actually asked me and my ex if we preferred fingers, tongue, or strap-on. I thought I would choke to death on the tea I was sipping at the time."

"What? It's a legitimate question," Erma stated.

"No preference, all have their time and place."

Codee's eyes went wide and she choked on the tea she'd just taken a sip of.

"See, Sawyer answered my question without me having to tear down the Great Wall of China. But isn't there one that's your go-to choice?"

Sawyer chuckled. "Okay, if I have to choose, tongue."

"Good choice." Erma smiled.

"Will you two please stop? I'd prefer the Spanish Inquisition regarding my accident."

"All right. What did the doc say about any permanent damage to her head? Not that she wasn't seriously warped prior to the injury, but I'm talking about any possible memory issues, or other things?"

"I guess I had what he referred to as a 'grade-five concussion' because I lost consciousness for more than ten minutes. The good news is that he gave me a guarded clean bill of health as long as I take it easy for the next week and do follow-up if I experience nausea, blurred vision, confusion, unusual behavior, or any other complications. He also mentioned something about watery discharge from my nose or ears." Codee shuddered.

"I suppose I'd better not develop a cold in the next few days, or it'll be back to hospital jail for me. Their biggest worry is that I might develop seizures later on. The doc referred me to a specialist in Seattle because they can't figure out how I managed to wake up after three days with relatively minor aftereffects from the trauma. Once the fog cleared from my head, I was able to rattle off the year, knew where I was, and even recognized the doc. I don't know why I still have some light sensitivity, but that's for the experts to decipher." Codee rubbed her eyes in an unconscious gesture after revealing this unusual reaction to her injury.

"Do you need someone to take you?" Erma asked.

"No, Sawyer has already offered to escort me."

Erma nodded and smiled. "Good."

"Erma, please don't laugh, but in my dream I had a twin sister, and I think it's possible I really do have a sibling. Sawyer is going to help me try to track her down."

"Now, honey, why would I laugh? If you believe you have a twin running around out there, you probably do. Oh God help us, though, if there are two of you gallivanting around Moses Lake." Erma grinned. "I'll do whatever I can to help," she amended.

"Codee, do you think your pain has subsided enough to stomach some food?" Sawyer asked.

"Maybe in a little bit after the medication kicks in."

"Oh, I can rustle up something for you girls to eat tonight. It would make me feel like I contributed in some way, even though Numbskull here didn't bother to ensure I could be there for her."

"I love you too, Erma," Codee quipped. She shifted in her seat and grimaced. The two little pills Sawyer had given her didn't seem to have the kind of impact she was hoping for.

Sawyer was looking intently at her. "You seem like a short nap might do you a world of good. Erma, I'd love a home-cooked meal from you, considering I don't possess that particular skill, but do you mind holding off for a few hours?"

Erma smiled. "It'll take me that long to create a masterpiece. You get Ms. Independent settled in for a nap, and if you want to come over and keep me company, that would be grand."

"Okay, will do."

Codee frowned. "Not that I'm not appreciative of all the love and care I'm receiving, but do you really have to treat me like a small child?"

"Getting someone settled after an injury that caused unconsciousness for three days is just providing the type of care the doctor ordered. Don't make me call Dr. Smith back to revoke your early parole."

"All right." Codee waved her good hand. "It's just that I haven't had to deal with a two-person tag team before. Erma's been the only one I've ever had to endure because my ex wasn't comfortable with the few times I did get sick. Hovering or caregiving wasn't really in her nature."

"One of the many reasons I didn't care for her," Erma added.

"Ooh goody, you can fill me in on all the juicy details when I visit."

Codee glared at Erma. "You are forbidden to tell stories while I'm resting."

"Yeah, yeah, yeah." Erma put her hand up. "Talk to the hand."

"Oh why do I even bother?"

Chapter Fifteen

Sawyer moved the block of cheese up and down the grater in a methodical rhythm as the square rapidly reduced in size. She noticed how Erma's arthritic hands were struggling with the frozen prawns as she began to peel them into the garbage can she'd retrieved from under the kitchen sink.

"Hey, why don't you let me do that after I've finished grating this cheese for you?"

Erma paused. "You really are a keeper and quite the catch. If only I was twenty years younger and gay. You like her, don't you?"

Sawyer cocked her head and hesitated as she gathered her thoughts. "Of course I like her. She's…."

"An easy person to love and yet not so easy to get to know," Erma finished for her. "Codee is complicated. She's never let anyone inside before, but then none of the others were worthy of her trust. I think you may be the one to break through her wall. I love her like my own daughter, but she is exasperating. I think she chooses a certain type of girlfriend so she doesn't have to commit and can legitimately walk away from anything that might develop into something long-term. She'll have a hard time doing that with you, but, then again, she probably won't let you push the door open even though you do have one foot in it."

Sawyer laughed. "We're a perfect match, then, because I fall in love with people who can't or don't love me back. It always ends in disaster with me holding the shattered pieces of my heart in my hand, ready to mold them back in place to try again."

"My advice, for what it's worth, is don't let her push you away and don't give up because I sense there's something special about you that even Miss Independent won't or can't ignore. Serendipity, that's what I'm seeing unfold."

Sawyer pushed the cheese she'd grated aside and then moved to the sink. She gently took the frozen crustaceans out of Erma's hands and began to peel them. "She briefly mentioned growing up in foster care, and that's where I'd like to start looking to track down her sister, unless you think revisiting that will be painful for her."

Erma nodded. "I'm sure it will be painful. She's never gone into great detail, but I suspect it wasn't all that pleasant for her, yet Codee is nothing if not strong. If it means finding her sister, she'll survive. How about I make you some coffee since you insist on doing all the prep work for dinner?"

"Oh what the hell. I'd kill for another cup, so I'll throw caution to the wind. I'd like to stay awake well into the evening to make sure Codee remains as pain free as possible."

Sawyer did want to remain alert and another cup of coffee probably wouldn't kill her, but the real reason she accepted was because she knew Erma would want something to do while she finished peeling the prawns and grating the other block of cheese she'd pulled from the refrigerator before retrieving the frozen shellfish.

"You don't think it's a wild goose chase to try to find a twin that might not exist except in her dreams?" Erma picked up the kettle and filled it with tap water.

Sawyer chuckled to herself imagining Erma chastising Codee for insisting on bottled water when good old tap would do just fine. She wasn't picky when boiling the tap water took out all the impurities, but had to admit that she preferred the cleaner bottled version.

"No, I don't. I learned long ago that sometimes our brains process certain memories in different ways, and I believe she's remembering her twin through the dream process. Besides, no harm, no foul. If a twin sister doesn't exist, all we've lost is a little time and energy doing some research. But if she does exist, what a wonderful feeling to discover you have family you never thought you had. I love my brother even though he drives me crazy sometimes. I can't imagine navigating this world without his love and support. I've done my fair share of crying on his shoulder, even though I had to restrain him from kicking every one of my exes' asses."

"You know, I've never seen Codee cry, not even once."

Sawyer's brow furrowed. "She cried when she woke up."

Erma raised her eyebrow. "She did? I need to hear exactly what happened. This is a very interesting development. I'm not saying Codee is some coldhearted bitch, but she is very careful about showing emotion."

"She said something about having a sister who was dead and that I was dead too. She called me a hallucination and then started spouting some crazy thing about David Trison being the president. I was very worried until we figured out she'd had some bizarre dream. I mean, can you imagine anything nuttier than David Trison as president?"

Erma poured a premeasured amount of ground coffee into the french press she'd retrieved from the cabinet, and Sawyer was secretly delighted she wasn't about to receive freeze-dried Folgers.

Erma turned around and shook her head. "Unfortunately I'm not sure how absurd that really is. He's gaining in popularity no matter what ridiculous thing comes out of his mouth. He's managed to piss off both sides of the equation by stating that women who get abortions should be prosecuted. He did backtrack, but the man has no filter and yet he still collects loyal followers. Somehow he says out loud what those asshole rednecks think and it spurs them on. It's mob mentality at its best. He encourages outrageous views and ridicules political correctness. God help us if the leader of the biggest superpower gives everyone license to think, feel, and act on those beliefs."

"Surely suggesting he would give someone bail money who punches out a person exercising their free speech rights when demonstrating against him is showing the nation what a terrible decision it would be to put him in office."

"You'd think so, but I'm beginning to wonder. Let's talk about something more fun. So what do you plan to do to woo our reluctant beauty?"

"You know her better than I do. What do you think I should do?"

"I'd say whatever you're already doing is working. I've never seen her this relaxed around someone. You seem to be a Zen magnet. I've noticed how you pick up every little nuance and just step in to help without being asked. That's very endearing, at least to me, and I don't think that has escaped Codee's notice either."

"There is something about her that has me transfixed. I'm willing to risk another heartbreak because I honestly think she's worth it. Maybe this time, I'll have found "the one." I know this sounds extremely cliché, but deep in my bones I feel this time is different. Perhaps it's wishful thinking, but the only truly missed shot is the one you never take."

"Good, I like a woman who perseveres. I'll remind you of this conversation if you begin to stray or get discouraged."

"By the way, are you making a less expensive version of lobster mac and cheese?"

"Bingo, give the woman a prize. Prawns work just as well. It's a little comfort food with panache."

Sawyer put the garbage back under the sink with the discarded shells and then returned to her stool at the kitchen counter. "Don't worry I'll take care of the trash after dinner. Right now my mouth is watering."

"Thank you. That would be good because they do tend to stink the place up."

"Everything smells glorious at this moment. The cheese alone would do it for me. This isn't some off-the-shelf, garden-variety cheese either. I'm going to watch what you do carefully because maybe I'll be able to replicate this without too much trouble. It seems easy enough."

"Oh it is. Half the battle with cooking is to start with the right ingredients. If you cut corners there, you're doomed to fail, so buy the good stuff and you're nearly guaranteed success. Well, most people are anyway. Codee used to be a horrible cook." Erma poured hot water into the french press, which sat on the counter next to the stove. "She would have starved to death when I went to visit my ungrateful children had I not shown her a few simple tricks. I think she lived at the bistro before I started bringing over leftovers and then began inviting her to dinner. It's only me, so I told her I loved cooking, but not for one. I tried to get her to believe she was doing me a favor. I don't think she bought it, but she pretended to because I'm sure after that first meal she craved home cooking."

Sawyer chuckled. "You are gloriously devious, and I mean that in a good way. I'm glad Codee has you in her life." She continued to grate the new block of cheese, catching a whiff of its nutty essence.

"And now she has you." Erma winked.

"For as long as she'll let me stay."

"Which I hope will be for a very long time." Erma pushed down the filter on the french press, poured the rich, dark liquid into a cup, and set it on the counter in front of Sawyer.

✝

Codee pried her eyes open as the wonderful aroma reached her nostrils. "Mmm, I smell my favorite comfort food," she said to the empty bedroom.

The blinds were closed, and she silently thanked Sawyer for making sure the light wouldn't irritate her sensitive eyes and bring back the pounding headache and accompanying nausea. She hadn't admitted that if she didn't lie down, the bile that felt close to the surface might erupt and interrupt the earlier conversation when they were having tea. She was afraid if she told them about it, they'd insist on her returning to the hospital.

She wasn't one hundred percent pain free, but her headache was now just a slight throb. *Tolerable.* She smacked her lips and felt the dryness in her mouth. After she shuffled into the bathroom attached to her master bedroom, she placed a ribbon of toothpaste on her electric toothbrush, stuck it in her mouth, and moved it around to cover her teeth. The tinkling of laughter floated from the kitchen, and she smiled, thinking that her two favorite people in the world were sharing some joy. *Wait, two favorite people? I barely know Sawyer.*

Codee rinsed and dried her toothbrush. She hated to stick the cap back on when it was wet because it always seemed to leave a little extra paste around the base that she'd have to constantly clean off. She touched the back of her head and felt the bandage that covered the bald spot. It brought her memory back to the part in her dream where she'd worried Sawyer was going to give her a buzz cut. Her hair was the only physical characteristic she believed was nice enough to draw attention. Maybe that was arrogant, but it was the one feature she remembered about her mother, and that brought a smile to her face. She didn't mind inheriting that trait at all.

She fluffed up her hair and stared at the dark circles under her eyes. *Time for a touch-up.* That was one feature she didn't appreciate acquiring and wasn't sure whom she'd gotten it from, her mother or father. Although she didn't wear a lot of makeup and tended to avoid using heavy foundation, she picked up a cover stick and swiped it under each eye, then carefully rubbed it in to cover up her flaw.

When she reached the kitchen, she barely managed to keep her laughter in check as the two women danced around the kitchen with The Staple Singers' "I'll Take You There" playing quietly in the background. It was strange she hadn't heard the music along with the laughter. She leaned against the doorjamb as she watched Sawyer's very fine rear end sway to the music while Erma tried to replicate her moves.

"No, you gotta put a little more soul into it. Just let your body feel the beat," Sawyer instructed.

"Easy for you to say, arthritis isn't plaguing your hips."

Codee cleared her throat, and Sawyer turned around and blessed her with a brilliant smile.

"Come on, Codee, show her how it's done, come dance with me," Sawyer encouraged.

"Oh no, you're not pulling me into this. I dance like a white boy."

Sawyer danced over and placed her hands on Codee's hips, stepped close, and gently shifted them in a syncopated movement that matched her own seductive swaying.

She let Sawyer rotate her body to the music, and for the first time in her life, she felt sexy as she danced with this beautiful and engaging woman.

Sawyer moved her hands to the small of Codee's back as Codee placed her hands around Sawyer's neck, and they continued to move in a perfect ballet of artistic motion.

"Now we're talking. That's it, feel the beat," Sawyer encouraged.

Codee was having fun dancing. *I'm dancing.*

When the song ended, they broke apart and stood looking at each other for a few seconds as dual smiles overtook their faces.

"I assume dinner is almost ready, because that heavenly smell permeated all the way upstairs and woke me from a deep sleep where I was ruler of the world after overturning Trison's evil empire."

"Part two of your dream? I really have to hear more about this. You should write a book; it sounds positively riveting. I can transcribe this new dream as well." Sawyer pivoted and picked up the plates that were on the island and placed them on the table in the dining room along with the silverware she'd grabbed in her other hand.

Erma bent over, opened the oven, and pulled out the large casserole dish filled with bubbling cheese, making Codee's mouth water. "I want to hear more about this dream, but I'd rather plot with you two about finding Codee's sister."

157

"Food first, plotting later. I'm starved. I always think better after dinner with a steaming cup of coffee in my hand." Codee grabbed the pitcher of ice water, with sliced lemons floating on top, in her one good hand as Sawyer went back to the counter to retrieve the three empty glasses.

✝

The three women sat on the wrap-around couch with their drinks in their hands. Sawyer had given up all pretense of avoiding more coffee because she wanted to remain awake a bit longer before succumbing to sleep. She thought it might be prudent to set her alarm to wake her every few hours to check on Codee throughout the night.

"Okay, let's talk strategy. Sawyer, where do you think we should start in our quest to find my sister, provided she isn't some mythical creature from my overblown imagination?"

Sawyer hesitated for a second until she saw the eager woman's expression. She decided she may as well take the plunge and, if it caused Codee brief discomfort, she could adjust her suggestion. "I think we should start by tracking down records from your first foster care placement, unless you can remember anything about where you may have been born. It's probably a long shot though."

Codee shrugged. "I know we spent some time in Bellingham, but I can't be sure where I was born. I can't even confirm I was born in this state. My mother didn't talk about the past. She was very future oriented, and I learned at an early age not to ask questions about a dad I barely remembered. I do vaguely recall her emotional reaction on the rare occasions I did ask. She always had tears in her eyes and her normally sunny disposition would become almost despondent, so I never pushed. I didn't like seeing her so forlorn, and after a couple of times, I stopped asking."

"Has your name always been Codee Sorenson? You don't recall anything different, do you?" Sawyer asked.

"Not while in foster care, no. For some reason, I dimly recall a different last name from when I was much younger, but I can't remember what it was. It's like the name is just out of focus for me."

"That's okay, maybe the foster care records will reveal something, or we can talk to someone involved in your first placement." Sawyer took a sip of her coffee.

"That was a very long time ago, and they might not even be alive. This is going to be like finding a needle in a haystack, isn't it?"

"Thirty years is kind of a long time, but that doesn't mean we shouldn't try."

"Try closer to thirty-five, but I do remember that the social worker involved in my first placement was a grumpy old woman. Even worse than Erma."

"If I thought you were serious, I'd walk right out and never cook for you again, you little imp."

"What about your first foster parents? Were they older as well? Did you get along with them? Do you think they'll remember you?"

Codee shrugged. "Don't know, I was pretty withdrawn at first. They were okay, I suppose. I didn't talk much and they didn't push. I was probably worse than Wednesday on *The Addams Family*. A very morose child is not a very delightful child. I can't imagine I was very memorable to them."

"I have a good friend who works with the Department of Children and Family Services. I'll contact her tomorrow as a starting point. I'm sure she can lead us in the right direction at the very least. She'll know what we need to do to obtain old records. How does that sound, Codee?"

"It sounds like as good a place as any to start." Codee leaned her head back on the couch and sighed. "So what's for dessert?"

"I hadn't really planned on anything because I didn't know if you'd show up, so I didn't have time to bake a pie," Erma explained.

Sawyer tried hard not to laugh as Codee's lips turned into a pout.

Erma chuckled. "Oh, stop pouting, I sent Sawyer to your home away from home before I put her to work, and she picked up those little cheesecakes you like from the bistro."

Codee's face instantly brightened. "Well, not as good as your dutch apple pie, but I'll take it. I do hope I won't drop any of those precious morsels on my clothes like I did with the mac and cheese. It's harder than you think to eat with your non-dominant hand. I felt like just burying my face in it like a pig at a trough. I might have, you know, if Sawyer hadn't been here to expose me to my colleagues at work, but all bets are off when it comes to dessert."

"I can feed you," Sawyer suggested.

"Oh no you don't. I'd rather be labeled a pig than treated as a baby. I already feel uncomfortable about you taking care of me."

"I could take over those duties, but I'd be nervous you might get dizzy and I couldn't catch you with my arthritis acting up. I think you should have Sawyer stay with you in your bedroom tonight, just to be on the safe side, you know." Erma winked at Sawyer.

"You are positively transparent, old woman. Stop trying to play matchmaker. You don't make a good Yenta." She remembered saying something very similar in her dream.

"It's a practical solution. I'm hurt that you don't trust me." Sawyer placed her hand over her heart and feigned indignation.

"Now don't twist my words, I did not say that. I have a king bed. I'm sure we can avoid our baser instincts for one night."

"Two, maybe three," Sawyer corrected with a cheeky grin. "Doctor's orders, remember, or straight back to jail, do not pass go, do not collect two hundred dollars."

†

Codee was secretly happy about this new turn of events, but she'd never admit it out loud. She wasn't sure she wanted to control her baser instincts. If only she could let go like she'd done in her dream.

Erma stood and stretched. "Well, girls, this old woman needs to head home and rest her weary old bones. Breakfast? I make a mean pancake."

"Blueberry?" Sawyer asked.

"Is there another kind?"

Sawyer glanced in Codee's direction and nodded. "I'd love for you to make us some pancakes. I'm an expert at reheating the syrup."

"How about I come by at around nine? Codee has the pancake mix in her pantry, and I'll bring my frozen blueberries I got from the farmers market last summer."

"Deal, I'll walk you out." Sawyer stood and tossed over her shoulder, "I'll be back in a minute."

Codee heard Erma and Sawyer whispering in the mudroom but couldn't quite make out what they were saying. She imagined she felt her ears burning and just knew she was the topic of their hushed words.

When Sawyer came back, her eyes briefly flicked her way before she inspected the tops of her feet. "Look, I don't want to invade your space any more than is necessary. A blanket and a pillow on the floor will work. I've had worse accommodations when traveling around with the rugby team."

Codee raised her eyebrow. "You're kind of small for a rugby player, aren't you? Besides, I'm guessing those team-bonding moments are a distant memory and you haven't had to share floor space in quite some time. Personally I won't even lie out in the sun anymore without a cushy little pad under my aging body. I'll be honest, I don't love the idea of sharing my bed with a virtual stranger who's come to my rescue, but I don't hate it either. I'm not very good at being a patient and letting someone take care of me, even if they are the embodiment of every lesbian fantasy in a clichéd romance novel. If only reality were half as good as those books, you and I would be naked, sweating, and having the most mind-blowing sex we've ever had in the span of a few minutes as we find it hard to resist each other in my huge king bed."

Sawyer laughed. "I don't even know where to start with a response. First, I am not that small for a position called 'winger.' Second, I only gave up my cleats two years ago, and third, would you settle for mildly pleasurable sex? After all, I did play the part of the chivalrous dyke who offered to sleep on the floor. I think that calls for some kind of reward."

"You're kidding, right?"

"Yes, of course I'm kidding. Your virtue and morals are safe with me. I really only want to make sure you don't have any side effects from your fall. What kind of person do you think I am, taking advantage of a woman who just woke from a three-day coma?"

"Could you at least fake making a pass at me so I can delude myself that my charms are irresistible to you?"

"Too bad you're joking. Come on, let's get you settled in for the evening, because tomorrow we're starting on our epic quest to find your long-lost sister. Can I just say, thank God for your neighbor, because I can't cook." She offered her hand to Codee, who took it and allowed the assistance.

Sawyer didn't let go after Codee had stood and started up the stairs to the bedroom. Holding on didn't feel natural, but it wasn't awkward either. She'd noticed Sawyer was a tactile person, always using her hand to calm someone and make a connection. It wasn't her way, but she was adjusting because she still felt a bit off, and Sawyer's touch did help her relax.

They each took turns in the bathroom, and since she had taken a nap earlier and changed into sweats and a T-shirt then, all she had to do was brush her teeth and wash her face. She assumed Sawyer already had a toothbrush and change of clothes in the bag she'd left in the hallway, presumably unsure of how the evening would unfold and where she would sleep for the night. Sawyer seemed like the organized type who wouldn't forget the little things.

Codee was already under the covers but sitting up when Sawyer came out of the bathroom in a pair of baggy shorts and long T-shirt. She got a chance to appreciate her finely toned legs. They looked like she ran a lot, and she had just the body type Codee was attracted to. Other lesbians could have the bulging muscles of a hard-core butch who could bench-press twice her weight. She liked women who were fit but not overly muscular. Not that there was anything wrong with the heavily muscled women who frequented the local gym, but they weren't her cup of tea. She jumped when Sawyer waved a hand in front of her face.

"Hey, are you okay? You're not having a mini seizure, are you?" Sawyer cocked her head and then grinned.

She'd been caught looking a little too long at Sawyer's very attractive body. "No, sorry, just spaced there for a bit."

"So a lefty, huh?"

"What?" Codee asked.

"You prefer the left side of the bed."

"I could move over if you want this side." Codee did prefer the left side. In fact, she'd reluctantly given that up for her ex and never quite got a good night's sleep when they were together because of it.

"Nope, we're a perfect match. I prefer the right side."

Codee was starting to think they would be a perfect match, and it was too bad they worked at the same hospital or she might be tempted to give it a whirl.

"Do you need anything before we slither down into the bed and turn the lights off?"

"Hey, that's my line. You stole it, you line thief." Sawyer smiled. "Can I get you a glass of water or maybe some more of your meds?"

Codee touched her head and felt the bandage again. "No, I'm good. I really don't like to take medications, so unless it gets unbearable, I'll be fine."

Sawyer pressed a button on her watch and nodded.

"You're wearing your watch to bed?"

"Yes, I need to feel the vibration of my alarm. I don't want the noise to startle you; I just want to double-check you're okay with a quick nudge and then you can roll back over."

"So you plan on checking if I'm still breathing, huh?"

"I'll try not to startle you, but, yes, I'll be checking every two hours."

"I suppose that makes sense." She scooted down until the sheet rested just under her chin and turned to face Sawyer, who followed her lead. "Good night, Sawyer, and thank you."

Sawyer brushed her hand lightly across Codee's face. "Good night, Codee. Sweet dreams...of me, of course." She chuckled and then turned off the lamp leaving only the light from the moon to shimmer across the otherwise dark room.

Codee closed her eyes but didn't fall asleep until she heard the rhythmic breathing of her bedtime partner.

Chapter Sixteen

Sawyer felt the haptic notification on her wrist and pried her eyes open to look at the time. It was just after midnight. When she realized she'd snuggled up against Codee and had her arm protectively wrapped around Codee's middle, she carefully disengaged herself.

"Mrgfh...." Codee seemed to protest as she rolled onto her back.

Sawyer pushed aside the wisp of hair that had fallen into Codee's face and stared at the woman beside her, whose nose and cheeks started to scrunch and lose that peaceful expression from just a minute ago when Sawyer had spooned against her body.

Should I or shouldn't I? Now there's a butchered Shakespearian question. Sawyer did a mental shrug and replaced her arm after the sleeping woman shifted back on her side again. She rationalized that she wasn't making a move on Codee; she was just recreating the calm that appeared to exist before she broke their connection. *Connection,* yes, that's what she felt no matter how much Codee tried to put the skids on whatever was happening between them.

166

As she lay there with her arm wrapped tightly around Codee, she began to realize just how much her feelings had developed during the short time they had come to know each other. Even though she passed off her flirtations as jokes, Erma knew how she felt. She'd been open with her about her growing emotions. Holding Codee simply felt right, and she would find a way to convince the guarded woman that taking their friendship in a slightly different direction was the right course of action.

Sawyer closed her eyes and willed herself back to sleep, because the alarm wasn't going to allow her an uninterrupted rest, and that was okay, as long as she was able to ensure Codee was safe. A few extra cups of coffee in the morning and she'd be good to go.

†

The room was still pitch-black with the blinds fully closed when Codee stirred and opened her eyes to find Sawyer's arm casually flung over her stomach as Codee lay on her back. She grimaced, wondering if she had disturbed Sawyer with her snoring. Whenever she slept on her back, light snoring sounds snuck out of her mouth and nose. It used to drive her former lover nuts because she'd insisted even those barely audible noises kept her awake. She knew giving her ex earplugs and suggesting she use them wasn't a very nice thing to do, but she was losing a lot of sleep every time the grumpy woman had woken her in the middle of the night asking her to turn over.

Codee smiled, wondering how Sawyer had managed to check on her without waking her up. She didn't want to wake the sleeping beauty after that, so she continued to lie there with the comfort of Sawyer's arm draped over her middle.

As the sun slowly began to rise, the light created a faint glow in the room, leaving just enough light to observe the beautiful young woman. Sawyer twitched after Codee felt her watch vibrate, and she watched as Sawyer opened her eyes and seemed startled when they landed on Codee's smiling face. She quickly removed her arm. "Oh, um, you're awake." Sawyer's face turned bright red as she turned her wrist to glance at her watch. "It's only six, you should probably try to get some more sleep."

Codee wasn't about to bring up the fact Sawyer's arm had been wrapped intimately around her stomach just a few minutes ago. "*You* should probably try to get some more sleep. I slept through the night, which I'm positive you did not. Besides, I'm an early riser and six is practically sleeping in for me." She grinned.

"No, I'm good, but how about I fix some coffee for us? I'm positively stupid until I have my first cup. Or do you prefer tea in the morning? I could fix you some tea," Sawyer amended.

"No, coffee, definitely coffee in the morning for me."

"What time do you think Erma will visit?"

"I suspect she'll pop over around seven thirty. She knows I get up early, but…." Codee wrinkled her face in thought. "She might wait because she doesn't know when you usually get up."

"Do you mind if I take a shower after we have our coffee?"

"Not at all."

Sawyer smacked her lips. "I'll brush before heading downstairs, even though for some it probably ruins the flavor of the roast. Honestly, though, I don't even like the taste of coffee. I only drink it in the morning for the effect."

"I'll bet you're one of those that have a drop of coffee with your cream."

"Guilty. By the way, do you have a computer I can use? I'd like to do a little research before I call my friend. I could use my phone, but the screen is so tiny."

"I have a laptop. Will that work?" Codee used her good hand to scoot up to a sitting position.

"As long as you have wireless access, it will work great. I'm just going to google a few things." Sawyer pushed the covers aside, swiveled her body, and stepped onto the rug. She brought her hands above her head and stretched.

Codee sat transfixed as Sawyer's T-shirt rose enough for her to get a good glimpse of her flat stomach. She wanted to touch it but tamped down that urge.

A quick yawn and Sawyer turned to head into the bathroom.

She remained sitting on the bed, trying to remember the details of her dream and what the dream sister had told her about her father. Maybe that tiny bit of information was something to work with.

When Sawyer walked back into the room, leaned over her bag, and started rummaging around, Codee had a front-seat view of her tight bottom. It had the perfect combination of roundness and width. The curve of her hips was just wide enough to scream *all woman* without over exaggerating the ratio between them and her waist.

She watched as Sawyer plucked a hair tie from an inner zippered pocket in her overnight bag and pulled her shoulder-length, wavy, blonde hair into a messy ponytail.

Codee remained transfixed by Sawyer's girl-next-door good looks. She wasn't stunning like the airbrushed models in the popular magazines, but when she smiled, it was if a beam of light highlighted her natural beauty. Codee wondered if Sawyer bleached her teeth because they were so white they nearly blinded the person she directed her smile to.

"Something wrong? You're staring at me. I know I don't have food between my teeth, because I just brushed and I would have noticed a booger hanging from my nose," she joked.

"Oh, sorry, just spacing out a bit. I was trying to remember my dream and hoping for a clue. Do you think it's odd that in my dream I bounced back and forth between seeing the events unfold through your eyes and then mine? Why would that happen in a dream? Shouldn't it unravel like a movie through only one person's perspective? Why in the world would I see through your eyes, Sawyer? I barely know you."

Sawyer cocked her head. "I don't know. I did spend my free time talking to you and sharing random things about my life, so maybe you heard me. Or it could be because you were heading to my pre-termination hearing, so maybe your subconscious was telling you to keep an open mind and try to walk in my shoes. You know, seek to understand rather than to be understood."

"Hmmm, interesting theory. I do try to keep an open mind, and, in your case, I was already predisposed to finding an alternative to involuntary separation. Everything in my dream seemed so real, including how I was feeling. It was a bit freaky seeing things through your eyes, especially experiencing your opinions and feelings about me."

Sawyer raised an eyebrow. "Did I have impure thoughts or something?"

"So, coffee?" Codee decided it was time to change the subject lest she reveal the intimate details of the dream.

"Shall I bring you a cup in bed?"

She scrambled from the mattress. "No, I'm up, but I need a few minutes in the bathroom. I'll be down when I'm done. You know where to find everything, right?"

"I do, and even if I don't, I can always snoop. It'll give me a chance to learn about the enigma before me." Sawyer winked. "Sanctioned snooping is becoming my favorite pastime."

"What? I don't think I've actually given you carte blanche to snoop." Codee's eyes went wide.

"Kidding. We really need to work on your sense of humor, or lack thereof. You let it leak out on occasion, but not enough. Although now my curiosity is piqued. You don't have various sex toys located in your kitchen drawers, do you?"

"Um, no."

Codee retraced part of the dream and remembered she was playful, flirty, and did possess a sense of humor. Too bad it was all part of a made-up world she'd conjured as she slumbered for three days. Maybe the universe was trying to tell her something more than she had a twin sister. Perhaps it was time to lighten up and take a less serious view of the world.

"Kidding again. Boy, you are just too easy." Sawyer chuckled as she exited the room.

Codee shook her head and went in search of her laptop. She was anxious to begin the hunt for her sister, and, if Sawyer had an idea of where to start even before contacting her friend, she wanted to provide her with whatever tools were needed. It was nice to have two people on her side who didn't think she was nuts for believing her crazy dream had some buried truth in it. She pulled her computer out and headed to the bathroom to empty her bladder and quickly brush her teeth, then joined Sawyer in the kitchen.

✝

Sawyer was leaning against the counter daydreaming about how nice cozying up next to Codee felt last night. She knew the guarded woman had caught her in the act, but she hadn't said a word, apparently preferring to ignore the arm draped across her stomach. She'd really wanted to caress Codee's skin and kiss her tempting lips, but that was clearly out of the question.

Codee strolled into the kitchen with a laptop clutched in her good hand. The computer pressed against her T-shirt caused it to stretch tightly over her breasts. Sawyer noticed she wasn't wearing a bra and could see every little detail of her breasts and nipples. Like a car wreck on the side of the road, she couldn't take her eyes off Codee as she set the laptop on the counter.

"Now who's staring? I might say the same things, because I double-checked my teeth and took a quick inventory of my nose for potential hanging items."

"Touché. Thanks for bringing the laptop. I wanted to look up the number for the Department of Children and Family Services here in Washington. I have a good friend, Yvette, who works there. I just want to prepare you, I'm not sure they have records back that far unless you were adopted."

"Older children are rarely adopted. Babies are generally preferred. Most of my time was spent in a group home with an occasional stint with either a do-gooder family or someone looking to make a few extra dollars. Foster family placement generally fell in one of those two categories. Most of the kids hoped for the former, but a majority of them got the latter. Kids with sunny dispositions sometimes won the lottery when the do-gooders adopted them. I lacked the requisite charming personality that would increase my odds," Codee stated without emotion.

"We'll have a nice breakfast, and then I'll make the call."

The teakettle whistled, and Sawyer filled up the french press and set the timer for exactly four minutes. A favorite barista at a shop she frequented had told her that leaving the water in the press too long was as bad as pressing before the coffee had a chance to percolate. The perky barista had railed against the over-roasted beans at Seattle's favorite coffee chain and how often people screwed up a great cup of coffee by leaving it to sit too long in the press.

Sawyer felt Codee's eyes on her. "You're very precise about coffee, aren't you?"

"Yes, I am, and wait until you taste it. You'll be singing my praises very soon. I have to do something to make it taste better. Some people—not me, mind you, but others—will drink my coffee black, it's that good. I prefer coffee that tastes more like a latte."

"I prefer coffee black with just a touch of cream and sugar, so I can definitely taste the difference between a good cup of joe and a great one. That's why I'm particular about the beans I purchase."

"I know, I could tell." The buzzer on the timer went off, and Sawyer pushed down on the press. She filled Codee's cup to the three-quarter mark, and when Codee motioned for her to continue, she poured until she left just a little room for a splash of cream. She left more than a quarter of her own cup free for cream.

Codee looked back and forth between the cups. "I just remembered something from my dream that's really odd. This morning scene is like déjà vu, only I'm the one who liked a little coffee with my cream, and you're the one that made a smart remark about it."

"Hmm, that's interesting. I will not apologize for creating my modified vanilla latte. I'm very happy you have the french vanilla cream for me. Good choice in coffee beans and creamer. I think I might have to ask for your hand in marriage now because you've just met two items in my top-ten list." Sawyer topped off her coffee with cream and added two spoons of sugar.

"I sure hope the other eight items are more discerning, because the first two might let in any old person." Codee added a little bit of cream and some raw sugar to her coffee, stirred, and took a sip. "Good job, you will make somebody a nice wife."

"There is hope for you yet. I do believe you're getting into the joking spirit now."

Knock knock

Erma burst through the door that connected the garage to the kitchen, carrying a bag of blueberries. "Hellooooo. I saw the lights on and figured you kids were up. Now I know you two are a match made in heaven, because Codee's an early riser too. You are an early bird, right? Or did this one push you out of bed at an ungodly hour?"

Sawyer chuckled. "No, she did not push me from the bed, and yes, I can be an early riser when properly motivated, but I have to admit it took my watch to wake me up this morning. You're already up, so why do you say it's an ungodly hour?"

"She set her watch to wake up every two hours and probably hasn't had a proper amount of rest," Codee interjected.

"Okay, you two, get out of the kitchen and argue about sleep over there." Erma pointed to the couch. "I'll have the cakes done in a jiffy. Do you still have some of that orange spice tea?"

Codee nodded as she led Sawyer to the couch. "I wish it was time to make the call already. I'm anxious to find out if we'll be able to track down those records."

"Not that we'll hit a dead end, but can you remember anything from your childhood that might give us a clue? What about other adults in your life that might remember something?" Sawyer asked.

"I had a favorite teacher that I remember. She seemed to be the only one who ever broke through the wall I put up. Mrs. Haverstone…that was her name. She was my fifth grade teacher. She wasn't very young, though, so I'm guessing she'd be in her late seventies, early eighties now."

"Okay, that's good. Do you remember where you went to school?"

Codee's face brightened. "Yes, I went to Washington Elementary in Mt. Vernon. The school, if I remember correctly, had been around since the early 1900s, but thank goodness they went through a remodel to modernize the building in 1983."

"That's excellent, Codee. You never know, maybe your old teacher remembers something."

She looked away and tears formed in her eyes. "I wish I'd gone back to see her after I graduated from college. It will be nice to finally tell her what an influence she had on my life."

Sawyer grabbed Codee's hand and held on. "Regardless of whether we find those foster care records or not, I think we should try to track down your teacher. What was her name again?"

"Mrs. Haverstone."

"Okay. I think we have plan B already worked out. I have a good feeling about this."

Codee smiled. "Thanks. I like your enthusiasm. It helps. Hey, Erma, how're those cakes coming? I'm starved."

"Culinary masterpieces take time," Erma called out. "Didn't I hear that Sawyer would be responsible for the heated syrup?"

"Yes, ma'am." Sawyer released Codee's hand, stood, saluted Erma, and winked.

Chapter Seventeen

Sawyer paced as she held the cell phone against her ear. Codee nibbled on her lower lip as she listened to one end of the conversation.

"So no records back that far.... I see.... So if there was a complaint issued against someone, they would keep that for thirty-five years.... No, she was never adopted.... I could ask, but I don't think there were any allegations made of abuse.... Yeah, we should get together soon.... Maybe after all this is over.... Sure, I can ask.... Yeah, she is.... Okay, enough or I won't introduce you.... Hey, I really appreciate you answering all my questions.... I know I really should brush up on my knowledge on your department.... Yeah, definitely keep me in the loop. Later, Vetti."

"I'm going to take a wild guess and say we won't be obtaining any records from my foster care placements that might help."

Sawyer was frowning. "No. I'm really sorry, Codee. They don't have foster records back that far. They only keep adoption records, and since you were never adopted, I'm afraid that will be a dead end. I do think it's worth pursuing your grade school teacher though."

Codee's frustration at this first set back was disappointing, but she tried very hard to mask her feelings. She sighed. "Plan B, then. Who's ready for a road trip?"

Sawyer stopped shuffling across the floor and grinned. "I'm always up for a road trip."

"Hey, you two love birds aren't going to cut me out of the fun, are you?" Erma asked.

Codee opened her mouth to speak, and Sawyer looked at Erma, wide-eyed.

"Um...," Sawyer began.

"Stop that, or we'll banish you from hanging out with us. Sawyer and I are just friends," Codee finished when she'd recovered from the initial notion of thinking about Sawyer as a lover.

"Um-hmm, well, you better stop looking at one another like you're ready to jump each other's bones, then, or one of you will get the wrong idea. I just call it like I see it. I better get to join you on your adventure, or no more home-cooked meals," Erma threatened.

"I can take a little ribbing if it means we can continue to benefit from her cooking. Please, pretty please, Codee, can we allow some grace here?" Sawyer batted her eyelashes and held her hands in front of her in a prayer position.

"Okay, who's driving and when can we get going? Mt. Vernon is at least three hours away." Codee stood. "I can be ready in less than a half an hour, so how fast can you move your wicked bones, Erma? Sawyer can use the other bathroom while I'm taking my shower."

"I'll be back here in forty-five minutes." Erma held up her hand. "Unless you want to get some greasy food for lunch, I'll need those extra few minutes to fix us something more nutritious."

Sawyer raised her hand. "I vote for the delay."

"Fine, but I want your chicken salad with craisens."

"Good choice. I just happen to have all the ingredients to whip it up for us." Erma made her way slowly to the garage door, leaving the two women staring at each other.

"How bad is her arthritis?" Sawyer's forehead creased with worry.

"It looks like it's really acting up. She has problems with her hands and knees. I know she's in a lot more pain than she'll ever admit to. I told her to go see a naturopath or an acupuncturist. I know that's sacrilege, given that I work for a health system that only recommends surgery and drugs as a treatment plan, but I really think that would be the better option for her."

"I noticed her having difficulty last night. I know a good practitioner. I'll suggest the same thing. Listen, I'm sorry if she's making you uncomfortable with her comments about, um…."

"It's okay, she means well. Besides the fact that we work in the same organization, I'm definitely not good relationship material. I have issues," Codee confessed.

"This conversation deserves more attention than we can currently give it. I don't want a few minutes of rushed explanation or simple statements. I reserve the right to fully explore this at a later date, but for now we better jump in the shower, or Erma will be able to legitimately chastise us for any delay to the road trip."

"Not to mention what her warped little brain will conjure up, and express without apology, for why we were delayed." Codee smiled.

Sawyer started to run up the stairs and called over her shoulder, "Last one out of the shower is a rotten turnip."

Codee enjoyed Sawyer's playful side as she quickly followed, pointing to the door at the top of the stairs. "You're on your own to find the towels." She shot Sawyer a self-satisfied grin as she turned the corner and headed into the master bathroom.

✝

Four hours later the three women pulled into the parking lot in front of a red brick building.

"I guess the city has really grown since I went to school here. I don't remember the library being this big. Do you really think it would be better to start here versus going directly to the school?"

"You're in human resources, can you imagine the school handing over records on their former employees? Libraries are wonderful resources and can provide a lot of background information, enough that maybe we'll get lucky and come across something to determine if your favorite teacher still lives in the community. If she was forty or so at the time, it would make her at least seventy now. She could have been any age when she taught you—everyone seems old when you're in grade school. Maybe she got some kind of teacher award that they recorded in the newspaper. If she made that much of an impact on you, it's certainly possible."

"She was by far the best teacher I ever had, so I hope she was recognized for how much she made a difference in my life and probably the lives of many others. I'll bet she had a knack for identifying those who had issues...."

"Tsk, tsk. I sure do hate when you imply you're some seriously damaged human being. Damn, you are so infuriating, Codee." Erma shook her head, opened the car door, and winced as she emerged into the misty, gray day, so typical of the weather on the west side of the state.

Sawyer shrugged. She wasn't about to interject her own thoughts into the matter. She wanted that chance to have a more serious conversation at a later date when Codee wouldn't feel like the two of them were ganging up on her. "You saw the grimace, right?"

"Yes, it was hard to miss, and I don't think it was related to her jab at me. I'm not really sure why she's struggling so much today. It's probably all the moisture and cold. I know it exacerbates her symptoms. After we're done here, I think we should figure out where to get toasty and dry while we enjoy the lunch she made. I'm sorry we agreed to that versus going out to eat."

Codee struggled to open the passenger-side door with her left hand.

"Wait, I'll get the door for you." Sawyer jumped out of the car and opened it.

"This cast is really starting to annoy me."

They followed Erma into the building, easily catching up with her as she ambled along the sidewalk.

Sawyer was glad there wasn't any snow on the ground to make Erma's path more hazardous, because she sensed the older woman wouldn't take kindly to an offer of assistance. *Damned independent women.*

✝

Codee noticed the pleasantly plump woman with the bright red hair sitting at the front desk as she greeted them with her small, even white teeth below her expansive gums. The jovial expression put her at ease right away.

"Hello, what can I help you with?" the woman asked.

"Is it possible to search for news articles on a specific person that date back twenty years or more?" Sawyer inquired.

"Yes, absolutely. Do you have a name?"

"Only a last name. I had a teacher who had a big impact on me a long time ago, and I wanted to find out if she'd ever been recognized by the school district. It's long overdue that I told her what her influence meant to me, and I was hoping I might be able to track her down. Her name was Mrs. Haverstone."

The woman's face brightened. "Oh my goodness, really? I had Mrs. Haverstone in fifth grade. I remember her." She lost her smile. "She was a big supporter of the library and was on the board until her.... Oh, I really shouldn't be telling you this. I always assume people have positive motives, and it gets me in trouble all the time."

"I promise we don't have any nefarious intentions. I'll admit we do have another reason to try to track down Mrs. Haverstone, but I promise it's not to cause her any grief," Sawyer explained.

The woman narrowed her eyes. "What's the other reason?"

"I'm trying to track down a twin sister I'm not even sure exists." Codee sighed. "I guess that doesn't sound so sane, does it?"

The woman looked at them, glanced back over her shoulder, and called to a young girl putting books on a cart, "Addison, would you mind watching the desk for a minute?" She turned back to Sawyer. "I'm going to need the whole story before I consider giving you any information, and I better not hear that you bothered Mrs. Haverstone later on, or I'll send my cousin, who's part of the Mt. Vernon Police Department, after you. Come on, we'll go over there in the reading area and have a seat. You better get out your driver's licenses, because I'm taking down all your information before I share anything."

Sawyer chuckled. "Okay, that's a fair deal. If you're going to trust us, we have to trust you with some sensitive information. I'm pretty good at reading people, so I'm willing to take a leap of faith and show you my license, but I can't speak for my friends."

Erma cocked her head to the side. "I don't have anything worth stealing, so sure, why not?"

Codee narrowed her eyes. "I'm not as trusting as these two, so I hope you won't hold it against me if I'm a bit leery. Lessons from foster care will do that to a person."

"No license, no info." The woman crossed her arms across her chest.

She didn't get a bad vibe from the woman, but she did sense a deep respect for Mrs. Haverstone and a fair amount of protectiveness toward her former teacher. She decided she wanted the information badly enough to take a chance, and so far in her life, her gut instincts about people, other than those she was attracted to, had not been incorrect.

"All right. I suppose that's fair. Besides, I know where to track you down, and I want the name of your cousin to double-check he's really on the force before we do this little information exchange," Codee insisted.

✝

Sawyer wasn't opposed to the extra layer of verification, but her insistence on confirmation of the cousin did add to her perception that Codee was exceptionally guarded. She came to the conclusion that breaking through her barriers would be more difficult than she originally assumed, but she was worth the extra effort.

They'd all given the library attendant their driver's licenses after Codee had called the police department to verify the woman's claim.

"Okay, you need to give me the whole story about why you want to find Mrs. Haverstone, and then maybe I'll tell you where you can track her down."

Codee took a deep breath. "Please don't pass judgment until you hear me out. Five days ago I slipped and fell on the ice, hit my head, and was unconscious for three days. In the time I was out, I had a very vivid dream that was so real to me. In it, I met a twin sister I didn't realize I had. I know this seems farfetched, but for some reason I believe my subconscious is trying to tell me something. I don't recall having a sister, but I do have this niggling sensation that she exists and is somehow tied to my vague memories of my father, and why my mother wouldn't talk about him."

"That doesn't explain why you want to track down Mrs. Haverstone," the woman interrupted.

"My mother died when I was young, and I was put in foster care. Those records aren't available anymore, and the only adult I remember ever opening up to was Mrs. Haverstone. I know it's a long shot, but I might have told her something when I was young that could help me find my birth records. I don't think my name is the same, and I don't even know if I was born in this state."

Sawyer glanced at Codee's hopeful expression. At that moment, she didn't think she wanted anything more than for Codee to be able to connect with her old teacher, who Sawyer hoped would miraculously have the information she needed.

The woman stared at Codee, seeming to study her. "Well, that's a really interesting story. I'm not sure why I believe you, but I do." She swiped a tear away. "I don't want to dash your hopes, but about eight months ago, Mrs. Haverstone suffered a major stroke. She's been in a rehab facility ever since. I don't know how far she's come in her recovery, but I know there were some cognitive issues. Her husband died six years ago, and she never had children. I don't think she could, which is why she was so good at her job. She loved every student she taught like they were her own. I haven't been to visit in a while." She looked down. "The library staff was like her second family. I could go with you after work."

"What's the name of the rehab center?" Sawyer asked.

"Mira Vista."

Sawyer was concerned about hanging around for several hours, especially since Erma seemed to stiffen up so much on the drive over. "We have a long drive back to Moses Lake, so I hope you don't mind that we'd prefer to visit with her right away instead of waiting."

The woman whistled. "Moses Lake, that's a long drive. Sure, go ahead. I understand. Will you let me know how it all turns out?" She walked over to the reception desk, pulled out a sticky-note pad, and scribbled something on the top paper. "Here's my cell phone number." She pulled off the sheet and handed it to Codee.

"I will. Thanks for helping us out, and I'll tell her you're coming to visit tonight."

The woman nodded. "Do that, because then I'll be sure to follow through and not make any excuses like my big baby of a husband wanting dinner on the table at a certain time." She grinned.

Chapter Eighteen

Sawyer took Codee's hand and held on, giving it a quick squeeze but making no effort to break their connection.

Erma winked as they waited for Mrs. Haverstone in the large recreation room. The front-office staff informed the trio she was just finishing up with her speech therapist and she'd expressed her delight that one of her former students was there for a surprise visit.

A tall, thin woman pushed a wheelchair as she entered the spacious area from a side corridor. Codee's heart fell when she saw the women lock the wheels after situating a frail-looking woman of about eighty in front of them. Not only was the woman before her drastically aged from what she remembered, but the stroke had clearly taken its toll on her beloved former teacher. The left side of her mouth drooped, and she was considerably thinner than when she'd taught her. *I guess thirty-five years is a long time.*

Codee was surprised to see a twinkle in the old woman's eyes as she slurred, "Codee."

She couldn't control the tears that formed in her eyes. "Mrs. Haverstone, how can you possibly recognize me after all these years?"

Mrs. Haverstone's lips attempted to curl up in a post-stroke smile.

She thought that if her fondness for the old woman wasn't so deep, the effort to smile might seem grotesque, but to her it was a welcome sight.

"Google," she managed to reply.

Codee tilted her head. "Google?"

"Favorites, computer."

"I think she's trying to say she googled you and you were a favorite student of hers." Sawyer released her hand.

Codee moved to the wheelchair and gently hugged the woman. "I should have tracked you down twenty years ago when I finally received my masters. That success was every bit yours to celebrate as it was mine. I never would have gotten there if you hadn't steered the boat in the right direction. You changed my life and I never thanked you."

"Why now?" Mrs. Haverstone lifted her arm and gave an awkward pat to Codee's good arm.

"God, I'm an ungrateful...."

"She's trying to find out more information about her first foster care placements and if her name changed so she can look up birth records. We were hoping you could re-member something that would help."

Mrs. Haverstone's eyes turned stormy. "Mean people, don't." She paused as if trying to find the right words.

"The foster parents?" Sawyer asked.

She nodded.

"You don't want us to try to find them, do you?"

She turned her sharp eyes in Sawyer's direction. "Who?"

"I'm a friend. Do you know something that would help?" Sawyer asked.

"Hard." Her pained expression reflected frustration. "Write."

Sawyer turned her head around and strode over to the front desk, where she collected a pen and a small notepad.

Codee patted her hand. "Thank you for trying to remember. Anything at all you can tell me...."

Sawyer handed the notepad and pen to Mrs. Haverstone, who slowly crafted a response. The writing was sloppy and the words choppy, but Codee understood.

Looked records. Needed know. Wanted help. Name Murphy.

Codee read the note. "So my name is Codee Murphy?"

Mrs. Haverstone nodded.

"Do you know where I was born and if my birthday is August 15, 1971?" Codee gave her back the paper, and she wrote one word.

Bellingham

Codee leaned over and read the upside-down word. "So I was born in Bellingham, Washington? Do you know if it was St. Luke's or St. Joseph's hospital? I know they merged, but they were separate in 1971."

Mrs. Haverstone scribbled, *Joseph.*

"I think I have a twin sister. Thank you." She kissed Mrs. Haverstone's cheek. "Are you hungry? Because Erma here"—she pointed at Erma, who was sitting quietly in a chair with a broad smile on her face—"makes the best chicken salad I've ever tasted, and I think a nice little picnic lunch is in order while we visit some more with you. Is that okay?"

The lopsided smile was all the answer Codee needed.

†

The bleak, overcast day was a sharp contrast to the mood in the car as the three women drove back home. Sawyer noted how slowly Erma moved as she folded herself into the backseat and gingerly clicked her seat belt into place. She made a mental note to discourage Erma from participating in future long-distance road trips. She needed to have a game plan on how to go about approaching that topic in a way that wouldn't offend her. Sawyer believed Erma would never admit to the level of discomfort she was undoubtedly experiencing.

Codee appeared so excited by the news and was fidgeting in her seat, already doing research on her smartphone regarding how to access her birth records. Although she was having a hard time holding the phone in her swollen hand and using the tiny keypad to type, she'd managed to access the information she needed quickly. Sawyer wanted to help and was almost ready to pull over to the side of the road to search the Internet herself when Codee joyously announced her findings. After fifteen minutes, they'd only made it to Highway 20 when she provided the information to her road trip cohorts.

"It's so easy. I'm on the Washington State Department of Health site, and I can just order the birth records online or by phone for fifty dollars if I want them to speed things up and ship it next day. Hmmm, do I want the process expedited?" Codee glanced at Sawyer and shot her an impish grin. "Hell yes I do."

"I'm pulling over so I can push the buttons on the phone to call the department. Your hand must be killing you. I'll bet you're causing it to swell some more." Sawyer neatly pulled the vehicle to the shoulder, not caring when the person behind her leaned on his horn.

"People are so dang impatient these days. Here, let me see." Sawyer accepted the phone, focused on the small screen, and called out, "Erma, you remember the first part of the phone number, and Codee, you're responsible for the rest. I think I can handle the one eight hundred part. Okay, Erma, can you remember five, two, five? Codee, your numbers are zero, two, one, seven." Sawyer pushed the first three buttons. "You're on, Erma."

"Five, two, five."

Sawyer entered those numbers. "Codee?"

"Zero, two, one, seven."

"It's ringing." Sawyer handed the phone back.

"Uh, hi, yes, I'd like to order my birth record.... Yes, my own.... so I can also order another birth record if I know the date and name? That's great...."

Sawyer nodded when Codee captured her eyes with the unspoken question. She definitely thought it was worth the chance to toss out the name she'd remembered from her dream.

"So Washington is an open-records state, and it's legitimate for me to find records for a twin sister, right...? What if I'm not exactly sure about the spelling of the first name...? Okay, I'll check that out.... Vital Chek, huh...? Yes, for right now I can give you my birthdate, name, and the hospital I was born in. I don't have the exact time.... Thanks so much.... Yes, Codee Murphy, *C* as is Cat, *O* as in orange, *D* as in dog, *E* as in elephant, and *E* as is elephant.... Yes, I guess that is an unusual first name.... Yes, Murphy with a *Y*.... The date is August 15, 1971, and the hospital was St. Joseph's in Bellingham...." Codee ended the call after providing her address.

"It sounds like you may be able to get the records for your sister." Sawyer was careful not to add, "If they exist," because she really wanted Codee's dream to have an element of truth.

"I guess Washington is progressive with their birth and death records, but not their foster care records. Interesting. Rather than try to give them different possible spellings of my sister's first name, the clerk suggested I use that Vital Chek site. Apparently people use that all the time for genealogy questions. Since Codee isn't a very common name, I wouldn't be surprised if there's an unusual way to spell China. What do you think?"

"China is an unusual name to begin with, but I've seen people get extremely creative with the spelling of common names, so it's entirely possible the logical way we might spell the name isn't the correct spelling." Sawyer held out her hand. "Can I see your cell phone for a second? I'd use mine, but... well, I can't really afford a robust data plan and I'm always running over."

Codee handed over the phone, and Sawyer's fingers flew over the keypad. "Okay, just a quick search shows the traditional spelling—you know, like the country—and then there's a different spelling with a *Y* versus *I*. There's two different spellings with *Y*, one with a single *N*, and one with a double *N*. I think we should try as many possibilities as we can."

"Okay, not to rush you or anything, but can we head back now? I'm anxious to access that site on my laptop, because I'll admit, doing it on a smartphone is challenging with one hand basically out of commission, and I can't ask you to spend hours on the Internet while we're precariously parked on the shoulder of a major highway. Besides, we should get Erma back home."

"Oh don't hurry 'cause of me. I've had more excitement this trip than I've had in years."

Chapter Nineteen

Codee stood over Sawyer with her good hand casually placed on top of her shoulder. As Sawyer clicked the mouse selecting the next button and the name blinked on the Vital Chek screen—*Chynna*—she stared at the monitor in wonderment.

"I have a sister. Can you type her name into Google and see what comes up?"

Sawyer quickly did the search, and several Facebook and LinkedIn options appeared on the screen. "Wow, I didn't think that many people would pop up." She started with the various Facebook options. "A lot of these are too young."

Codee had to verbalize the next roadblock to her quest. "She might not have the same last name; mine is different. She could be married by now."

"What about asking for some help from a private investigator? You have a lot of information now, and at least you have a place to start."

"I guess." She couldn't mask the profound defeat she felt at not finding her sister after all the legwork they'd already done. She should have expected the search for her sister wasn't going to be all smooth sailing. Codee stepped back and turned away from the screen. She couldn't stand to see the setback blinking ominously from the laptop.

The chair scraped softly against the wood floor, and Sawyer's gentle hands turned her around. The embrace was a welcome distraction, and she molded herself into the strong body. She let Sawyer stroke her hair and whisper comforting words.

"We're going to find her. I'll help. I promise. Vetti's ex is in the business, and she comes highly recommended. I met her once, and she left a positive impression. They're still friends, so I'm sure she would take on the case."

Codee pushed back and looked into Sawyer's compassionate eyes. She had an overwhelming desire to kiss those lips, and before she realized what was happening, she closed the distance and brushed them against Sawyer's irresistible mouth.

Sawyer opened her mouth, and Codee felt the acceptance of her tentative entrance inside. Her lips were so soft and pliable, and the kiss was more sensual than desperate—a slow tease. She melted into the sensation before the realization hit that she was kissing a colleague. She reluctantly pushed herself away.

"Oh God, I'm so sorry, Sawyer. I shouldn't have done that."

"Why not? I'm definitely not complaining. I'm single, you're single. Yes, we work in the same place, but you don't supervise me, so in my mind that doesn't violate any reasonable nepotism policy I've ever heard of."

"I'm a senior leader. I'm held to a much higher standard, and I'm in human resources for God's sake. No one in the organization would be appropriate for me to date. It's an unwritten rule."

"I'll quit or you can terminate me. Maybe my termination was meant to be. I can get another job. I want to explore this, us," Sawyer pleaded.

"I can't let that happen. I couldn't terminate you in a dream or in real life, so that's not an option. I'm not a good bet for a healthy relationship, so I'm definitely not worth giving up a job you just got that is perfectly suited for you."

"That's my choice to make...."

Knock knock

Erma walked in carrying a large, rectangular pan. One of the thick, green hot pads was on the bottom and the other was gripping the side of the baking dish. "I want to know what you discovered and I've brought the entrance fee. I had sauce in my freezer and cheese in the drawer for my family's secret manicotti recipe." Her eyes darted between the two women. "Did I interrupt something important?"

"I'm going to be five hundred pounds if I don't stop indulging in your cooking, Erma," Sawyer commented.

"Well then, none for you," she teased.

Sawyer grabbed the pan and placed it on the stove. "No, no, you'll still love me when there's a tad more of me to hang on to, won't you, Codee?"

Codee felt her cheeks flush.

"Oh I do love that shade of red, and I definitely disrupted something juicy. I want to hear all about it after you tell me what you found in your Google-thingy search."

"That does smell wonderful." Codee ignored Erma's teasing and steered the conversation into safe territory. "Eat first and update later. Remember, coffee lubricates my brain."

†

Erma had poked and prodded, but Codee stubbornly refused to reveal anything about the kiss, and finally she'd reluctantly made her way to the kitchen to retrieve the leftovers after she feigned the need to retire because of a headache. It wasn't exactly a lie; she had pinched the bridge of her nose as she felt the impending pressure on her temples, but it wasn't that bad—yet.

Sawyer had sent Codee a worried look and walked Erma to the back door.

Erma took her half-empty pan, and Codee heard Sawyer provide a brief update to "Project Chynna," the apt name she'd given to the most important search Codee had ever done.

Sawyer had even excused herself right after the meal to call her friend, get a contact number, and arrange a meeting for the very next day. It was beyond thoughtful, and she wondered if letting herself get close to someone else besides Erma would really be so awful.

They could be friends, she rationalized. She could use another good friend. Sharlie didn't count, even though she had invited her staff out for drinks on a few occasions to celebrate the success of a new initiative or some other special event. In a rare move she had once invited Sharlie along with her entertaining husband over for a glass of wine one night.

Her immediate dilemma was what to do about sleeping arrangements post *incredible kiss*. She'd been the one to initiate it, so would Sawyer expect something tonight? Certainly she'd made it clear they couldn't go there again. Hadn't she?

Codee supposed the conversation hadn't quite ended. She sighed, knowing they would need to finish *the chat*. She wasn't looking forward to that, but she'd made clear that being friends was the only thing on the table—at this time.

At this time? Why did I just amend my position?

195

She was sitting on her bed when Sawyer startled her from her musings.

"Sorry, I didn't mean to scare you. It looks like you're in the process of solving all the great mysteries of the universe."

Codee cleared her throat. "We need to talk."

"'Sawyer, you're a nice woman, but the kiss was a mistake. Can we just be friends?'" Sawyer paused. "Did I cover all the bases? Is that about right? Oh wait, I probably missed the argument about me being too young for you. I'm getting the friend sermon before you'll allow any emotion to sneak in. Too late, Codee, I already have feelings for you, so there isn't really an easy way to let me down." She held up her hand. "I'll find my own way to the guest room. If you need something, I hope you'll let me know. I'll check on you every few hours." She spun on her heel and left Codee with her mouth open and guilt crawling all over her body. She didn't know how to fix this, and once again her tears fell. Bitterly she wondered if perimenopause was the cause of all this emotion that had suddenly invaded her previously impervious mind. Sawyer was the last person she intended to hurt, but it was too late; she'd already royally messed things up.

"Damn, damn, damn." She fell back on her bed and cried herself to sleep. She didn't bother changing her clothes, brushing her teeth, or washing her face. She simply didn't have the energy to move.

†

Sawyer splashed cold water on her face and glared at her reflection. "Shit, you just had to pop off, didn't you?" She hadn't meant to sound so angry or flippant, but when she'd stalked out of the room without her bathroom supplies, or clothes to sleep in, it hadn't registered with her because she was spouting her honest feelings. She wore her heart on her sleeve. She knew that, and her love life always turned out exactly the opposite of how she wanted it to.

Sawyer tiptoed back to Codee's bedroom, metaphorically holding her tail between her legs, but when she heard the soft crying, she stopped outside the door and mentally whipped herself for causing more grief when she'd only wanted to shower her with love.

Friends. She bounced the word around on her tongue and thought if that was all Codee offered, she'd gladly accept it over nothing. Sawyer didn't think she'd fallen in love, *yet*, but there was something different about the beautiful woman, and that something was worth fighting for.

She was still chastising herself for acting like a three-year-old who hadn't gotten her way after asking to stay up just a little bit longer with the adults. Heading back to the guest room, she decided to wait an hour or so and then sneak back in to gather her bag and toothbrush. Maybe Vetti would have good advice for her, but maybe she'd only yell at her for falling, once again, for the wrong woman. She had said on more than one occasion it was Sawyer's special skill. Still, it was better to endure Vetti's reprimand and her soothing words afterward than suffer in silence. Sawyer wasn't interested in relationship advice from her friend who was also single. A shoulder to cry on, though, even if it was through the air waves, was better than nothing.

Sawyer remembered that she'd left her cell phone in her jacket pocket, so she crept downstairs to retrieve it. Once she'd closed the guest bedroom door, she called her friend and held her breath for the tongue-lashing before the salve. It was still early, but that didn't matter to Sawyer. She'd woken Vetti in the past after midnight when her last girlfriend had unceremoniously dumped her for a younger, better-looking model.

"Hey.... I did it again.... Yes, Codee.... I know, I know, but this time it's different. She's different.... No, I'm pretty sure I just blew it.... I made her cry.... No, I stalked away, and when I went back to get my bag, I heard her crying in her bedroom.... I got the friend speech, well not exactly, but she was just about to deliver it.... We kissed—correction, she kissed me, and I felt it all the way down to my toes before she pushed me away and said she can't get involved because she's the HR exec or some such bullcrap.... You're not helping. Isn't it time for the *best bud, I'll support whatever bonehead move you made* stage of our conversation...? I love you, too, but you know, not in that *lesbian drama, fall into bed with your best friend* way." Sawyer took a deep breath. "Nah, I'm okay. I'll check her every couple of hours, apologize tomorrow, and hope for the best. By the way, thank you for helping to set up the meeting. At least that's on track.... Yeah, I'll keep you informed."

After ending the call, Sawyer inched her way into the hallway, listening intently. She didn't hear the soft sobs, so she took a chance and lightly pushed open the door. Her heart broke to see Codee in the fetal position, clutching a pillow as if the soft object might be her savior. She desperately wanted to replace it and be the one to offer that protection and sense of security. After tiptoeing into the room, she quickly grabbed her overnight bag and left, gently pulling the door to leave a small crack for later when she would check on her. No matter what had transpired earlier, Sawyer needed to make sure the sleeping woman continued to remain free from any lasting effects from her fall.

As she'd promised herself, Sawyer crept into Codee's bedroom every two hours to check on her. She wasn't able to resist spending a few extra minutes standing over her and imagining what it would be like to enter her inner sanctum on a permanent basis.

At four, she watched as Codee tossed and turned, and in an effort to calm her, she brushed her hand against her forehead and down her cheek. Her eyes fluttered open for a few seconds before closing again, and Sawyer's heart warmed when a small smile appeared on her face.

Maybe it wasn't too late to repair the damage she'd done. It wasn't as though her master's program hadn't trained her thoroughly in good communication skills. Yet mastering those skills was so much easier when you weren't personally involved. Strong emotions were never logical.

Sawyer vowed to temper those emotions and finish that conversation like an adult.

†

It was still early when Codee opened her eyes and heard movement downstairs. She marveled at the possibility that Sawyer was an early riser, considering in her dream that wasn't the case. She assumed Sawyer was up, probably making coffee. The explanation for why she couldn't get involved hadn't gone well, but she didn't know how to fix it. She'd have to pull up her big-girl panties and give it another shot.

After dragging herself into the bathroom and releasing her full bladder, she peered at herself in the mirror. Red-rimmed eyes stared back at her. She looked like a pitiful mess. She touched her cheek, vaguely remembering when Sawyer had come into the room to check on her. She knew it wasn't a dream, and she hoped Sawyer could tell how she'd not only accepted the brief touch, but settled after feeling the gentle caress.

She couldn't delay the inevitable, so she made her way downstairs prepared to accept whatever punishment was in store for her after impulsively acting on her attraction. She half expected the cold shoulder or another round of protests.

Sawyer was pouring beans into the coffee grinder and turned around when Codee stepped up to the island. She looked Codee in the eye. "I'm sorry about last night. You don't owe me any explanations. Friends?"

Sawyer blew out a breath. "No, I'm sorry. I was the one that crossed the line and gave you mixed messages. It won't happen again. I could use another friend, thanks."

"Vetti and Jacque will be here in another hour and a half, and then we can get the ball rolling. Jacque is very good at what she does. If anyone can track down your sister, I know she can. I'd like to be there with you on this journey if you'll allow it. I kinda want to see the happy ending unfold."

Could it be that simple? The conversation had gone a lot more smoothly than she'd thought it would, and she didn't have to go into a lengthy explanation of why considering anything more than friendship was impossible for them. A part of her wanted Sawyer to protest, to fight for something more, but wasn't this what she wanted? No, if she were honest with herself, what she wanted was something entirely different. She wanted Sawyer in her bed; she wanted that part of the dream to come true. The rest she could do without, but Sawyer making love to her was something she craved no matter what she declared.

"Earth to Codee. Hey, where did you just go?"

Codee shook her head. "Oh sorry, coffee will help lubricate my brain cells."

"Your wish is my command." Sawyer bowed, turned back around, and pressed the button on the grinder.

Chapter Twenty

Codee opened the door and ushered in a tall, muscular woman with short, dark hair and chocolate eyes. She flashed back to her dream, and this handsome woman reminded her of someone in it, but with each day, the details were fading. Her companion stood to the side, patiently waiting for an invitation to step inside. Standing next to her tall friend, she looked less intimidating but still had a supremely confident air about her.

"Hi, I'm Codee. Please come in and we can make proper introductions."

Both women responded with a brisk nod.

Her companion broke into a wide smile and then charged over to Sawyer and enveloped her in a warm hug. "Hey, Trouble, it's been far too long since we last spoke." She winked.

Codee felt a tinge of jealousy at the familiar way the attractive woman spoke to Sawyer.

"Ha-ha, very funny. It wasn't that late when I called last night."

Had Sawyer called this woman last night, and why? Her interest in Sawyer's relationship to this woman was definitely piqued.

"This not-so-funny person is Vetti, my best friend. Jacque, stop looking so serious. You're scaring poor Codee with that badass expression."

The tall woman smiled, and it transformed her face. "I'm trying to look professional. Jeez, you've ruined everything. She's gonna think I'm some hack now."

"Nah, I told her you were very good at your job."

The woman stuck out her hand. "I'm Jac. No one gets away with calling me Jacque, except for the little pipsqueak over there."

Codee jumped when she heard the woman introduce herself as Jac. It was a familiar name, but she didn't know why.

Jac touched Codee's arm. "Hey, are you okay? You look like you just saw a ghost. I'm really sorry, I didn't mean to scare you."

"No, you didn't scare me. It's just that in my dream, I think there was a woman named Jac, and for some reason I think she was linked to Chynna."

Jac raised her eyebrow. "Chynna is the sister we're trying to find, right?"

"Yes, twin sister."

Jac wiggled her eyebrows. "Well then, I'm single, and if she looks like you, I could probably marry her on the spot."

Vetti whispered something in Sawyer's ear, and Sawyer responded by smacking her on the arm. Codee would find out what she'd said even if she had to pin Sawyer down and make her spill the beans. A brief vision of straddling Sawyer and pinning her hands above her head flashed in

Codee's mind, and she chastised herself for letting that mini-fantasy sneak in.

"What? I'm sorry, what did you say about marriage?" Codee asked.

Jac raised an eyebrow. "Yes, I see you were distracted by the two adolescents over there whispering secrets. Hey, you two, no secrets." She leveled her smoky gaze at Codee. "I was giving you a backhanded compliment and probably making a bad joke in the process."

"Oh, uh, sorry I missed that. I have no idea if my sister is a lesbian."

Sawyer glared at Jac. "Stop flirting with your client."

Jac held her hands up. "Fine, but when I find the twin, she won't be my client, so I get to flirt with her." She grinned.

"And that is why we split up...." Vetti laughed.

"Hey, I never touched, only looked. Don't let them think I was a cheater."

Vetti laughed again. "I know, just kidding." She turned to Codee. "Jac's the best. It was the damn army that was the culprit. I couldn't handle the stress of being an army wife when Don't Ask, Don't Tell was in full swing, and by the time they'd overturned the stupid thing and Jac went in the Reserves, we'd settled on a friendship. I also worried too much when they sent her to Afghanistan. You do need a wife to keep you out of trouble though."

"Are we going to get down to business now?" Sawyer snipped.

Codee couldn't help smiling inside. She shouldn't be happy that Sawyer seemed to feel her own bout of jealousy, but she was. This time she did hear Vetti when she whispered in Sawyer's ear, "Green is not your color." Codee pretended she hadn't heard as she led everyone into the living room and motioned for them to sit on the couch and chairs.

"Can I get anyone some coffee or tea?"

"Why don't you let me take care of that since I have two good hands compared to your one? You can fill Jac in on the details so she can get moving on this right away." Sawyer stood and looked expectantly at Jac and Vetti.

Vetti waved her arm in the air. "Nothing for me, thanks. I had a latte on the way."

"Do you have tea?" Jac asked.

"I do. Any special preferences?" Codee sat on the recliner closest to Jac.

"Do you have anything like apple cinnamon or orange spice?"

Codee smiled. "I have both. They're favorites of mine."

"Oh, well then, we're a match made in heaven. You have to become my wife after I finish this job for you and you're no longer my client."

"How about some mint tea to cool you off?" Sawyer crossed her arms.

Jac looked up. "Oh sorry, am I encroaching on your territory? I didn't know you two were an item."

"No, we're friends," Codee and Sawyer said in unison.

"Okaaaaay. I'll take orange spice, then."

Sawyer stomped into the kitchen, and Codee swiveled in her chair, watching Sawyer grab the teapot.

Vetti sat back and smiled after darting her eyes back and forth between Sawyer and Codee.

Codee thought Sawyer's jerky movements and clanging of the teapot as she filled it and put it on the burner was a surefire sign of her irritation. She stifled a chuckle as she turned back to face Jac, who'd apparently asked a question while she was watching Sawyer's exaggerated movements.

"I'm sorry, what?" Codee asked.

"Let's go over everything you've found out so far and also anything at all you can remember from childhood." Jac grabbed a notepad and pen from a bag sitting on the couch. In the blink of an eye, her demeanor had completely shifted, and she sensed Jac was in professional mode now.

"I know she was born on August 15, 1971, because that's the date of my birth. We were born at St. Joseph's in Bellingham. As with a lot of healthcare systems, they merged in the late eighties, I think, and changed their name to PeaceHealth. It's a Catholic system with other hospitals in the state and also in other states. That's about all I've learned so far about my sister."

"Vetti says her first name has an unusual spelling. Is that correct?"

"Yes, it's Chynna with a *Y* and two *N*s. Murphy is a pretty common last name, though, and I'm not even sure hers is the same. Mom changed mine to Sorenson, and I can only take a guess at why. I can't even tell you my father's first name until I get a copy of my birth certificate."

"Of course if we had Chynna's social security number, I'd have her location in a heartbeat, but what's the fun in that? I've always preferred a small challenge." Jac grinned. "Is there anything else you can remember, anything at all?"

"I think my father was in the armed forces. For some reason, I think I remember a man in fatigues with a buzz cut. He was handsome." Codee wasn't sure where that last comment came from. She wasn't even sure about the statement that he was a military man; stating that just felt right.

Jac closed her notebook. "Okay, I've got enough to start. If we're lucky, she stayed in Washington State and never changed her name. Give me a week or two to prepare a full report, and then we can set up another meeting and I'd be happy to help you decide how to proceed." Jac took Codee's hand and gave it a gentle squeeze.

Codee recoiled from the touch as she looked up and registered Sawyer's steely gaze. She couldn't tell if Sawyer was angry, sad, or a little of both.

Sawyer set the cup of tea down on the coffee table in front of Jac and captured Codee's eyes. This time, Codee clearly saw the pain reflected in her gaze.

"I need to pack my bag. Codee doesn't need me to hang around and get in her hair anymore. There haven't been any side effects in the last two days, so I think you're safe on your own now."

"Jac, you promised me that we could check out that place that serves brunch every day. We'll find our own way out." Vetti tugged on Jac's arm.

Jac looked confused for a minute and then seemed to gain an understanding of the subtle maneuvering. "Oh right. I did, didn't I? Um, I can send you the details of my fee via e-mail, unless you'd prefer we go over that right now."

Vetti smacked Jac across the stomach. "What? You're not charging Codee. She's a friend."

Jac raised her eyebrow.

"Okay, she's a friend of Sawyer's, who is my best bud, so can't you do this pro bono?" Vetti batted her eye-lashes. "Please. For me?"

"All right. I have a feeling this day is going to cost me a lot more than a measly brunch."

"Oh no. Please send me a bill for whatever the going rate is. I'm not hurting for money and can definitely afford your services. I insist."

"Well, if you insist." Jac shrugged. "It was a pleasure to meet you. I'll be in touch."

It seemed like an afterthought as Vetti turned around and casually tossed out, "Hey, would you mind telling Sawyer there's an opening now in the children's division and she should hurry up and submit her application? The ancient in that department just submitted her resignation yesterday. Good timing, huh?"

Codee wasn't sure what Vetti meant by the "good timing" comment, but it probably had something to do with the boundaries she'd drawn regarding not dating someone from the same organization. She had to think about that a little more before she would agree this was indeed good timing. She'd just assumed Sawyer was interested in transferring to the social services department at the hospital because Codee knew she was completing her masters in social work, but maybe the hospital wasn't really the best match. She'd never really asked Sawyer about her dreams or passions. The naked truth was she didn't know a whole lot about Sawyer, but she wanted to, and right now Sawyer was getting ready to leave without giving her the opportunity to learn about this wonderful woman who'd been so unselfish with her time and attention.

✝

Sawyer scooped up her discarded clothes from the guest bedroom and quickly stuffed them into her bag, then gathered the remainder of her personal items and tossed them on top. After that she quickly zipped it shut. The teeth on the zipper vibrated and filled the air with the sound of closure.

With the bag slung across her shoulder, Sawyer began her descent to the main living area, prepared to say goodbye to Codee and protect the fragile pieces that were left of her breaking heart. Midway down the stairs, she nearly ran into her. Sawyer couldn't meet Codee's eyes as she attempted to sidestep around the object of her desire.

"Sawyer, please stop. You haven't even said goodbye to Erma, and she'll wonder why you suddenly ran off.

You said we could be friends. This doesn't feel like a friendly departure."

Defeated, Sawyer sat in the middle of the stairs. She kept her head bowed.

Codee used her hip to nudge Sawyer over just a little and sat down next to her. "Will you please talk to me? I still need you in my corner."

Tears glistened in Sawyer's eyes as she admitted, "I behaved positively infantile. Yes, I've been known to fall very quickly, but I've never once let the little green monster completely take over my body. It felt like an alien was in charge. I just need a little time and space to adjust to a new fantasy. You know, the friend fantasy. It isn't nearly as fun as the other one I cooked up in my head." A partial smile appeared.

"I will be fine on my own for the next few days and then will probably return to work on Monday. Maybe we can plan to get together on the weekend. How does a sappy romantic comedy sound?"

"At the theater or here with homemade popcorn and a cozy couch?" Sawyer asked.

"You make the popcorn, bring the movie, and I'll offer up my couch and entertainment center."

"You have an entertainment center? Why, Ms. Sorenson, you've been holding out on me."

"It's upstairs in my bonus room. I rarely use it, but it's got all the latest and greatest gadgets—fifty-inch flat-screen TV connected to a high-end surround-sound system. I bought it for my ex, who spent an enormous amount of time vegetating in front of it while I read. It comes in handy when Erma and I are in the mood for movie night."

"Well, that is a deal I cannot refuse. We should invite Erma."

"Of course we'll invite her. I need something to bribe her from having a temper tantrum over missing out on meeting the PI we hired."

"You hired," Sawyer clarified.

"I still hope you're in this with me. I've been comforted by your presence. Are you?"

"Am I what?"

"Are you still in this with me?" Codee asked.

"Always, for as long as you need me."

Chapter Twenty-one

Sawyer held two of the DVDs she'd brought behind her back, dancing around and laughing as Codee attempted to snatch them from her.

"Nope. I'm saving one of these little gems for last. Kind of like that last, perfect bite of food. It's my all-time favorite, and I don't want you making any snide comments about the old classics."

"Hey, I just thought maybe you'd pick at least one from this decade. I know *Casablanca* is a classic, but God, hasn't everyone seen it a thousand times?" Codee made another grab.

"They don't make movies like they used to."

"True, but how many old classics featured lesbians getting a happily ever after?"

"Okay, good point, which is why I just happen to have the perfect choice as our next movie. Erma wouldn't be offended by a lesbian love story, would she?" Sawyer frowned. "Do you think that's why she made that lame excuse about needing to do laundry?"

Codee rolled her eyes. "No, I believe she had another motive." She didn't want to reveal that she'd had a heart-to-heart with Erma the night before where she'd told her about the kiss and explained why she couldn't start anything with Sawyer. Erma kept trying to convince her that her logic was faulty.

"Oh?" Sawyer raised her eyebrow.

"So...what is this perfect lesbian movie you've brought?"

Sawyer held up one of the DVDs while keeping the other hidden behind her back. "One of my favorites, *Imagine Me and You*."

"I heard that was a good one. I've never seen it."

"Lena Headey was smoking in the movie." Sawyer tilted her head. "You look like her."

"Yeah, right."

"No, you do."

"So do you think it would be totally decadent to order a pizza, considering we've already devoured mega quantities of popcorn dripping with butter?"

Sawyer set the DVDs on the floor next to the open case and pushed the button on the player to eject the movie they'd just watched. "How long will it take for them to deliver?"

Codee inched closer and tried to see the title for the third DVD. "Probably an hour."

"Back away from the movies, Miss Nosy. No, I think that's perfect timing. We devoured the popcorn over an hour ago, so we're due for more junk food." She placed the movie back in its case and shuffled the other two DVDs until she'd selected her next choice, popped it into the empty slot, and covered the secret movie with the one they'd just watched.

"Fine, I'll just mosey on back to the couch and order the pizza for us. Have you always liked old classics?" Codee plopped down on the couch and grabbed her cell phone.

"Yeah. Mom and I would waste away our Sundays watching the oldies movie channel. It was a tradition while my dad and brother went on their *manly outings*. Depending on the season, their activities ranged from fishing to hunting. I didn't like watching living things die, even the slimy fish." Sawyer grabbed the remote and joined Codee on the couch, where she sat close by, leaving just enough room so their legs didn't touch.

"Let me order the pizza, and then do you mind if we talk a little bit before starting the movie? I'd like to hear more about life in a normal family. I suppose you would prefer a vegetarian pizza? Cheese is okay, though, right?"

"There're not too many cheeses I don't adore."

Codee handed Sawyer the phone. "Would you mind finding Guido's in my contacts list? My passcode is 0871." She held up her casted arm. "I still struggle a bit with those tiny buttons with one hand somewhat out of commission."

Sawyer set the remote on the coffee table and accepted the smartphone. "You know, you really shouldn't use your birthday or any parts of your birthday as a passcode. It's too easy to break into things." She deftly navigated to the contact and handed the phone back.

"Yeah, can you deliver a medium Margherita.... Codee Sorenson.... Yeah, I'm at the same address.... Okay, thanks, Carl." Codee set the phone on her thigh, pushed the End button, and set it on the side table. "One hour. So tell me what it was like growing up with a brother."

"You're on a first-name basis with the pizza delivery guy?" Sawyer shook her head. "Never mind. Before I spill all about my pig of a brother, you need to tell me what's in the pizza you just ordered. No little fishes, right?"

212

"What! You don't like anchovies? Better give me the phone back." Codee held out her hand.

Sawyer's arm brushed against hers, and it sent a jolt through her body.

"I'm kidding. Now who needs to take a few lessons in anti-gullibility?" Codee laughed at Sawyer's grimace as she grabbed for the phone. "I ordered us a pizza with a pesto base, ricotta, mozzarella cheese, tomato, basil, and a drizzle of fresh lime juice. It's delish."

"Now that is something my brother would do to me and worse. Although he wouldn't just threaten to order a pizza with anchovies, he'd do it and eat the damn thing with a big grin on his face. I do love my big brother and I know he loves me, but I think I'd rather have a sister. You just can't talk about your first sexual experience with a brother, at least not with mine. He was very overprotective. Didn't any of the kids you grew up with in foster care fill the role of a sibling?"

Codee shook her head. "My first sexual experience was with an older girl in one foster home. She was overprotective all right, but not in a good way. It was a confusing time for me, and, well…."

When Sawyer draped her arm across Codee's shoulder and brought her in close, Codee didn't pull away. She let herself mold into Sawyer for just a few minutes.

Sawyer moved her hand along Codee's shoulder, rubbing gently.

Codee reluctantly shifted, and Sawyer removed her arm. "I'd rather learn more about you. What made you decide to go back to school for your masters? I know you took the admitting job because it worked with your school schedule, but I'm guessing you had some kind of career before the hospital."

"Not really. There isn't a whole lot you can do with a bachelor's in women's studies. I worked as a clerk at the Department of Social and Health Services with Vetti. She encouraged me to go back to school. I wanted to work with children, and I've been waiting for the right opportunity to come up. Vetti assured me a retirement was in the wings, but when Sharlie offered the chance to transfer versus getting fired, I took it. I don't want a termination on my record."

"Oh crap. I forgot to tell you Vetti mentioned there was an opening now. Some woman did retire. I'm sorry, I was supposed to tell you that, and then I got distracted that day you were upset."

Sawyer smiled. "I know, she told me. I submitted my résumé on Friday and I have an interview on Monday at nine. I'm a little nervous about it, and if I don't get this job, I may have irritated my new boss to the point the hospital will follow through with a termination after all is said and done. After I just got the job, she hasn't been too happy about me taking so many days off."

"But you took off the time to help me out. I'll talk to—"

"No, please, don't do that. You've already gone out on a limb for me. I think maybe I'm not meant to work for the hospital. The universe must have other plans for me, and maybe for you as well." Sawyer grinned.

"It certainly does feel as though strange things are shifting in this universe. You seem to bring out a side of me I didn't know existed, and I like that. Maybe I don't have to be so guarded all the time. I don't want to be that way with a brand-new sister I never knew I had, so I better start practicing the kind of warmth and openness that seems to just ooze from your pores. I could learn a lot from you, Sawyer."

"Does that mean you'd hold open the possibility of something a little more than friendship if I do get the job in children's services?" Sawyer turned her body to face Codee.

Codee gazed at her hopeful expression and one more brick tumbled from her carefully erected wall. She wanted more than anything to take that leap of faith and venture into uncharted territory. It was time she let someone in and gave them a fighting chance at the kind of intimacy she'd only read about but never experienced first-hand.

"I suppose the expression, 'never say never', applies in this situation. I could crack open the door, if the right pieces fall into place."

Sawyer pulled Codee into an embrace and kissed her on the cheek. "When I see the crack, you'd better be prepared for my boot in the door, because I'm going to kick it wide open. Hey, I meant to ask you if you really have a cabin like in your dream. Wouldn't that be a great place for our first date?"

"I wish. That was the only part of the nightmare that could be classified as a dream. I've always wanted a romantic cabin in the woods. Although it does seem out of character for someone whose heart has an emotional padlock to consider wanting anything romantic in their life. I suppose it's all part of this re-occurring fantasy of mine that's appealing about it. You know, roaring fire, no one around for miles…." She could feel her face turning a bright shade or red..

"Hey, you're remembering something in that dream that you haven't revealed to me, aren't you? I'm guessing something very fun occurred in that romantic, imaginary cabin of yours."

"Hey, are we going to watch *Imagine Me and You* anytime this century?"

"Funny. Nice redirection." Sawyer chuckled, picked up the remote, and started the DVD. "Just don't fall asleep on me, because the best is yet to come."

Chapter Twenty-two

Codee was spinning her pen around on her desk and daydreaming about the movie marathon with Sawyer. She was surprised Sawyer brought *An Affair to Remember*. It was her all-time favorite classic, iconic flick.

She secretly cheered when Erma had said she was busy that night, leaving her alone with Sawyer. She had learned a great deal about her as they watched movies and devoured junk food. She wasn't exactly envious of Sawyer's normal childhood, but she was wistful about what she'd missed growing up in the system.

Sawyer never pushed for more information and seemed to have a sixth sense for when Codee began to feel uncomfortable. She'd make a joke about a certain someone always changing the subject, but she never pressed for more than Codee was ready to reveal. In time, she could see herself removing all her self-imposed barriers. She might even share the grizzly details and the culprit of her intimacy issues.

She mused that even in her dream she hadn't fully confessed to Sawyer about Sue and that first sexual experience that felt more like a violation than a welcomed encounter, though it hadn't necessarily been violent. Her experience in foster care could have been a whole lot worse, and for that she'd always felt some level of gratitude for Sue and her protectiveness.

The bottom line was she felt guilty for letting that experience influence her so much, because it shouldn't have been a big deal in the grand scheme of things. She imagined others would simply tell her to get over it and that it was just a lame excuse for being a frigid bitch.

Sharlie poked her head in the doorway and startled Codee from her daydreams. "Sorry, did I scare you?"

"Just a little. I'm being rather unproductive today, and I can't even use the excuse of too many good drugs, because I decided I better follow the policy I helped craft about a drug-free workplace. I stopped taking the pain pills on Sunday. What can I do for you?"

"Sawyer is out in the lobby and was wondering if you had a few moments."

"Sure. Send her in. I don't have anyone else needing to see me today, do I?"

"Nope, I'll take care of the new grievance in admitting, but we really need to talk about Hilda. Can't we consider giving her a settlement agreement? She's killing our turnover stats."

Codee sighed. "I'll make an appointment to talk with Tim again about her, and maybe this time I can convince him that we need to do something. Can you please block some time out this afternoon for you to give me an update? I might need to use that information in my meeting with him."

"Okay, will do. By the way, no one would care if you started dating Sawyer...just saying."

Codee narrowed her eyes. "I am officially gonna kill Erma. When you find her dead body, will you at least plead my case and tell the police it was justifiable homicide?"

Sharlie chuckled. "Please don't kill her. How will we benefit from her baked goods then? We depend on her stopping by every week with those tasty treats. I'll send Sawyer back, and if she's offering lunch, you'd better take her up on it. I'm tired of seeing you eat at your desk day in and day out. Get out, live a little."

Codee listened to the tinkling of laughter that reminded her of a gentle caress to a piano as it faded down the hallway. She realized she liked the way Sawyer laughed. It was genuine and musical, not an irritating guffaw or fake titter.

Sawyer poked her head in the doorway first. "Hey, stranger, how about some lunch? I'm buying because I want someone to celebrate with me."

"I don't know. I've been distracted all day and haven't gotten a darn thing done. I haven't even managed to sort through the thousands of emails overflowing my mailbox. I swear they're like little bunnies, propagating all over the place."

Sawyer stepped inside and sat on the chair in front of Codee's desk. "Sharlie assured me that you have nothing pressing in the immediate future. Please, I really want to share my good news, and it's not the kind of thing that lends itself well to a dump and run. Besides, I need your sage HR advice."

"Sharlie is a terrible busybody. It's about the job, isn't it?"

"Yes. Will you take an hour and come with me?" Sawyer leaned slightly forward. "I really do need your special expertise."

"Oh all right, but if anyone is paying, it'll be me. Promotions and dream-job offers have special rules. The person receiving the offer never pays for the celebratory party afterward." Codee stood and gathered her bag lying on the cabinet to the right of her large, L-shaped desk. It was made of the same cheap material as her monstrosity of a desk, and she hated it all.

"Is the bistro okay?"

"Is there anywhere else?" Codee grinned. "I sure wish this town would get in the capitalist spirit and open up some competition."

"The sushi restaurant used to be surprisingly good for the middle of the state. I was sad when the owner sold it. The new place has bastardized the California roll with that imitation crabmeat. I know that's how most places prepare it, but I miss the real crab they used to serve."

Codee raised her eyebrow. "You like sushi?"

"You say that like I'm some unsophisticated hick. Yes, I do like sushi, quinoa, and many other ethnic foods. Just because I've lived in Moses Lake all my life, doesn't mean I don't enjoy trying different things, and new foods are at the top of my entertainment list."

"Duly noted. I didn't mean to offend, but you strike me as the meat-and-potatoes sort—minus the meat."

Sawyer crossed her arms. "Well, I'm not, and just for that, you will have to accept an invitation to at least one of my favorite out-of-the-way places. They have the kind of amazing food that will blow you away."

Codee chuckled. "I sense that's the excuse you'll use to get me to go on a date with you."

"I've already finagled a way for you to go on a date with me—solid career advice from a seasoned professional. I'm going to consider our lunch today a date. Still as friends but hoping for a status change in the very near future."

"You don't give up easily, do you?" Codee began walking out of the office, grabbing her coat from the rack on the wall.

"Nope, not when something is really worth fighting for and when I sense that destiny is playing a major role, regardless of how serendipitous it is." Sawyer smiled as she followed her.

"I like that word, *serendipitous*. Don't take this the wrong way, but it sounds sexy coming out of your mouth. And no, that wasn't the crack in the door, so keep your booted feet to yourself."

When Codee and Sawyer reached the outer reception area, Codee informed Clare, "I'll be out of the office for about an hour. Sharlie mentioned that I don't have anything pressing, but you can reach me on my cell phone if you need to get ahold of me."

Clare scowled. "Didn't Sharlie tell you about her grievance meeting?"

"She did, and she also told me she had it covered. See you in an hour." Codee pushed open the door and squinted into the sunshine as the biting cold hit her face.

"She's a bit of a prune for an HR receptionist," Sawyer whispered.

Codee sighed. "In my dream she was the *traitor* that turned us in and got you and Chynna executed. That should tell you something about how my unconscious views her. I know I really should work on that with her. Was she rude to you?"

"Nah, Sharlie was grabbing something from the printer and intervened before Clare had a chance to ask me what I needed. I've just had other, less positive interactions with her in the past. I think she gets along with Hilda, so *that* should tell you *something*."

"I wish people would give me the details on her rude behavior, but so far there hasn't been anything specific. Failure to smile isn't exactly grounds for termination. I shouldn't really be sharing this with you." Looking around, she wondered who would drive to the bistro. "Um...."

"We can take my car, it's right here. That way we don't have to schlep up to the gravel parking lot." Sawyer pulled her key from her pocket and unlocked the door to her older-model Toyota Camry. "And don't worry, your secret is safe with me. Besides, everyone knows Clare skates along the edges, and you'll probably never have a justifiable reason to let her go." Sawyer pulled open the passenger door.

Codee slipped inside and settled into the seat. "Enough about that. I'm looking forward to hearing all about your good news."

"And I'm looking forward to sharing it with you."

✝

The bistro was a flurry of activity, and conversation buzzed around them like a busy hive. Sawyer tried to lead Codee to a quiet corner after they'd ordered their food at the counter, but the place was so busy, finding an intimate spot was nearly impossible. Finally, she settled for a table in the center of the room.

The wooden chair scratched across the floor, but the noise barely penetrated the buzz of conversation.

"I'm sorry, I guess anytime around noon was bound to be crowded." Sawyer placed her elbows on the table and leaned in.

"If it wasn't so cold out, we could escape the wall-to-wall people and sit outside. I wish my house was a little closer." Codee's voice barely rose above the din.

Sawyer wiggled her eyebrows. "I guess playing hooky is out of the question."

"We could take our food and go back to my office. You *were* seeking my professional counsel, so that might be the more appropriate place."

"No way, we are not going to take the chance of our lunch date being interrupted by some HR emergency." Sawyer grinned.

"Well then, be prepared to shout out your questions."

"So, in a nutshell, I was offered the job at the Department of Children and Family Services, and I'll be working with the foster care program and Child Protective Services. It's what I've wanted to do since I started my masters, but when Sharlie offered up the job at the hospital, I felt like I should take it in lieu of termination. It was very kind of her to make the transfer happen so quickly, and I know she bent the rules because the job did not get posted for seven days like the contract dictates." Sawyer paused as if to collect her thoughts.

"I don't really understand your dilemma. Are you saying you might not take this dream job because you feel obligated to stay at the hospital?"

Sawyer nodded.

"Okay, that's just silly. I'd advise you to do what is best for *you*."

"There are so many reasons to jump ship, at least that's how I'm viewing this, and only one reason to stay."

"What's the one reason to stay?"

"I don't want to disappoint you or cause problems because you vouched for me."

Codee waved her hand in the air. "Oh posh. People take jobs and leave before the ninety days are up all the time. That's what the probationary period is for. It's a time for both parties to check things out and make sure it was the right decision. I'm sad to see the hospital lose such a great employee, but happy you'll be the one to advocate for those kids, and, believe me, they need a strong advocate."

"So you think I should accept the job? Funny thing is that it's not even more money, it's a lot less, but it's what drives my passion. I need to do something I consider worthwhile work, and honestly, getting people out of the hospital in the quickest way possible does not feel like it's all that valuable. Sure, it protects the hospital's bottom line, but it doesn't really safeguard the patient when they're discharged to a less than ideal place."

"I do think you should take the job. I still feel like I'm doing something that's worthwhile every time I help someone find their right place in the world, like right now. Employees truly are the most valuable resource, and if I always remember to do the right thing by the employee, they pay me back tenfold. When you come across a colleague more suited for hospital work, I know you'll send them our way."

Sawyer smiled. "I will, I promise. Thank you so much for easing my guilty conscience."

"The only other advice I would give is that you never want to burn any bridges, so I'd give at least three weeks' notice."

Sawyer clapped her hands together. "Now that all the business is over, have you heard anything yet from Jac? I know it's only been a short time, but I'm very excited for you."

Codee sucked in her right cheek and bit the inside.

"No, nothing yet. I'm usually a very patient person, but I'm a nervous wreck."

Sawyer brushed her hand lightly against the cheek Codee was gnawing on. "I know, I can tell."

"You can?" Codee kept chewing.

Sawyer chuckled. "Yes, you have a tell."

"A tell?"

"Yeah, like in poker. It's like a habit or facial expression that tells the other players when you're bluffing. Police often look for tells. By the way, you should never play poker. How do you possibly get through union negotiations? You are very expressive."

"What's my tell?"

"You nibble on the inside of your cheek and sort of at the edge of your lower lip. It's adorable. It makes me want to kiss that corner. I'm surprised you don't cause sores on the inside of your mouth though."

"Oh. For some reason, I get into a zone when I'm in negotiations, so I think I'm safe there, but now I have to ask Sharlie about it. I would think either she or the attorney would have told me if I was giving up our position at the table. Maybe they've just been too kind to correct me." She shrugged. "I guess I always thought I hid all my emotions. No one else has ever accused me of showing my feelings before."

"I guess I'm just good at reading people and picking up on the subtle cues. So...what are your plans after Jac tells you how to find Chynna?"

"God, I have no flippin' idea. You're awfully optimistic. What if Jac can't find her or..." Codee's eyes went wide "...she isn't alive?"

Sawyer gathered Codee's hands that she'd rested on the table. "Don't think like that. I have a good feeling about everything. I truly believe the universe sends us messages through our dreams for very specific reasons. I don't think you would have dreamed about a sister you weren't sure you had only to learn she'd passed. I can't really explain my beliefs, but then again, neither can anyone who has a deep faith in God. Sometimes we all just have to take that leap."

"Thanks, you always seem to calm me. I suspect I'm no longer biting that lip of mine."

"No, you're not, and you've just blessed me with one of your glorious smiles. You could melt the ice caps with the brilliance of your smile."

"Flatterer."

"Nope. Truth-teller."

"It's weird that some of the things in my dream were true to real life and other things were slightly off. At least I got the fact I have a sister right."

"Maybe other things in your dream will also come true. I get the feeling I played a bigger part than you've fessed up to, if your periodic blush is any indication." Sawyer smirked. "Oh, here comes our food." She looked up and released Codee's hands as the server placed Sawyer's portobello mushroom sandwich in front of Codee, and Codee's turkey on focaccia at her place setting.

They giggled and switched plates after the server left.

"You know, I've never tried that, but it looks and smells wonderful. Maybe I should have left the inadvertent swap as is, but you probably don't eat any kind of living thing. I got that impression when you talked about your father and brother and their hunting escapades."

"I don't eat red meat, but on occasion I eat fish or poultry. It's better for you, and I don't see those mournful cow eyes as I take a big bite." Sawyer picked up her sandwich, chomped down, and moaned, "Mmmm."

"So do you have any advice on how to approach a long-lost sister who is probably as equally ignorant of my existence as I was of hers prior to the dream, nightmare, whatever you want to call it?"

Sawyer quickly chewed. "I always prefer the direct, face-to-face approach, but in this case, it might be a bit of a shock. I'm a processor; let me ponder this and get back to you."

"I think if someone showed up on my doorstep at this point in my life, I'd probably think it was a scam." Codee sighed and picked up her turkey sandwich.

"Using intermediaries is usually a fairly safe approach. It allows the person to get used to the idea of a face-to-face meeting. Maybe you can use Jac or Vetti in that manner. She's a wonderful social worker and has a way with people."

"So do you. Maybe you should approach Chynna."

"I could do that, or Jac and I can do it together. Jac is kind of intimidating on her own, huh?" Sawyer laughed.

"Oh, I don't know. At first she was a bit stiff, but then she was downright charming."

Sawyer frowned. "You aren't interested in her, are you?"

Codee laughed. "No, relax. You are so easy. I was just yanking your chain. Speaking of tells, you broadcast the little green monster the other day. I thought I'd have to put a cast on my teakettle."

"I know, not one of my finer moments. I'm sorry. I'm not really like that usually." Sawyer focused on Codee. "In all seriousness, though, do you think I could ask you on a proper date once I don't work for the hospital anymore?"

"Yes, I think I'd like that."

"So the age difference isn't a problem?"

"Are you calling me old?" Codee asked.

"No never, can you forget I even brought that up?"

"Hmmm, you better think of a way to wipe that completely from my mind then."

Sawyer beamed. "Perfect. I'm going to plan something spectacular."

"I look forward to it."

Chapter Twenty-three

Codee felt the vibration of her phone as she was meeting with the CFO about Hilda, and she was tempted to pull it out of her jacket pocket. All week long, Sawyer had sent little texts and periodic hand-written notes with mini chocolates. Or she would find a fresh flower at least once a day on her desk after coming back from a meeting. That always made her smile. She knew Sharlie was an accomplice in Sawyer's elaborate wooing plan. She felt special with Sawyer courting her. It was old fashioned, and she'd never experienced that kind of targeted attentiveness. Every day she was more comfortable with the notion of dating Sawyer and the invisible shield was slowly disintegrating.

Tim's bobbing head distracted her from her pleasant thoughts.

"Okay, I understand. Yes, I'm just as concerned about the turnover in the admitting department. I'll talk to her."

"Tim, you've been talking to her for months, and I haven't seen any improvement. That department will be the primary reason we don't meet our turnover goal. We skated by last year by the skin of our teeth. Turnover is now twenty-five percent of our overall bonus, so do you want to be the one who explains to the board why we haven't met our goal? Or to the employees when their bonus is much less this year?" Codee pushed.

Tim leaned back against his chair. "So what do you suggest?"

"A settlement agreement. We offer six months' severance in exchange for her voluntary resignation. That is more than generous given she's also head of the leading department in employee grievances."

"Will you be there in the meeting when we offer this?" Tim asked.

"Of course. If you're in agreement, I'll prepare the document and we can give it to her today. Fridays are the preferable day to do this sort of thing. Tim, you know I don't suggest these things lightly. I know we're affecting someone's livelihood, but in this case I really don't think we have the option. Too many employees have suffered the consequences of her poor management,"

"All right. Do it. I'll have my secretary set up the meeting for four. Will that work for you?"

"Yes, I'll make it work." Codee stood. "Thanks, Tim. I know this is hard for you, and I do appreciate having a CFO who has a conscience and compassion for employees."

She quickly exited his office, pulled her phone out of her pocket, and frowned when she didn't recognize the number of the missed call. She kept walking as she scrolled through her smartphone and noticed a voice mail. As she walked outside into the wintry blast, she continued to mess with her phone so she could access the message.

"Hey, do you want another mishap? Stop obsessing over your phone while you walk in the slick parking lot. There are still some icy spots," Sharlie warned.

Codee looked up to see her concerned, hazel eyes. "You're right, I do not want to slip into that weird alternate universe again. Once was enough."

She had given Sharlie the broad strokes of her dream, without admitting to the blossoming love affair with Sawyer. Sharlie had made clear her opinion about Sawyer and how perfect she thought she was for her, but Codee still felt a little uncomfortable revealing much about her personal life to coworkers.

"Stick that weapon of mass distraction back in your pocket, please, until you're settled into your chair back at the office."

"Yes, Mom,"

†

Codee picked up the single purple rose laid out on her desk and placed it under her nose as she breathed in the flowery scent. She retrieved the note that lay underneath the flower.

Science fiction marathon tomorrow? I'll bring the movies and popcorn. And no, this is not the official first date. I have something more creative in mind.

She was looking forward to finding out what Sawyer had planned for her. She was such a big tease, and the buildup was excruciatingly pleasant.

She lowered herself into her chair, still smiling from the note. Leaning back against the cushion, she remembered the voice mail. After she pulled her phone from her pocket, she pushed the button to listen to the message from the unknown number.

"Hey, Codee. This is Jac. I caught a lucky break, and I'm relatively confident I found your sister. She lives in Washington, which is quite a fluke because she's moved around quite a bit as a result of her military career. Can we meet up tomorrow?"

Codee's heart raced. Nothing had prepared her for this news. It tore at her sense of calm to hear the update and not know exactly how to proceed. It was almost too much to process all at once.

Without thinking, she pressed the number for Sawyer. She was probably with a patient and couldn't answer her phone, but she needed to hear her calming voice. "Hey, Sawyer, I know you probably aren't able to answer right now, but can you call me back as soon as you get this message?" she said after Sawyer's voice mail greeting finished.

She was chewing on the inside of her lip when Sharlie poked her head in the doorway a few minutes later. "Hey, Sawyer is outside and said you called. She came right over. She sounds worried. Anything I can do to help?"

"No, I did call. Uh…it's personal."

"Okay, I'll send her right back." Sharlie grinned and left the office.

Sawyer was breathing heavy as she burst into the office. "What's going on? Are you okay?"

"Jac called. She found Chynna."

"That's good, right?" Sawyer crossed the room and sat in the chair in front of the desk.

"She wants to meet tomorrow. Can you come over?"

"Of course. You just tell me the time and I'll be there with bells on my toes. Codee, I have a really good feeling about this. Everything is going to work out perfectly. Look, I know you don't talk much about your experience growing up in foster care, but it doesn't take a rocket scientist to figure out it's had a huge impact on you and your ability to trust. I just want you to know I may have a boatload of faults, but I do have the patience of Job and I've been told I'm an exceptional listener. Whenever you're ready, I'll be there to hear your story."

"For right now, can we just start with you helping me navigate this uncharted territory?"

"You bet. Now stop chewing a hole in the side of your cheek, because I'll be right there with you every step of the way."

"You better get back to work now. I'll call and leave a message regarding the time."

Sawyer exited the office with a small wave and a bright smile.

She picked up her phone again and pushed the button to return Jac's call. "Hi, Jac, this is Codee.... Thanks for calling.... Yes, tomorrow would work out well for me.... Yes, nine is great.... I asked Sawyer to come by. Is that okay...? Thank you. I'll see you tomorrow."

Codee couldn't believe how much the dream had affected her life over the past week and a half. She was on the precipice of entering into two different relationships, and both scared the crap out of her. She supposed this was what one might consider positive fright, but to her fear was fear and even good stress was hard on a person.

Chapter Twenty-four

When Sawyer got the message from Codee that Jac was coming by at nine, she decided to get up early and swing by at eight thirty. She suspected Codee was past the point of nervousness and was on the verge of a mini panic attack.

In the short time she'd gotten to know the reserved woman, she'd seen an incredible amount of growth. Bit by bit, the pieces of her self-imposed wall were crumbling down.

Sawyer wasn't surprised to see Erma sitting in the chair when Codee answered the door and led her to the living room. Erma was the other person Codee trusted. Perhaps not implicitly, but as far as Codee was inclined to trust another person. She now counted herself in that tight circle, and she'd thanked the universe profusely for that small development.

"Hey, Erma. What did you bring over for breakfast?" Sawyer grinned.

"Oh, I see, you just love me for my cooking ability," Erma teased.

"And...?" Sawyer shot back.

"I made some quiche with feta and olives, you know, Greek style."

"Yummy, I'm already drooling. I'm like one of Pavlov's dogs. I take one look at you and start salivating." Sawyer winked.

"You go ahead and serve yourself. It's in the oven. I'm too comfy here, and Codee still has that wounded paw."

"I'm not an invalid, you know," Codee huffed.

"Did you two already have a slice?"

Codee shook her head. "We were waiting for you. Somehow I just knew you'd arrive ahead of time. Erma just got here."

Sawyer grinned. "Go on, sit down. I'll serve both of you. It's the least I can do since I continue to mooch food off you. Your kitchen and I are on a first-name basis now. I can find everything on my own. I presume coffee is waiting for me too." She set her backpack down next to the coffee table.

"Of course," Codee answered.

Sawyer made quick work of serving up three healthy slices of the quiche and set them on the coffee table with cutlery. She went back into the kitchen and poured herself a cup of coffee, and then prepared it to her liking. When she came back into the living room, she set it in front of the open spot on the couch next to Codee's plate.

Erma and Codee picked up their forks when Sawyer sat down and settled into the couch, grabbing her own utensil.

"Mmm, this turned out better than I thought, if I do say so myself," Erma said after finishing her first bite.

"Thanks for leaving out the ham. I always think of Babe the pig and can't ever bring myself to eat either ham or bacon, even though I love the smell of both. Turkey bacon and sausage quells my cravings." Sawyer broke off a large chunk of the delicious-looking pie. "Oh. My. God. Please be my surrogate mother so I can drop by anytime I want for a home-cooked meal," she exclaimed after chewing the delectable morsel.

"Thank God I didn't break my leg as well as my arm or I'd be in trouble. I can still use my exercise cycle, even if I can't row at the moment. It is the only thing that keeps me from expanding like a blowfish."

Ding-dong ding-dong

Sawyer turned her wrist over to glance at her watch. "I guess we aren't the only early birds. I think I'm starting to like Jac. I do respect people who are early or right on time. Whenever someone is late, I think that's a sign of disrespect."

Codee jumped up, and Sawyer heard the front door creak open. She wondered what caused the noise and if she could fix that for Codee. *Maybe the noise doesn't bug her.*

"Come on in. Thanks, Jac, for finding out the information so quickly. I'm a little nervous."

Jac and Codee rounded the corner and entered the living room. Jac frowned. "You do want the information, right?"

"Oh yes. I'm sorry. I can't believe I'm just blurting my insecurities to anyone standing in front of me." Codee gestured for her to sit in the open chair.

"No worries. This is a big deal. Hey, Erma and Sawyer." Jac flashed them her bright smile.

Sawyer was happy to see Jac the Charmer instead of Jac the Professional. She thought if Jac displayed her severe side, she might make Codee more flustered than she already was.

Before sitting, Jac handed Codee a folder.

"Go ahead and open it. Chynna has moved around quite a bit in the military. She's a bright star in the Navy. The rumor is that she's being considered for a promotion to rear admiral. That's the equivalent of a one-star general and is quite an accomplishment for a woman. Regardless of the progress in the Navy over the last several years, there still aren't many women in the higher ranks. There are only seven women who are rear admirals, and a total of twelve combined rear, vice, and full admirals right now. She's currently stationed on Whidbey Island. She also has an interesting specialty—explosive ordnance."

Codee shifted her gaze up after scanning the pages.

Sawyer watched as joy spread across Codee's face. The pride was evident in her wide smile.

"She looks just like me but with short hair. Just like in my dream," she said in amazement.

"Yeah, she's quite the looker all right. No romantic entanglements at the moment. She's had some short-term relationships, but nothing permanent. I think the longest was two years. It didn't end well, and from what I understand, the bitch threatened to tell during the Don't Ask, Don't Tell era." Jac grimaced. "I'm not sure what happened to change her mind, but it never got that far."

Codee's eyebrow rose to her hairline. "How'd you find all this out?"

"I'm very thorough. Besides, I wanted to know if she was single. Sorry, that extra effort is definitely not part of my fees." Jac shot everyone a mischievous grin.

"I don't know what to do now. I am so out of my element here."

"May I make a suggestion?" Jac lost her smile and her expression turned serious.

"Please do."

"Let me approach Chynna and explain the circumstances so she doesn't think you're some crazy stalker. I'll take a picture of you to show her how much you two look alike. There's no question you are twins. I promise I will remain professional when I give her your background. I can relay my meeting with you after I've given her all the information. What do you think?" Jac asked.

Codee turned to Sawyer. "Should I let Jac be the intermediary?"

"I think that's a great idea, and then when she wants to meet you, we…" Sawyer pointed to Erma and Jac "…can all go with you."

"How does this work? Will you call her or just show up at her door?" Codee asked.

"I prefer the face-to-face approach. I can gage reactions better that way. I'll show her my credentials and allow her to check me out if necessary. She didn't get as far as she has without an ability to size up any situation quickly."

"Okay. Of course I'll pay you extra for that."

Jac waved her off. "All part of the fee. Trust me, I'm charging plenty. I love Whidbey, so a trip there will be a pleasure."

Sawyer grabbed Codee's hand and squeezed. She kept their hands clasped and noticed Jac's hawk-like stare. A subtle nod let her know Jac wasn't a threat to her plans to win Codee's affections. Now Sawyer thought Jac was on a mission of her own to try to ingratiate herself with Codee's twin. *Providence*. Sawyer thought the events would unfold the way the universe intended. Codee's dream was the spark to ignite the coming of the future.

✝

"*The Hunger Games* is not science fiction," Codee declared.

"Dystopian society, science fiction—it's all semantics. Besides, Katniss is positively yummy," Sawyer defended.

237

"Hey now. I thought you were trying to woo me?"

"You don't think Katniss is attractive?"

"Deflection. Nice." Codee grabbed a handful of popcorn and tossed a few kernels into her mouth.

"In all seriousness, she doesn't hold a candle to your beauty."

Codee pushed her shoulder against Sawyer. "Charmer."

Sawyer opened her mouth and showed all her teeth in an exaggerated grin. "Is it working?"

"Oh yes, it is, and you know it."

Codee was glad Sawyer had brought *The Hunger Games* series of movies as they waited for Jac to call with an update. She knew Sawyer was doing everything in her power to distract her. Erma had decided *The Hunger Games* wasn't her cup of tea. She couldn't stomach a movie about kids killing one another. It was "disturbing," she'd announced on her way out.

Codee's phone blared her ring tone, and she pressed the Answer button when she saw who the call was from. Picking up the phone and then placing it against her ear, she answered, "Hi." Her voice trembled. "What?" she squeaked.

Sawyer was motioning with her hand, and Codee didn't know what she wanted.

"Speaker, put it on speaker," Sawyer ordered.

She fumbled with her phone, and Sawyer gently retrieved it and pushed the Speaker button.

"Codee, are you still there?" Jac's voice blared through the tiny speaker in the phone.

"Hey, Jac. I just put you on speaker. This is Sawyer."

"Oh, hi, Sawyer. I just told Codee that Chynna is with me and we're on our way to Moses Lake. She wants to meet Codee in person and says she remembers her. She has quite a story to tell. Oh and Sawyer, I think I just met my future wife."

"Does that line work on anyone?" a musical voice filtered through the speaker.

Jac laughed. "We'll be there in about thirty minutes. Don't panic, Codee, it's all good."

"Yes, please don't panic. I've been searching for you, and clearly I hired the wrong person. I can't wait to meet you."

"Thank you," Codee whispered.

"Gotta go, too many distractions to deal with right now with this beauty sitting beside me," Jac announced.

Trailing laughter was all she heard as the call disconnected.

Codee stared into space. "She remembers me," she softly declared. "Why didn't I remember her?"

Sawyer wrapped her arms around Codee. "I don't know, hon. Memories are unique to everyone. She didn't say when she remembered you. Maybe her revelation is new like yours was."

"I know you've been here all day, practically babysitting me and calming my nervousness, but will you consider staying, please?"

"I wouldn't dream of going anywhere until you kick my sorry ass out for overstaying my welcome."

"Never." Codee laid her head on Sawyer's shoulder.

"Music to my ears." Sawyer began weaving her fingers through Codee's hair.

Codee transferred her attention to Sawyer's gentle strokes and forgot all about Katniss's final confrontation with President Snow. They hadn't gone on an official date yet, even though she'd acted rashly and kissed Sawyer, yet in this instant she felt thoroughly loved. A feeling she hadn't experienced in a long time, perhaps ever. She'd vaguely remembered how much her mother had loved her, but that was long ago and nearly forgotten as the memories faded with each passing year.

After five minutes of silence, Codee unraveled herself from Sawyer's protective embrace.

"I want to explain why I'm so guarded...," Codee began.

Sawyer shifted and then reached for her hand and held it lightly. It was the perfect response. She didn't want Sawyer to say anything; she just wanted to get it out and expel the demon once and for all.

"I wasn't ready. I was only twelve when she crawled into my bed and started touching me. I didn't know what to do. It wasn't like with the boys who I would kick, punch, and scream at until she came and beat them to a pulp. Sue was my savior until she became something else. I was so confused. She always came to my defense, but something about her touch felt wrong and yet it also felt so right. At first I tried to tell her no, but I guess my body betrayed me. I had my first orgasm before I got my period." Sawyer squeezed her hand.

"She was possessive and so angry most of the time. Angry at the world, at me because I didn't know how to respond, and livid I wasn't quite ready to fall in love. She became more insistent and rough. It got to the point where I'd do things to her that I wasn't comfortable with, but it was the only way to make it stop for the night. If I could get her to climax, she'd leave me alone for the remainder of the night. It's had a profound effect on every relationship I've ever attempted. Sex is important to people, and I've established a mechanical, almost clinical approach to it. My lovers could tell that emotion didn't accompany the act. I'm a great lover that is devoid of emotion. You should run now, far and fast."

"Codee, you're a bright woman, so I know you realize none of your earlier experiences are your fault. Everyone copes with abuse in different ways. For the record, I'm not going anywhere, because regardless of how much you insist you don't show your feelings, I absolutely feel emotion from you. I'm in no hurry to add intimacy to the mix, and when it happens, I'm convinced it will be everything I've ever dreamed of. Thank you for trusting me with your story." Sawyer pulled her into another embrace and kissed her forehead.

Codee tilted her head forward and telegraphed her need. She wanted Sawyer to kiss her. She wanted to accept someone's first move without feeling like she wasn't in control. "Please…," she pleaded.

Sawyer brought their lips together. Her kiss was tentative, exploratory.

Codee felt a rush of emotion as the kiss became more insistent. Their tongues rolled against each other as Sawyer carefully sucked on her bottom lip, sending a pleasurable shiver along her body. An involuntary moan escaped her as Sawyer continued her loving attention to every part of her mouth. Eventually she broke free and gasped for breath.

"Scary, but if my long-lost sister wasn't on her way, I do believe I would let you take me to bed and break my own rule of not dating hospital employees."

"Rain check?"

"Yes, in two weeks."

Sawyer flipped her wrist. "Actually three hundred forty hours, twenty minutes, and thirty seconds."

Codee laughed. "Do you have a countdown app for your watch?"

Sawyer grinned. "I do, and this is the first occasion I've had to use it."

"How could I not fall for you?"

241

Sawyer pressed her mouth against Codee's again for just an instant. "Yep, how could you not?"

The two women sat together on the couch in perfect harmony as the credits rolled on the second part of the final *Hunger Games* movie.

Chapter Twenty-five

The sound of the doorbell blasted into the living room and broke the tranquility as Codee remained leaning against Sawyer. Even though she was expecting the bell, it shattered the perfection of the moment.

This was it, what she'd anxiously anticipated for over a week. She opened the door, and the warm smile of her double was like a ray of sunshine bursting through the clouds. Chynna instantly gathered Codee into an enthusiastic hug.

Codee grunted.

"Oh God," Chynna's voice pierced the air. Codee marveled at how much she sounded like her sister.

"Jac told me you broke your arm. I didn't hurt you, did I? It's just that I've dreamed of this moment. It's so much more satisfying in person," Chynna blurted out.

Codee noted Chynna's casual outfit: a pair of jeans and a fleece pullover underneath her jacket. She wondered if she'd had other plans Jac had interrupted with the startling news.

"Oh no, it's okay. Please come in. Did Jac tell you I had a dream about you and that's what started this whole…God, what do I call this?"

"Miracle," Chynna supplied.

"Yes, miracle. I didn't remember anything. I have a family," Codee said wistfully as she led them into her cozy living room. "Can I get you something to drink? Coffee, tea, wine? Sorry I don't have any beer."

"None for me. I don't drink and anything with caffeine this late in the day just gives me the jitters," Chynna answered.

"Nothing for me either," Jac added.

Sawyer stood and held out her hand. "Hi, I'm Sawyer. Um, I'm a…."

"My good friend that will morph into something else in how many hours?" Codee teased.

Sawyer chuckled and glanced at her watch. "Three hundred thirty-nine hours, two minutes, and fifty seconds."

"Inside joke?" Chynna asked.

"Yeah, something like that," Codee answered with a small smile. When she turned her head, in her peripheral vision, she caught Jac giving Sawyer the thumbs-up.

Chynna and Jac each sat in the chairs opposite the couch.

"I answered my door, and at first I wondered why this serious-looking woman was standing there. She had a military presence about her, but I know every single person on base and I would have noticed her. Yes, she's someone I definitely would have taken note of. I admit, my initial response was very guarded. I made her give me her driver's license, and then I called a friend who owes me to check her out, even though my gut told me she was the real deal. I thought maybe someone was taking advantage of my desperate attempt to find you," Chynna explained.

"She made me wait until her friend called back, even though I had that picture of you on my phone as additional proof," Jac added.

"I knew I should have hired a woman." Chynna winked. "Pop wouldn't even give me Mom's maiden name, even when I pressed him. Stubborn old bastard." Her eyes watered briefly.

"Is...is...he still alive?" Codee asked.

Chynna shook her head. "Rotten timing. He died two weeks ago. I pushed for the assignment to the Whidbey Naval Air Station when I learned about how far the cancer had spread. He lived in Anacortes with Uncle Frank. He's another stubborn old fart. I don't blame Mom for kicking Dad out. He could be downright scary during one of his episodes, but I learned how to deal with him. Most of the time he was the most loving man, except when I brought up Mom. I learned early on to shut up about that. I remember following him around when we were younger while you clung to Mom's leg."

"I have an uncle?" Codee asked in wonderment.

"Yep, an uncle, an aunt, and six cousins. I don't think there is anyone on Mom's side of the family though. I did overhear Pop talking to Uncle Frank one night, and he said something like he couldn't take you away because Mom didn't have anyone else, and no matter what, he just couldn't be that cruel. I thought that was ironic since he'd had no qualms about squirreling me away in some backwater camp for paranoid vets. We were off the grid and so far into the woods that I'm sure Mom didn't have a prayer of finding us. At first it was fun, like camping, but not the kind of place fit to take a young child."

Sawyer had a concerned look.

"Chynna, so you think you can start from the beginning? I think all this information is a little overwhelming.

245

Did Jac explain that Codee grew up in foster care?" Sawyer interjected.

Chynna brushed away a tear that erupted. "Yeah. That stubborn old man let his bitterness get in the way and never even checked up on Mom and Codee. We could have been a real family a lot sooner had he pushed aside his pride. Although, maybe you had it better. Growing up with Pop and his vet friends was interesting, but very unusual. Maybe you got the better end of the deal. I cried for Mom that first month, and then I toughened up. Will you tell me about her?" Chynna pleaded.

"All I can tell you is what I remember. I was so young when she died. I remember how she used to get sad. I think when Dad took you away, it broke her heart, and I could never quite fill the void. I'm so sorry, but I'd blocked your existence until just recently. I think the memory of you was always there, but it was hidden just beneath the surface." Codee shook her head. "What a waste of time."

"Better late than never. When did you have your dream?" Chynna asked.

Codee shifted in her seat. "I had my accident about two weeks ago."

"That's the same time I, all of a sudden, felt this need to try to find you. It felt almost like a compulsion. I knew I shouldn't badger Pops in his last moments, but I just couldn't help myself. He remained mute to the very end and wouldn't tell me a single thing to help. Finally I got Uncle Frank to talk, and that's when I hired the useless PI who had the details of my birth as a starting point. I guess Uncle Frank thought that since Pops was dead, he didn't have to keep all the secrets anymore."

"How did Dad die?"

Chynna sniffed. "Lung cancer. Pop was a heavy smoker and drinker. If the lung cancer hadn't killed him, I'm sure his liver would have eventually. That's why I don't drink or smoke. I'm not interested in playing Russian roulette."

"Is that what you meant by one of his episodes? Was he a mean drunk or something?" Codee asked.

"Oh no, he was actually better when he was drunk, but I still knew it would eventually kill him. No, Pop suffered from PTSD. The Vietnam War took a huge toll on him. He kept a gun under his pillow, and when he woke with that wide-eyed look waving the gun in the air and spewing profanities at an unknown enemy, it was downright terrifying. From a young age, I learned to hide under the bed until one of the guys came and calmed him down. Otherwise, he was as gentle as a kitten," Chynna explained.

"I'm sorry, it sounds like your life wasn't a picnic either. I wish we'd had each other to weather all the storms growing up, including all those confusing feelings during puberty."

"You're a lesbian, right?"

Codee nodded.

"I've only been able to come out recently. That was a very trying and confusing time for me as well. Pop eventually accepted it, but once again his bitterness rang through. He insinuated I'd gotten the gay gene from Mom and he let his disgust surface." Chynna sighed. "I finally accepted that his revulsion wasn't necessarily about me being gay, but more of a remnant of his paranoia that Mom kicked him out to go gallivanting around with some woman. I tried to explain to him once that she'd probably booted his ass out because of her inability to deal with his PTSD, and if he ever wanted to have another meaningful relationship with anyone, he needed to get his shit together and go through the intensive counseling the Veterans Administration eventually offered to vets. Of course I was only eight when I told him that, so I don't think I quite communicated it in those exact words. I think I might have hinted at wanting a new mother."

"Did he?" Codee quivered with emotion.

"Yeah, he did, but I don't think he ever got over Mom and never pursued anything with anyone else—at least not that I knew about. I assume he sought care more for me than for himself. He knew how frightened I got when he had an episode."

Codee felt Sawyer's quiet presence beside her while she talked with Chynna well into the evening. Erma's timing was perfect when she brought over a delicious variety of Greek dishes to go along with her earlier quiche.

Her yawn was a dead giveaway of how tired she was, and when Chynna hinted at getting a hotel room in the area so they could continue to visit on Sunday, she had insisted both Jac and Chynna stay. She'd picked up on their comfortable banter and thinly veiled looks of interest, so she didn't think sharing the guest bedroom would be a problem for them.

Codee didn't really want Sawyer to leave, and when Sawyer had whispered in her ear that she'd like nothing better than to hold her all night after this emotional day, she accepted her kind offer.

Chapter Twenty-six

The last few days of Sawyer's employment were extremely hard on Codee. She wanted to ignore all her rigid rules and let nature takes its course. The smoldering looks and mild flirtations amused everyone around them, but Sawyer had been the one to steadfastly refuse to arrange the date until she no longer worked at the hospital.

Chynna had found a way to take some personal time off, and they'd spent the last few weeks getting to know one another. Chynna had also spent quite a bit of free time with Jac while Codee was at work. She admired Jac and thought they made the perfect pair, even though they jockeyed for dominance and she never knew which one would ultimately win out. Perhaps neither would and they would alternate as true partners should. Codee wondered if she and Sawyer would find that perfect balance. For the first time in her life, she was optimistic that she'd found her perfect mate.

Finally, the day had come for their first date. Codee thought this was such an odd way to describe their outing because she already felt like she knew Sawyer on a level so deep that it scared her sometimes. They'd been spending a lot of time with one another, and she knew in reality this wasn't their first date, but they had both pretended they'd spent all that time together strictly as friends. It was ridiculous—she knew that—especially after allowing a few passionate lip-locking sessions. Some she started and others Sawyer initiated.

Chynna had opted to spend the night with Jac, so Codee decided an early morning call to her sister was appropriate payback because she'd refused to reveal any details on the mysterious first date Sawyer had planned for them today.

"So this is what it's like to have an older sister," Codee lamented after Chynna refused to answer her questions.

"She made me promise, and I never break a promise. Besides, don't you want to be surprised?"

"No. Surprise is overrated. She's been teasing for two weeks now." Codee pouted.

"Good things come to those who wait."

"Whatever happened to 'blood is thicker than water'? Come on, just a little hint." Codee moved around in her kitchen while she waited for her coffee to brew.

"Nope. You'd think you were ten, rather than a forty-five-year-old going out on an amazing first date."

"See, it's comments like that that pique my interest and demolish any patience I ever had, which was slight to begin with. Sawyer is the one with all the patience; I've never had any."

Ding-dong ding-dong

"Hey, Chynna, can you hang on? That's the doorbell."

Chynna's evil laugh rang through the line. "It's begun. I'm going to let you go now, because you're going to need every ounce of energy and brain power today."

"Fine, be that way." Codee pressed the End button and traversed through the kitchen and into the foyer on her way to the front door.

Jac was on the other side with a single red rose. "I've been asked to deliver this to you with the following message; she made me memorize it. 'Ice can be treacherous, especially to you, but it can also be quite romantic. When you figure out this clue, the first part of the date will ignite those muscles you probably haven't used in ages.'" Jac handed Codee the rose and pivoted to leave. "Good luck."

"Wait. That's all I get?"

"Aw, come on, Codee, it's not that hard to figure out. While it rhymes with *stink*, it is definitely far from it. I wish Chynna and I were joining you guys. It sounds like a blast."

She shut the door and began mumbling to herself. "Hmmm blink, think, sink, kink." She chuckled. "No, I know she wouldn't drum up something kinky with ice, although…rink. Ice rink. Oh man, she's like a steel trap. She remembered me talking about one of my favorite memories, when I used to sneak out and slide on the ice, pretending I was a famous ice skater."

Just as she was about to grab her coffee, the doorbell rang again. Vetti stood on the other side. She handed Codee another single red rose with a hand-painted card. Codee opened it.

"Knowing how intelligent you are, I'm sure you've figured out the first clue already, but don't come until ten. Bring a hat and gloves. Relax and have your coffee, and don't forget to eat a healthy serving of Erma's french toast. XXOO Sawyer"

Erma's smiling face peered out from behind Vetti, as the older woman held out a large pan. "Here's your french toast."

"Get in here and tell me everything you know about this date."

Erma laughed. "No way, and ruin the surprise?" She got a dreamy look on her face. "Oh, to be young again and fall in love for the first time. If you do not hang on to this woman and make her a permanent fixture in your life, I will personally wring your scrawny little neck." She handed Codee the pan.

"Oh Erma, I think I've fallen in love for the first time in my life. It's such a glorious, yet absolutely terrifying feeling."

"Really?" Vetti and Erma said together.

"Have you told her that?" Vetti asked.

"Oh goodness, no. I don't want to scare the poor woman," Codee confessed.

"I've known Sawyer a long time, and yes, she falls for women easily, but I've never seen her this…I don't how to describe it, other than perfectly tuned to the world around her. She is without a doubt madly in love with you, but afraid to tell you." Vetti patted Codee's good arm. "Please don't break her heart. Sawyer is one in a million."

"I really don't plan to. I've even started working on myself to overcome…um…my issues. I'm sure she's told you." Codee leaned against the door.

"No, she hasn't, but I've seen enough damage to young kids who haven't had the best early childhood experiences to recognize the signs, and you're different now, so whatever you're doing to resolve those demons, it's working. Maybe it's the love or potential love of a good woman." Vetti grinned.

"Hey, do you two want to come in and visit for a bit?"

"Nope, we gotta go help with something else." Vetti tugged on Erma's arm.

Codee closed the door and decided she needed to tell Sawyer how she felt about her. They'd probably done things all the wrong way—getting to know one another and falling in love before the first official date—but she wouldn't have it any other way.

✝

Sawyer peeked out the window at the Larson Recreation Center. "She's here. Okay, do you have phase two set up?"

Vetti, Jac, Chynna, and Erma all nodded.

"I am so glad you all pulled some strings for me. I never would have been able to accomplish all of this without you. Thank you." Sawyer touched her hand against her heart.

Sawyer had transformed the indoor ice skating rink into a winter wonderland. All of the walls were covered in butcher paper and painted to look like a snowy, magical mountain retreat. Buckets of evergreens dotted the ice in a random pattern, and in the center a pile of red rose petals added the perfect touch of color.

Her heart beat loudly, and she marveled at Codee's youthful appearance as she seemed to take in the setting all at once. Her eyes sparked against the backdrop of the silvery ice.

Sawyer held out a single red rose. "You made it."

"This is amazing." Codee leaned in and pressed her lips against Sawyer's. "Thank you for remembering. If you don't mind, I'd like to keep on my slick tennis shoes and forego the skates."

"I wouldn't dream of sticking those blades of destruction on either of our feet. There's only so much I'm willing to do for love. I don't know how people don't destroy their ankles standing on top of that sliver of steel."

"How did you manage to reserve the rink? Saturdays are their biggest days."

"I have friends in high places." Sawyer winked. "Besides, we only have it for an hour, and then my accomplices will clean up the place and they can open at noon."

Sawyer led Codee out onto the ice, and they slid around, laughing and hugging one another when the other started to slip. Sawyer was careful not to let her tumble and managed to be the one to always land on her behind, pulling the woman she'd fallen for on top so she had a soft place to land. Each time she took the opportunity before her and captured Codee's lips, with each kiss more passionate than the one before.

A few minutes after eleven, Vetti and Erma entered the rink with several young men and women in tow.

Erma was carrying two thermoses. She nodded at Sawyer. "It's all ready. They're just outside waiting for you."

Sawyer picked up her backpack that she'd stored on the side of the rink and stuffed both thermoses inside. "Okay, time to bundle up. You have a hat and gloves, right?"

Codee nodded and pulled her gloves from her down jacket. "I read the note. I don't have a hat, but the hood on this coat is extra warm."

After Sawyer put on her own coat, hat, and gloves, she grabbed her backpack and took Codee's hand, leading her outside.

Two large Clydesdale horses were shaking their heads as their bells tinkled in accompaniment to Chynna and Jac's laughter. Jac was flicking Chynna's large top hat as Chynna pulled her in for a kiss.

Sawyer cleared her throat. "Um, are you two ready?"

Chynna turned her head. "Oh sorry." She pointed at Jac. "This one was distracting me from my appointed duties. Ma'am, would you like some help into the carriage?"

Codee chuckled. "No, I think I'd rather have Sawyer's hand on my butt guiding me into the seat."

"Oh yeah, I'm gonna love this ride. It's starting out perfectly," Sawyer declared.

Codee lifted her leg to bring her foot onto the wood step, grabbed the edge of the carriage with her good arm, and pulled herself up while Sawyer gave her a gentle push.

"Um, you can let go of my butt now." Codee slid into the seat and moved over, leaving room for Sawyer to join her.

Sawyer grinned and toppled into the seat next to her. She tossed the backpack between her legs, grabbed the blanket lying on the floor of the carriage, and pulled it over their laps. "You warm enough?"

"Um, yeah, that extra little caress certainly heated up my core."

"You two all settled now?" Chynna asked.

"Yep," Sawyer and Codee answered.

Chynna clicked her tongue, and the horses moved the carriage forward.

Sawyer retrieved a thermos from her backpack, and then opened the steaming container. After she poured the sweet chocolate mixture into the cup, she handed it to her date. She retrieved the other thermos, poured herself a cup, wrapped her free arm around Codee, and settled back into the seat.

Codee blew across the cup and took a sip. "Oh, this is heavenly."

Sawyer frowned. "Wait, before you take another sip. I know you don't drink a lot, but I thought a small amount of Irish Cream wouldn't hurt. But if you'd prefer the virgin version, I think Chynna has another thermos stashed somewhere on this rig."

"Nope, this is good. It's noon somewhere. It's time to live on the edge a little. I've never done anything as decadent as drink alcohol before noon."

The clip-clop of the horses' hooves on the smooth, black pavement continued to lull both women into a relaxing ride.

Sawyer had rented a cozy cabin for the day and arranged for a gourmet campfire lunch complete with a gas bonfire pit in the center of the room surrounded by potted evergreens that looked suspiciously like the ones at the rink. She'd decided that ignoring the dangers of having an open flamed makeshift campfire was worth the risk to see the complete joy on Codee's face.

As they roasted their marshmallows over the pit, Sawyer brushed a lock of Codee's hair back and barely skimmed her lips against Codee's in a hint of the love she felt for this woman, who literally had blossomed before her very eyes in the last two weeks. The floodgate had opened, and then the emotion came pouring out after she'd trusted her enough with her fragile insecurities.

"The last part of the date is something that's a little unusual. I've written you a love letter, but it's a love letter I've imagined I might write twenty years from now on the anniversary of our first date. It's a future love letter." Sawyer pulled a lilac envelope from the front zippered pocket of her backpack and handed it to Codee.

February 5, 2036

Hello, My Beloved Wife,

It's the anniversary of our first official date, and I can honestly say I fall just a little more in love with you each day. I never thought that was even possible.

I'll bet you think I fell in love with you on the day of our first date, because that's when I had the courage to tell you, but you'd be wrong about that. I fell in love with you when you opened those beautiful eyes of yours and said, "And you're dead too," and started to cry. Somehow I knew those words were spoken with a depth of emotion that neither one of us understood at the time but learned very quickly about. I've never wanted to share my life with someone as much as I wanted to share my life with you at that particular moment, but somehow, even though it defied all logic, it made sense.

Every single heartbreak that occurred before I met you was worth it, because I knew that just around the corner something special was waiting for me, and then you showed up in my life. You are like the air that I breathe, essential to my well-being.

Happy anniversary, sweetheart. I will love you forever.

Sawyer waited patiently for Codee to finish her love letter. She wondered if this was the best way to tell her she'd fallen head over heels in love, but it was too late now if it was the wrong decision.

Codee looked up with tears in her eyes. "I've fallen so in love with you, I can't imagine living another day without you by my side. Thank you."

The passion and love between the two mingled like smoke from a real fire as their lips came together one more time, sealing the eternal flame.

Epilogue

One year later

Sawyer held the TV remote loosely in her hand as she relaxed on Codee's couch. She was flipping through the major network channels and frowned each time she listened to the reporters' updates.

She considered herself fortunate Codee hadn't run screaming for the hills yet, but then she had been extremely purposeful in her courting plan—taking things excruciatingly slow. They hadn't made love for the first time until six months after their first date, but that didn't bother Sawyer because she was in for the long haul.

Three months ago Sawyer had borrowed money from her parents and made an offer on a rundown cabin in the woods. She spent a lot of her free time working on the remodel to make sure that before winter set in, it had the basics to ensure it was livable.

Sawyer smiled as she recognized the silver lining to the completely disastrous condition of the cabin—it meant more time with her lover in the evenings. Codee had taken pity on her deplorable living conditions and invited her to stay at her house until the cabin remodel was complete. The setup was win-win for everyone. Sawyer was able to take her time to complete the repairs the right way, and eventually she hoped they would split their time between the two places, giving Codee her dream cabin in the woods. She would bring Codee all the samples and ask her opinion about tile, wood floors, and other materials for the upgrade of the country getaway. The cabin was turning into quite a cozy place, and Codee had described it as "rustic elegance." She'd beamed with pride when Codee coined that phrase.

Neither of them ever specifically defined their relationship, but for all intents and purposes, they were living together full-time and Sawyer had zero doubt Codee would make the ultimate commitment with her when the time was right and she got up the courage to ask. Sawyer was in no hurry; they would get there.

Codee had said the three words that were most important to her. Saying she'd fallen in love on their first date was a milestone for sure, but when she'd blurted out, "I love you," seemingly out of the blue, Sawyer knew this was forever. That was enough for her to wait ten years if that was how long it took to accept her proposal of marriage.

Codee walked into the room holding a bottle of wine and two glasses. "Liquid courage. Either we'll be celebrating the first woman president or drowning our sorrow, knowing we live in a country where a complete idiot such as Trison managed to get himself elected to the highest office in the most powerful nation. How're the numbers?"

Sawyer stopped pressing the button on the remote. "I keep looking for a news channel that is reporting different results, but I'm afraid you may be some kind of seer, because the unbelievable is about to occur. They just declared Trison the winner in Florida."

Codee set the bottle and the two glasses down on the coffee table. "I don't want to be a prophet, but this is bad, really bad. Is it at least close?"

"It's close. We're waiting for Georgia now, and if he wins there, it's all over. Carlson won't have enough to win, even if she takes every other state that hasn't yet declared a winner."

The recognizable sound of breaking news interrupted the conversation. "It's official, Georgia has just declared David Trison the winner. Carlson is about to make her concession call to him. The Trison camp is going wild...."

"God help us," Codee groaned.

"Any chance you'd like to move to Canada with me?"

"I think that's about the best offer I've received all year, but to be honest, I don't want to be anywhere that you're not, and even if we have to stay here in the United States, being with you makes everything so much better. If I have to endure four years of that idiot, I'm glad you'll be by my side while I'm doing it."

"I love you," Sawyer declared as she moved to Codee and kissed her sweetly.

"I love you too, and together we'll ride out this nightmare."

Author's Note

When I first wrote this story, it was many months prior to the results of the 2016 election. I never thought in a million years (yes I know that's an exaggeration), that President-elect Trump would win. I've joked about not being comfortable in the role of a seer, and I was certainly as surprised as the rest of the country regarding the outcome.

This story was intended as an outrageous satire, so take a deep breath with me and trust that I am really not a predictor of the future. We've come too far to let anyone push us back into the closet, and I refuse to go to that dark, scary, place. I will remain optimistic, yet I will be prepared to act and not stay on the sidelines. What we as a country permit, we promote.

About the Author

Annette Mori

Annette is an award-winning author and healthcare executive living in the beautiful Pacific Northwest with her wife and their five furry kids. Well, actually, it might be more than five, but they do not count the ones they only feed. Annette believes it is not too late to try something new.

As an avid reader, she is pleased there are thousands of good books to choose from, and hopes that one day hers will be one of the many for readers to consider. She reads at least three to four books a week, so please, keep them coming. She has a habit to feed, after all.

No matter if you loved one of her books or hated it, Annette would love your comments. Feel free to e-mail her at annettemori0859@gmail.com. She believes she will always be a WIP (work in progress—she just learned that), so feedback is a gift. Please follow Annette's blog at: https://annettemori0859.wordpress.com/.

Other Books from Affinity eBook Press

The Termination by Annette Mori
Codee is having a bad day and it's only going to get worse. Sawyer, a compassionate young woman, is resigned to her fate. Her only question is what fate is that? Enjoy this satirical romance, with all of its twists and turns, that just might make you go hmm...

The Next Time by Erin O'Reilly
What if you had the chance to make history stop repeating itself? Would you sacrifice today for a chance at a better tomorrow? There is a moment in everyone's life that defines their future. For Jac and Carol, that time is now. Jump ahead twenty-five years and meet Carol's granddaughter Livvy. She is ready for a challenge and is fleeing the nest and getting on with her life. Read this wonderful love story that spans several lifetimes.

Open Your Heart a Sensual Collection by Ali Spooner
Excite your senses, rejuvenate your memories and best of all flirt with the edge of eroticism. Allow us to help you relive that first kiss, flirting with young love, your dream come

true, surprise encounters, and your wildest desires... Enjoy these stories of love, sweet seduction, and steamy encounters. Open Your Heart...a sensual collection.

Secret of Stone Creek by Natalie London
Jennifer Cameron arrives in Stone Creek, Wisconsin to sell her grandparents' large Victorian home. While there she is intrigued by a twenty-four-year-old never solved murder. Her attraction to the lovely and mysterious librarian, Diana vies for her attention. Follow this suspenseful whodunit to its conclusion.

The Promise by JM Dragon
An accidental meeting with Melissa Grant, leads to an unexpected offer for Kris Lake—refurbishing a beach cottage, with the help of Melissa's granddaughter Claire. Do outer imperfections prevent them from reaching the beauty that lives inside and the chance of a happy new life? Find out in this lovely romance that will fill you with heart-warming sensations throughout the story.

Christmas at Winterbourne by Jen Silver
The Christmas festivities for the guests booked into Winterbourne House has all the goings-on of a traditional holiday. The only difference is that this guesthouse is run by lesbians, for lesbians. Join the guests and staff at Winterbourne for a Christmas you'll not soon forget.

The Review by Annette Mori
Silver Lining, a successful lesbian romance writer, has the crazy idea to sponsor a contest where the first reader who posts a review wins a home-cooked meal with an offer to fly

the winner to Washington State. Jasmine, the winner, has engaged in subtle flirtations with Silver. Bizarre messages from the unknown fan has Silver questioning the wisdom of a relationship with Jasmine.

South of Heaven by Ali Spooner
Kendra Drake has taken over as Captain of her father's shrimp boat. As a favor to her father, Kendra has agreed to give fellow shrimper, Lindsey Bowen, a chance to work on the boat but first must prove herself to Kendra and her crew. Lindsey finds a way into Kendra's heart. Will it only last for the summer?

Catch to Release by Lacey Schmidt
On the verge of success, lesbian folk-rock star, Shay Greenaura, finds herself caught up in more than just her music. Threats have her manager hiring a security firm for protection. Addison Weller, a former Diplomatic Security Services agent is called in to assess the threats against Shay. Their undeniable attraction, brewing silently between them, could prove to be a fatal distraction. Follow this fast-paced adventure to its surprising romantic conclusion.

Ready for Love by Erin O'Reilly
Kylie Wilcox's life dramatically changed with the death of her husband. Dr. LJ Evans, a renowned archaeologist, needed and wanted nothing but her work for her happiness. Their worlds are about to collide and lives will be altered forever.

Neptune's Ring by Ali Spooner
In the sequel to *Venus Rising*, Nat and Liz, owners of Venus Rising, invite Levi and Vanessa to join them in a venture for

a new club on another island. They find the perfect place in an unfinished resort, Neptune's Ring. While on the island, Levi is drawn into a mystery involving secret compartments and a murder. Join the characters in this page-turning adventure, filled with steamy romance, intrigue, and an unsolved murder.

The Ultimate Betrayal by Annette Mori
Lara is a successful, beautiful, charming, financier. She is also a total control freak, so whatever Lara wants, Lara makes sure she gets. Rachel is Lara's fun-loving, charming, irresistible wife. Sophia's surprise visit to see Lara sets in motion a number of life changing events for them all. Hell has no fury as a woman scorned.

Keeping Faith by TJ Vertigo
You loved them in the previous novels, Private Dancer, Reece's Faith, and Reece's Star, now join the antics of Reece, Faith, Cori, Vi, and even The Animal, one last time in *Keeping Faith*.

Bound by Ali Spooner
A rogue, master vampire threatens the existence of the New Orleans vampire clan. Lord Jordan enlists Devin Benoit, sister of the Baton Rouge Alpha, and her witch lover, Tia, to assist with cleansing the city from potential disaster.

The Circle Dance by Jen Silver
Jamie Steele has moved to another town, trying to forget the heartbreak of losing her lover of six years. Sasha Fairfield finds her thoughts taken up with her ex-lover and thinks she wants Jamie back. Follow this captivating romance as love

dances through the lives of these women to its surprising conclusion.

Search for the White Moon by Natalie London
Kathryn Austin, a government agent, is given opera singer Adriana Desi as her new assignment. Their lives and futures are in danger as the White Moon terrorists hunt them. Immerse yourself in this fast-paced, romantic thriller by debut author Natalie London.

Take Me as I Am by JM Dragon & Erin O'Reilly
When Jo Lackerly and Thea Danvers meet, an unexpected friendship develops, proving a catalyst for both women to change their lives irrevocably. Follow them on a journey of discovery that will have your heart smiling, blood boiling, and senses entangled in a wonderful romance.

Carved in Stone by Jen Silver
Join the characters from *Starting Over* and *Arc Over Time* in this final book from the Starling Hill trilogy. Ellie Winters thinks she might be going mad when the ancient queen wants a proper burial for herself and her consort. *Carved in Stone* has romance, adventure, a treasure hunt, and happy endings for all, living and dead.

Anywhere, Everywhere by Renee MacKenzie
Gwen Martin's life in the Ten Thousand Islands area changes irrevocably when Piper Jackson comes into her life. Without trust, can the budding relationship between Gwen and Piper survive? Or will the answers to these questions continue to haunt them?

E-Books, Print, Free e-books

Visit our website for more publications available online.

www.affinityebooks.com

Published by Affinity E-Book Press NZ LTD
Canterbury, New Zealand

Registered Company 2517228

www.ingramcontent.com/pod-product-compliance
Lightning Source LLC
Chambersburg PA
CBHW060529260626
47161CB00003B/819